The newscast confirmed that the 'Autarchy of United Babur' had reiterated its claim. Because Mirkheim was located so near, as interstellar distances went, and because the supermetals were of incalculable strategic importance, Babur could not and would not tolerate possession of that globe by any power which had demonstrated hostility to Babur's legitimate activity in space. 'Yesterday,' the cast continued, 'we received a tape of an address by Prime Minister Lapierre of the Solar Commonwealth. He maintained that his government is willing to negotiate, but that Babur thus far has made none of the normal preliminary moves. At the same time, he said, the Commonwealth will under no circumstances yield to naked aggression. The Commonwealth will stand firm, and if necessary will take, quote, "forceful measures" . . .'

Mirkheim

POUL ANDERSON

SPHERE BOOKS LIMITED
30/32 Gray's Inn Road, London WC1X 8JL

First published in Great Britain by Sphere Books Ltd. 1978
Copyright © Poul Anderson 1977

To Jerry Pournelle

Printed in Great Britain by
Hazell Watson & Viney Ltd
Aylesbury, Bucks

To Jerry Pournelle

Prologue

Y minus 500,000.

Once there had been a great proud star, bright as a hundred Sols. Through four hundred million years its blue-white fire burned steadily, defiance of the darkness around and challenge to those other suns whose distant brilliances crowded the sky. Orbiting it afar was a companion worthy of its majesty, a planet whose mass equaled fifteen hundred Earths, redly aglow with the heat of its own contraction. There may have been lesser worlds and moons as well; we cannot now say. We simply know that the giant stars rarely have attendants, so this one was due to a curious ordainment of God, or destiny, or chance.

The giants die young, as arrogantly as they have lived. A day came when the hydrogen fuel at the core was exhausted. Instead of swelling and reddening as a lesser sun would do in its old age, this fell in upon itself. Energies beyond imagination broke free; atoms crashed together to fuse in strange new elements; the star exploded. For a short while, in its fury, it shone well-nigh as radiant as its entire galaxy.

No ordinary world could have endured the storm of incandescence which then swept outward. Something the size of Earth must have perished entirely, the very iron of its core made vapor. Even the huge companion lost most of its mass, hydrogen and helium bursting forth into endlessness. But this drank so much energy that the metallic heart of the globe was only turned molten. Across it seethed the matter cast out by the star in its death struggle.

More of that matter escaped into space. For tens of millennia the wrecks of sun and planet whirled in the middle of a nebula which, seen from afar, glowed like faerie lacework. But it dissipated and lost itself across light-years; darkness moved inward. The remnant of the planet congealed, barely aglimmer where its alloys cast back the gleam from distant constellations.

For half a million years, these ruins drifted alone through the deep.

Y minus 28.

The world men call Babur will never be a home to them. Leaving his spaceship, Benoni Strang grew violently aware of weight. Upon his bones lay half again the drag of the Hermes which had bred him or the Earth which had bred his race. Flesh strained against the burden of itself. The armor that kept him alive became a stone on either shoulder, either foot.

Nevertheless, though he could have activated his impeller and flitted from the airlock, he chose to stride along the gangway to the ground, like an arriving king.

At first he could barely see that beings awaited him. The sun Mogul was high in a murky purple heaven where red clouds roiled, and its radiance was more fierce than that of Maia or Sol; but it was tiny at its distance. Hoar soil gave back some light, as did an ice cliff a kilometer away and the liquid ammonia cataract toppling over its sheerness. Yet his vision did not reach to the horizon. He thought a grove of low trees with long black fronds stood at the edge of sight on his left, and that he could make out the glistening city he knew was to his right. However, this was as unsure as the greeting he would get. And every shape he discerned was so alien that when he glanced elsewhere he could not remember it. Here he must learn all over again how to use his eyes.

A hydrogen-helium atmosphere turned shrill the boom of the falls, the thump of boots on gangway and afterward their scrunch across sod. By contrast, his breath within the helmet, the slugging of blood

2

in his ears, came to him like bass drumbeats. Sweat dampened his skin and reeked in his nostrils. He hardly noticed. He was too exultant at having arrived.

The blur before him gained form with each step he took, until it was a cluster of a dozen creatures. One of them moved to meet him. He cleared his throat and said awkwardly, through a speaker: "I am Benoni Strang. You wanted me to join you."

The Baburite carried a vocalizer, which changed hums and mumbles into Anglic words. "We required that for your sake as well as ours. If you are to maintain close relationships and do research on us, as we on you, then you must often come to the surface and interact directly with us. This visit will test your ability."

It had already been tested in the environmental chambers of the school that had trained him. Strang didn't say so. That might somehow give offense. Despite two decades of contact, trade which had culminated in exchanging spacecraft technology for heavy metals and a few other goods, humans knew little about Baburites. *We're absolutely ignorant of how much they know about us,* he recalled.

"I thank you," he said. "You'll have to be patient with me, I'm afraid, but eventually I should be in a position to reward your efforts."

"How?"

"Why, by finding new areas where we can do business to our mutual benefit." Strang did not admit his superiors had scant expectation of that. He had barely gotten this assignment, mainly to give him a few years' practical experience, he a young xenologist whose education had concentrated on subjovian planets.

He had uttered no hint of the ambition he nourished. The hour to do so would be when he had proof the scheme was possible—if it ever would be.

"After our experience on Suleiman," the native said, "we question what we may gain from the Polesotechnic League."

The flat artificial voice could convey none of the resentment. And did such an emotion lie behind it? Who could read the heart of a Baburite? It did not even have anything like a heart.

"The Solar Spice & Liquors Company is not the whole League," Strang answered. "Mine is entirely different from it. They've

3

nothing in common but membership, and membership means less than it used to.''

"This we will study,'' the being told him. "That is why we will cooperate with your scientific team. We mean to get as well as give knowledge, information we need before our civilization can claim a place by yours.''

The dream in Strang flared upward.

Y minus 24.

Both moons of Hermes were aloft, Caduceus rising small but nearly full, the broad sickle of Sandalion sinking westward. High in the dusk, a pair of wings caught light from the newly set sun and shone gold. A tilirra sang amidst the foliage of a millionleaf, which rustled to a low breeze. At the bottom of the canyon it had cut for itself, the Palomino River rang with its haste; but that sound reached the heights as a murmur.

Sandra Tamarin and Peter Asmundsen came out of the mansion onto a terrace. Halting at the parapet, they looked down to where water gleamed through shadow, then around them to the forest which enclosed Windy Rim, and across to violet silhouettes of the Arcadian Hills. Their hands joined.

She said at last, "I wish you had not to go.''

"Me too,'' he replied. " 'Tis been a wonderful visit.''

"Are you positive you can't handle the matter from here? We have complete equipment, communication, computation, data retrieval, everything.''

"Ordinarily that would be fine. But in this case—well, my Traver employees do have legitimate grievances. In their place, belike I'd threaten a strike myself. If I can't avoid giving preferential promotions to Followers, at least I can try to hammer out a set of compensations for Travers, as might be extra vacations. Their leaders will be in more of a mood to compromise if I've taken the trouble to come meet them in person.''

"I suppose you're right. You have a sense for such things.'' She sighed. "I wish I did.''

4

He regarded her a while, and she him, before he said, "You do. More than you realize." Smiling: "You'd better—our probable next Grand Duchess."

"Do you believe so in truth?" On the instant, the question they had been thrusting aside throughout this holiday was with them. "I did once, oh, yes. Now I'm not sure. That's why I've, well, retreated here to my parents' home. Too many people made plain what they think of me after seeing the consequence of my own damn foolishness."

"Brake that nonsense," he said, perhaps more roughly than intended. "If your father had not those business interests that disqualify him, there'd be no doubt of his election. You're his daughter, the best possibility we own—equal to him, maybe better—and for precisely that reason, you're intelligent enough to know it. Are you telling me you've let a few prudes and snobs hurt you? Why, you should be bragging about Eric. Eventually your youngling will be the best Grand Duke Hermes ever had."

Her eyes went from his, toward the darkling wilderness. He could barely hear her: "If he can curb the devil that's in him from *his* father."

Straightening, she met his gaze again and said aloud, "Oh, I've stopped being angry at Nick van Rijn. He was more honest with me, really, than I was with him or myself. And how could I regret having Eric? But of late—Pete, I'll admit to you, I wish Eric were legitimate. That his father were a man who could bide with us."

"Something of the kind might be arranged," he blurted. And then his tongue locked, and they stood long mute, two big blond humans who searched each other's faces through a twilight that half blinded them. The breeze lulled, the tilirra chanted, the river laughed on its way to the sea.

Y minus 18.

A ship hunted through space until she found the extinct supernova. Captain David Falkayn beheld the circling planetary core and saw that it was good. But its aspect was so forbidding that he christened it Mirkheim.

Soon afterward, he guided other ships there, with beings aboard who meant to wrest hope out of desolation. They knew the time granted them would be slight, so while they could they must labor hard and dare much.

Falkayn and his comrades did not linger. They had lives of their own to lead. From time to time they would come back, eager to learn how the work had gone; and always the toilers would bless them.

Y minus 12.

When he descended on Babur, Strang no longer walked, but traveled about at comparative ease, held in a harness atop a gravsled. The natives knew he could handle himself sufficiently well on their world to merit their respect. He had proved that over and over— occasionally at mortal risk, when the violent land suffered an outburst, a quake, or an avalanche. Today he sat in a chamber built of ice and talked for hour after hour with one he called Ronzal.

That was not the Baburite's true name. There was a set of vibrations which the computer in a vocalizer decided to render as "Ronzal." Conceivably it was not nomenclature at all. Strang had never found out for certain. Nonetheless, in the course of time he and the bearer had become friends, as nearly as was possible. And who could tell how near that was?

Which language they used during their discussion depended on what either wanted to say. Anglic or League Latin lent themselves best to some concepts, "Siseman" to others. (Those three syllables were another artifact of the vocalizer.) And still, every now and then they must grope about for a way to express what they meant. They were not even sure always what they thought. Though they had spent their careers patiently trying to build bridges across the differences of their brains and their histories, the endeavor was far from reaching an end.

Yet Ronzal could say what wakened trumpets in Strang: "The

final opposition has yielded. The entire globe is meshed in the Imperial Band. Now we are ready to look outward.''

At last, at last! But years lie ahead before we—Babur and I—can do more than look. Calm, Benoni, lad, calm. The human hauled back down his soaring thoughts. ''Wonderful,'' he said. That was about as much enthusiasm as he saw any point in showing. The two races did not rejoice alike. ''My colleagues and I have been expecting it, of course. You've rolled up victories till I was puzzled why any society dared resist you. In fact, I'm just back from a conference with my''—he hesitated—''my superiors.'' *They aren't really. No longer. As events here gathered momentum, as it grew more and more likely that Babur can in fact become the kind of instrument I foresaw, and I am now their vital principal liaison with Babur: I have become their equal. In the end, I am going to be their chieftain.*

No matter now. No sense in boastfulness. It's a weary way yet till I stand again on Hermes.

''I'm authorized to begin talks about creating a space navy for you,'' he said.

''We have considered among ourselves how that can be an economic possibility,'' Ronzal responded. ''How can we meet the cost?''

Fighting for coolness against the thrill that went through him, Strang spoke with caution. ''It may be our relationship is ready to go beyond the immediate value-for-value we've exchanged hitherto. Obviously you can't buy weapons development from us with the resources you have to offer.''

(Gold and silver, cheap on Babur because, at its temperatures, solid mercury filled their industrial roles better. Plant secretions which were convenient starting points for organo-halogen syntheses. Some other materials that formed links in a chain of trades, from planet to planet, till the traders finally got what they wanted. Commerce between worlds so mutually foreign would always be marginal at best.)

''Our races can exchange services as well as goods,'' Strang said.

Ronzal fell silent, doubtless pondering. How deeply dared it trust monsters who breathed oxygen, drank liquid water, and radiated

7

oven-hotly from their armor? Strang sympathized. He had passed through the same unsureness; he would never be quite at ease either. As if to remind himself how out of place he was here, he squinted through gloom at the Baburite.

When both stood erect, Ronzal's head reached the man's waist. Behind an upright torso stretched a horizontal barrel, tailless, mounted on eight short legs. It seemed to bear rows of gills. Actually those were the opercula protecting tracheae which, given a dense hydrogen atmosphere, aerated the body as efficiently as Strang's lungs did his. From the torso sprang a pair of arms terminating in lobsterlike claws; extending from the wrists above these were strong tendrils to serve as fingers. The head consisted mostly of spongy snout, with four tiny eyes behind. The smooth skin was striped in orange, blue, black, and white. A filmy robe covered most of it.

The Baburite had no mouth. It ground up food with its claws and put this into a digestive pouch on the abdomen to be liquefied before the snout dipped down to absorb the nourishment. Hearing and smell centered in the tracheal organs. Speech arose from vibrating diaphragms on the sides of the head. The sexes were three, and individuals changed cyclically from one to the next according to patterns and circumstances which Strang had never managed to elucidate fully.

An untrained human would only have perceived grotesqueness. He, looking at the being in its own environment, saw dignity, power, and a curious beauty.

A humming behind the vocalizer asked, "Who of us will gain?"

"Both of us." Though Strang knew his words would have no meaning to the listener, he let them clang forth: "Security. Mastery. Glory. Justice."

Y minus 9.

Seen from an activated transparency in Nicholas van Rijn's penthouse atop the Winged Cross, Chicago Integrate was a godland of spires, towers, many-colored walls, crystalline vitryl, gracefully curving trafficways, flickering emblems, here and there a stretch of trees and greensward, the sky and the lake as aglitter with movement

8

as the ground itself. Whenever they visited, the Falkayns never tired of that spectacle. To David it was comparatively fresh; he had spent most of his life off Earth. But Coya, who had been coming to see her grandfather since before she could walk, likewise found it always new. Today it beckoned their attention more than ever before: for they would soon be embarked on their first shared voyage beyond Sol's outermost comets.

The old man was giving them a small, strictly private farewell dinner. The live servitors whom he could afford didn't count, they were well trained in discretion, and he had sent both his current mistresses to his house in Djakarta to await his arrival in a day or so. Knowing that van Rijn's idea of a small dinner took a couple of hours, from the first beluga caviar to the last magnificently decadent cheese, the Falkayns brought good appetites. A Mozart sonata lilted them welcome; tankards of beer stood beside icy muglets of akvavit and a dozen varieties of smoked seafood; incense from Tai-Tu drifted subtle on the air. Their host had in their honor put on better clothes than he usually wore, full-sleeved shirt, lace at his throat and wrists, iridescent vest, plum-colored trousers—though his feet were in straw slippers—and he seemed in boisterous good humor.

Then the phone chimed.

"Wat drommel?" van Rijn growled. "I told Mortensen no calls from anybody less rank than the angel Gabriel. That porridge brain he got is gone cold and pobbery with lumps in, ha?" His huge form slap-slapped across an expanse of trollcat rug to the instrument at the opposite end of the living room. "I give him his just deserts, *flambé*, by damn!" A hairy finger poked the accept button.

"Freelady Lennart is calling, sir," announced the figure in the screen. "You said you would speak to her whenever she answered your request for a conversation. Shall she be put through?"

Van Rijn hesitated. He tugged the goatee which, beneath waxed mustaches, ornamented his triple chin. His beady black eyes, close set under a sloping forehead on either side of a great hook nose, darted toward his guests. It was not really true what many asserted, that the owner of the Solar Spice & Liquors Company had a cryogenic computer as prosthesis for a soul. He rather doted on his favorite granddaughter, and her newly acquired husband had been his protégé

9

before becoming his agent. "I know what she got to honk-honk about," he rumbled. "Grismal. Not for our happy fun gas-together."

"But you'd better grab the chance to contact her when it comes, right, Gunung Tuan?" Coya replied. "Go ahead. Davy and I will admire the view." She didn't suggest he take the call in a different room. That he could trust them as he did himself went without saying. As confidence dwindled in public institutions, those of the Solar Commonwealth and the Polesotechnic League alike, loyalties grew the more intensely personal.

Van Rijn sighed like a baby typhoon and settled himself into a chair, paunch resting majestically on lap. "I won't be long, no, I will currytail discussion," he promised. "That Lennart, she gives me indigestion, *ja*, she makes my ghastly juices boil. But we got this need for standing back to back, no matter how bony hers is. . . . . Put her through," he told his chief secretary.

Falkayn and Coya took their drinks back to the transparency and looked out. But their glances soon strayed, for they found each other a sight more splendid than anything below or around them.

He might have been less in love than she, being eighteen years older and a wanderer who had known many women in many strange places. But in fact he felt that after all that time he had finally come to a haven he had always, unknowingly, been seeking. Coya Conyon, who proudly followed a custom growing in her generation and now called herself Coya Falkayn, was tall and slender in a scarlet slack-suit. Her dark hair fell straight to her shoulders, framing an oval face where the eyes were wide and gold-flecked green, the mouth wide and soft above a firm little chin, the nose snubbed like his own, the complexion sun-tinged ivory.

And she could not yet sate her gaze with him. He was tall, too; his gray outfit showed off an athletic build; his features were lean in the cheeks and high in the cheekbones, his eyes the blue and his hair the yellow common among the aristocratic families of Hermes. He also had the erect bearing of that class; but his lips denied their heritage, creasing too readily into laughter. Thus far he needed no meditechnic help to look younger than his forty-one years.

10

They touched tankards and smiled. Then van Rijn's bellow jerked their minds willy-nilly across the room.

"What you say?" The merchant reared where he sat. Black ringlets, the style of three decades ago, swirled about his beefy shoulders. Through Falkayn flitted recollection of a recent episode when a rival firm had mounted an elaborate espionage operation to find out if the old man was dyeing his hair or not. It might be a clue to whether age would soon diminish his rapacious capacities. The attempt had failed.

"You shouldn't make jokes, Lennart," van Rijn bawled on. "Is not your style. You, in a clown suit with a red balloon snoot and painted grin, you would still look like about to quote some minor Hebrew prophet on a bad day. Let's talk straight about how we organize to stop this pox-and-pestilence thing."

Across several thousand kilometers, Hanny Lennart's stare drilled into his. She was a gaunt and sallow blonde, incongruously wearing a gilt-embroidered tunic. "You are the one acting the fool, Freeman van Rijn," she said. "I tell you quite plainly, the Home Companies will not oppose the Garver bill. And let me make a suggestion for your own good. The popular mood being what it is, you would be most ill-advised to turn your above-ground lobbyists and your under-cover bribe artists loose against it. They would be bound to fail, and you would gain nothing except ill will."

"But—*Hel en verdoeming!* Can't you see what this will bring? If the unions get that kind of voice in management, it won't be the camel's nose in our tent. No, by damn, it will be the camel's bad breath and sandy footprints, and soon comes in the rest of him and you guess what he will do."

"Your fears are exaggerated," Lennart said. "They always have been."

"Never. Everything I warned against has been happening, year by year, clomp, clomp, clomp. Listen. A union is a profit-making organization same as a company, no matter how much wind it breaks about the siblinghood of workers. Hokay, no harm in that, as long as it stays honest greedy. But these days the unions are political organizations as well, tied in with government like Siamese twin octopuses.

11

You let them steer those funds, and you are letting government itself into your business."

"That can be reciprocal," Lennart declared. "Frankly—speaking personally for a moment, not as a voice of the Home Companies—frankly, I think your view of government as a natural enemy of intelligent life, I think it belongs back in the Mesozoic era. If you want a clear-cut example of what it can lead to, look out beyond the Solar System; see what the Seven do, routinely, brutally, on world after world. Or don't you care?"

"The Seven themselves don't want open competition—"

"Freeman van Rijn, we are both busy. I've done you the courtesy of making this direct call, to tell you not to waste your efforts trying to persuade the Home Companies to oppose the Garver bill, so you may know we mean it. We're quite content to see the law pass; and we feel reasonably sure it will, in spite of anything you and your kind can do. Now shall you and I end this argument and get back to our proper concerns?"

Van Rijn turned puce. He gobbled a few words which she took for assent. "Goodbye, then," she said, and switched off. The vacant screen hummed.

After a minute, Falkayn approached him. "Uh, that seemed like bad news," he ventured.

Van Rijn slowly lessened his resemblance to a corked volcano. "Wicked news," he mumbled. "Unrighteous news. Nasty, sneaking, slimy news. We will pretend it was never spewed out."

Coya came to stand beside his chair and brush a hand across his mane. "No, talk about it, Gunung Tuan," she said quietly. "You'll feel better."

Between oaths and less comprehensible phrases in various languages, van Rijn conveyed his tidings. Edward Garver, Lunograd delegate in Parliament, had introduced a bill to put the administration of private pension funds credited to employees who were citizens of the Commonwealth, under control of their unions. In the case of Solar Spice & Liquors, that meant principally the United Technicians. The Home Companies had decided not to oppose passage of the measure. Rather, their representatives would work with the appropriate committees to perfect it for mutual satisfaction. This

12

meant that the Polesotechnic League as a whole could take no action; the Home Companies and their satellites controlled too many votes on the Council. Besides, the Seven In Space would likely be indifferent, such a law affecting them only slightly. It was the independent outfits like van Rijn's, operating on an interstellar scale but with much of their market in the Commonwealth, which would find themselves hobbled as far as those monies were concerned.

"And when United Technicians say where we invest, United Technicians got that much extra power," the merchant finished. "Power not just in our affairs, but in finance, business, government —and government is getting more and more to be what runs the show. *Ach*, I do not envy the children you will have, you two."

"Don't you see any hope of heading this off?" Falkayn asked. "I know how often you've played skittles with whoever got underfoot. How about a public relations effort? Pressure on the right legislators; logrolling, oh, every trick you know so well . . ."

"I think no chance, with the big five against us," van Rijn said heavily. "Maybe I am wrong. But . . . *ja, ja,* I am thirty years your senior, Davy boy, and even if I got long-life chromosomes and lots of good antisenescence treatment, still, in the end a fellow gets tired. I will not do much."

He shook himself. "But hoy, what fumblydiddles is this I am making? We are supposed to have a happy evening and get drunk, before Coya ships out with your team and finds me lots of lovely new profits." He surged to his feet. "We need more drink here! Mars-dry we are. Where is that gluefoot butle ? More beer, I say! More akvavit! More everything, by damn!"

Y minus 7.

The sun Elena was a dwarf, but the nearness of its planet Valya made its disc stand big and red-orange in an indigo heaven. At midmorning it would not set for almost forty hours. The ocean sheened calm as a lake. Land rolled away from it under a russet cover of shrubs and turf. Tiny, glittery flyers which were not insects rode a warm, faintly iron-tangy breeze.

Outside the headquarters building of the scientific base, Eric Tamarin-Asmundsen spoke his anger and his intent to the commander, Anna Karagatzis. Beside them, long-limbed, spindly, blue-furred, head like a teardrop with antennae, crouched the native they called Charlie.

"I tell you, you can do nothing there but waste your time," the woman said. "Do you think I haven't gone from protests to pleas to threats? And Wyler laughed at me—till he grew irritated and threatened me in turn if I didn't stop pestering him."

"I didn't know that!" Eric stiffened. Blood heated his face. He tried to calm himself. "A bluff. What would they dare do to any of us? What could they?"

"I'm not sure," Karagatzis sighed. "But I've been to their camp and seen how well armed they are. And we, what are we but a community of researchers and support personnel who've never been shot at in their lives? Stellar's men can do anything they want. And we're outside every civilized jurisdiction."

"Are we? The Commonwealth claims a right to punish misdeeds by its citizens wherever they are, not?"

"True. But I suspect many, perhaps all of this group have different citizenship. Besides, we'd get no police investigation here, across more than two hundred light-years."

"Hermes isn't so far."

Karagatzis gave him a probing look. He was large. His weather-browned features seemed older than his twenty-one standard years: broad, Roman-nosed, square-jawed, hazel-eyed, ordinarily rather pleasantly ugly but now taut with wrath. In the style of men on his home planet as well as Earth, he went beardless and cropped his black locks above the ears. His garb was plain coverall and boots; however, a shoulder patch bore the insigne of his ducal family.

"What could Hermes do?" Karagatzis wondered. "What would it? Valya is nothing to your people, I'm sure."

"Stellar Metals trades with us," he reminded her. "I don't think Wyler's bosses would thank him for provoking a good trading partner."

"Would one more set of outrages on one more backward world really annoy anybody? If you were back there, if you'd never served here, and heard the story, would you care that much? Be honest with yourself.''

He drew breath. "Freelady, I am here. I must try. Not?''

"Well . . ." She reached a decision. "Very well, Lord Eric,'' she said carefully, addressing him as if she too had been born to the dialect of Anglic which they spoke on Hermes. "You may go and see if your influence can help the situation. Don't bluster, though. Don't commit us to something reckless. And don't make any promises to natives.'' Pain broke through her shell. "It's already hurt too much, having them come bewildered to us when they'd thought humans were their friends, and . . . and having to admit we can do zero.''

Eric cast a glance down at Charlie. The autochthon had sought him out on his return. They had gotten acquainted when the Hermetian was doing field work in the mountains from which Charlie had since become a refugee. Taken aback, he could merely say, "I haven't built up this lad's hopes on purpose, Freelady.''

Karagatzis gave him a bleak smile. "You haven't mine, at least.''

"I oughtn't be gone long,'' Eric said. "Wish me luck. Goodbye.'' He strode quickly from her, Charlie beside him.

A few persons hailed them as they went. The greetings were not cheerful. Directly or indirectly, the invasion jarred on everybody's projects. More to the point, maybe, was the fact that these workers liked the Valyans. It was hard to stand helpless while the mountain folk were being robbed.

Helpless? he thought. *We'll see about that.* At the same time, the back of his mind told him that this had been going on for weeks. If it was possible to curb Stellar, wouldn't someone already have acted?

He and his partners had been on a different continent, mainly to observe dance rituals. Everywhere on the planet, choreography was an intimate, intricate part of life. To minimize the effect of their presence, they had parked their car well away from the site. The risk in thus cutting themselves off from radio contact had not seemed worth worrying about. But then he came back to a woe that he might have been able to prevent. . . .

Outside the base stood half a dozen knockdown shelters, their plastic garish against the soft reds and browns of vegetation. Karagatzis had told Eric how the Stellar Metals men had chased the few earlier independent gold miners—whose activities had been harmless, as small as their scale was—out of the mountains along with every native who resisted. The victims were waiting for the next supply ship to give them transportation.

Of the several men whom he saw sitting idle and embittered, one rose and approached him. Eric had met him before, Leandro Mendoza. "Hello, Freeman Tamarin-Asmundsen," he said without smiling.

For a split second, in his preoccupation, the Hermetian was startled. Who? Surnames were not ordinarily used in conversation with his class; he was "Lord Eric" when addressed formally, otherwise plain "Eric" or, to close comrades, "Gunner." He remembered that Mendoza was using Earth-style Anglic, and swore at himself. "Hail," he said as he came to a reluctant halt.

"Been away, have you?" Mendoza asked. "Just got the news, eh?"

"Yes. If you'll excuse me, I'm in haste."

"To see Sheldon Wyler? What do you think you can do?"

"I'll find out."

"Be careful you don't find out the hard way. We did."

"Uh, yes, I heard his razzos ordered you off your own digs, with guns to back them up. Where's your equipment?"

"Sold. No choice. We each had a nova's worth of investment in it, and not yet enough earned to pay for shipping it elsewhere. He bought us out at a price that leaves us only half ruined."

Eric scowled. "Was that wise? Haven't you compromised your case when you bring it to court? You will sue, of course."

Mendoza rattled forth a laugh. "In a Commonwealth court? If Stellar itself hasn't bought the judge, another company will have; and they swap favors. Our plea would be thrown out before we'd finished making it."

"I meant the Polesotechnic League. Its ethics tribunal."

"Are you joking?" After a few breaths, Mendoza added, "Well, run along if you want to. I appreciate your good intentions." Head drooping, he turned away.

Eric stalked on. "What did your other self say?" Charlie asked—a rough translation of his trilled question. Psychologists were still trying to understand the concept of you-and-me which lay beneath the upland language. And now, Eric thought, the whole upland culture was in danger of disruption by the operations in its country.

His own vocabulary was meager, the result of sessions with an inductive educator. "He is among those who were taking gold before the newcomers drove them off," he explained.

"Yes, ourselves know himselves well. They paid generously in tools and cloths for the right to dig a few holes. The newcomers pay nothing. What is much worse, they scatter the woods-cattle."

"The man who spoke to me did not expect my success."

"Do you?"

Eric didn't respond.

At the garage, he chose a car and motioned Charlie in ahead of him. The Valyan's antennae quivered. He had never flown before. Yet when the vehicle rose on silent negagravity, he regarded the land through the bubble canopy and said, "I can guide you. Steer yonder." He pointed north of east.

A human with a corresponding background could not have interpreted an aerial view so fast the first time, Eric thought. He had come here about a year ago prepared to feel a little patronizingly amicable toward beings whose most advanced society was in a bronze age. He had progressed to admiring them. Technologically they had nothing to teach a starfaring species. However, he wondered what eventual influence might come from their arts and their philosophies.

If their societies survived. The foundations of existence are often gruesomely vulnerable. As an immediate example, the uplanders got most of their food from leaf-eating beasts, not wild, not tame, but something which neither of those words quite fitted. By filling the choicest territory with seeking, gouging, roaring machines, the Stellar Metals expedition broke up the herds: and thus became akin to a plague of locusts on ancient Earth.

By all three blundering Fates, jagged through Eric, *why does gold have to be an important industrial resource?* The mature part of him said dryly: *Its conductivity, malleability, and relative chemical inertness.* He protested: *Why does an outsider corporation have to come plundering it here, when they could go to thousands of worlds that are barren?* The response came: *A rich deposit was noticed by a planetologist, and word got out, and a minor gold rush started, which the corporation heard about. The prospecting had already been done; and on Valya men need no expensive, time-consuming life support apparatus.*

Then why did the lode have to occur right where it is? That question had no answer.

The car flew rapidly over the coastal plain. Land wrinkled upward, turned into a range clad in trees. An ugly bare patch hove in view beside a lake. Charlie pointed, Eric descended.

On the ground, a pair of guards hurried to meet him as he emerged, a human and a Merseian. "What're you doing here?" the man snapped. "This is a no trespassing zone."

Eric bristled. "Who gave you property rights?"

"Never mind. We have them and we enforce them. Go."

"I want to see Sheldon Wyler."

"He's seen enough of you slopheads." The guard dropped hand to the blaster holstered at his waist. "Go, or do we have to get tough?"

"I don't believe he'd appreciate your assaulting the heir presumptive to the throne of Hermes," Eric said.

The mercenaries could not quite hide nervousness. The Grand Duchy was not many light-years hence, and it did possess a miniature navy. "All right, come along," said the human at length.

Crossing the dusty ground, Eric saw few workers. Most of them were out raping the forest. Stellar was not content to pick at veins and sift streams. It ripped the quartz from whole mountainsides, passed it through a mobile extractor, and left heaps of poisonous slag; it sent whole rivers through hydraulic separators, no matter how much swimming life was destroyed.

Inside a prefab cabin was a monastic office. Wyler sat behind the desk. He was bulky and heavy-featured, with a walrus mustache, and at first he was unexpectedly mild of manner. Dismissing the guards, he invited, "Have a chair. Smoke? These cigars are Earth-grown tobacco." Eric shook his head and lowered himself. "So you're going to be Grand Duke someday," Wyler continued. "I thought that job was elective."

"It is, but the eldest child is normally chosen."

"How come you're being a scientist here, then?"

"Preparation. A Grand Duke deals with nonhumans too. Uh, xenological experience—" Eric's voice trailed off. *Damn! The illwreaker's already put me on the defensive.*

"So you don't really speak for your world?"

"No, but—no—Well, I write home. In time I'll be going home."

Wyler nodded. "Sure, we'd like you to have a good opinion of us. How about hearing our side of the case?"

Eric leaned forward, fists on knees. "Freelady Karagatzis has, uh, told me what you told her. I know how you got your 'charter for exploration and development.' I know you claim real property is not a local institution, thus you violate no rights. And you say you'll be done in a year or two, pack up and leave. Yes. You needn't repeat to me."

"Then maybe you needn't repeat what your leader said."

"But care you not what you're *doing*?"

Wyler shrugged. "Every time a spaceship lands on a new planet, you get consequences. We knew nobody had objected to mining by free lances, though they had no charter—no legal standing. I was ready to bargain about compensation for the jumpies . . . the natives. But for that, I'd need the help of your experts. What I got was goddamn obstructionism."

"Yes, for there's no way to compensate for ruining a country. Argh, why go on?" Eric snarled. "You never cared. From the beginning, you intended being a gang of looters."

"That's for the courts to decide, wouldn't you say? Not that they'd try a suit, when no serious injury can be shown." Wyler put elbows on desk and bridged his fingers. "Frankly, you disappoint me. I'd hoped you wouldn't go through the same stale chatter. I can claim to be doing good too, you know. Industry needs gold. You'd put the convenience of a few thousand goddamn savages against the needs of billions of civilized beings."

"I—I— Very well." Eric lifted his head. "Let's talk plainly. You've made an enemy of me, and I have influence on Hermes. Want you to keep things that way, or not?"

"Naturally, Stellar Metals wants to be friends, if you'll allow. But as for your threat—I admit I'm no expert on your people. But I do seem to remember they've got their own discontented class. Will they

19

really want to take on the troubles of a bunch of goddamn outsiders, long after these operations are over and done with? I doubt it. I think your mother has more sense.''

In the end, Eric went bootless back to his car. It was the first absolute defeat he had ever known. As Karagatzis had warned, telling Charlie made it doubly painful.

Y minus 5.

That moon of Babur which humans had dubbed Ayisha was of approximately Lunar size. From a viewport in one of the colony domes, Benoni Strang looked out at dimly lit stone, ashen and crater-pocked. The sky was black and stars shone unwinking through airlessness. The planet hung gibbous, a great amber shield emblazoned with bands of cloud whose whiteness was softened by tints of ocher and cinnabar. Rearing above the near horizon, a skeletal test-pad support for spacecraft seemed like a siege tower raised against the universe.

Within the domes were more than warmth, Earth-normal weight, air that a man dared breathe. Strang stood on velvety grass, among flowering bushes. Behind him the park held a ball court, a swimming pool, fountains, tables where you could sit to dine on delicate food and drink choice wines. Elsewhere in the base were pleasure facilities of different kinds, ranging from a handicraft shop and an amateur theater to vices as elaborate as any in the known worlds. Folk here did not only need distraction from exacting work. They needed offsets for the fact that they would spend goodly portions of their lives on Ayisha and Babur and in ambient space; that they got no leaves of absence, were allowed no visitors, and had their outgoing mail censored. Those who eventually could endure it no longer, even with high pay accumulating at home, must submit to memory wipe before departing. The agreement was part of their contract, which colony police stood ready to enforce.

Strang's mind returned to early years, the toil and peril and austerity when men first carved for themselves a foothold in this waste; and he almost regretted them. He had been young then.

20

Though I was never especially merry as the young are supposed to be, he thought. *I was always too driven.*

"What're you brooding about?" asked Emma Reinhardt.

He turned his head and regarded her. She was a handsome woman from Germania, an assistant engineer, who might well become his next mistress; they had lately been much in each other's company.

"Oh," he said, "I was just thinking how far we've come since we began here, and what's left to do."

"Do you ever think about something besides your . . . your mission?" she asked.

"It's always demanded everything I had to give," he admitted.

She studied him in her turn. He was of medium height and slim, graceful of movement, his face rectangular in outline and evenly shaped, his hair and mustache sleek brown, his eyes gray-blue. In this leisure hour he wore an elegantly tailored slacksuit. "I sometimes wonder what'll become of you when this project is finished," she murmured.

"That won't be for quite a while," he said. "I'm presently estimating six standard years before we can make our first major move."

"Unless you're surprised."

"Yes, the unpredictable is practically the inevitable. Well, I trust that what we've built will be sound enough that it can adjust—and act."

"You misunderstand me," she said. "Of course you've got a lot of leadership ahead of you yet. But eventually matters will be out of your hands. Or at least many other hands will be there too. Then what?"

"Then, or actually before then, I'm going home."

"To Hermes?"

He nodded. "Yes. In a way, for me, this whole undertaking has been a means to that end. I've told you what I suffered there."

"Frankly, it hasn't seemed very terrible to me," she said. "So you were a Traver born, you couldn't vote, the aristocrats owned all the desirable land, and— Well, no doubt an ambitious boy felt frustrated. But you got offplanet, didn't you, and made your own career. Nobody tried to prevent you."

21

"What about those I left behind?"

"Yes, what about them? Are they really badly off?"

"They're underlings! Never mind how easy the conditions may seem, they're underlings. They've no say whatsoever in the public affairs of their planet. And the Kindred have no interest in progress, in development, in anything but hanging onto their precious feudal privileges. I tell you, the whole rotten system should have been blasted away a century ago. No, it should have been aborted at the start—" Strang curbed himself. "But you can't understand. You haven't experienced it."

Emma Reinhardt shivered a bit. She had glimpsed the fanatic.

Y minus 1.

Leonardo Rigassi, spaceship captain from Earth, was the man who tracked down the world for which several crews were searching. Astonished, he found that others were present before him. They called it Mirkheim.

Thereafter came the year which God, or destiny, or chance had ordained.

I

Under a full moon, Delfinburg was making its slow way over the Philippine Sea. A thousand colors flared and jumped, voices resounded, flesh jostled flesh through the streets of the pleasure district. There were those who sought quieter recreation. Among places for them was the roof garden of Gondwana House. At the starboard edge of a leading pontoon, it offered a sweeping overlook of the ocean city on one side, of the ocean itself on another. By day the waters were often crowded with boats, but usually after dark you saw only the running lights of a few patrolling fish herders and, in tropical climes, pumpships urging minerals up from the bottom to keep the plankton beds nourished. They resembled fireflies that had wandered far from land.

The garden's own fluoros were dimmed tonight and the live orchestra muted. It played dance music of the Classical Revival, waltzes, mazurkas, tangos leading couples to hold each other close and glide softly. Flowers and shrubs surrounded the floor, setting fragrances of rose, jasmine, aurelia, livewell adrift on the mild air. Stars overhead seemed almost near enough to touch.

"I wish this could go on forever," Coya Falkayn murmured.

Her husband attempted a chuckle. "No, you don't, sweetheart. I never knew a girl who has less tolerance of monotony than you, or more talent for driving it off."

"Oh, I wish a lot of things would be eternal—but concurrently, you understand," she said. He could hear how she, too, strove for lightness. "Life should be a Cantorian aleph-one. An infinity of infinities to you, my dear mathematical hobblewit."

Instead, he thought, *we move through a single space-time on our single tracks, for a hundred years or thereabouts if we have the best*

23

antisenescence régimes available to us—or less, of course, if something happens to chop a particular world line short. I don't mind my own mortality too much, Coya; but how I resent yours!

"Well," he told her, "I used to daydream about an infinity of women, all beautiful and accessible. But I found that you were plenty, and then some." He bent his head to lay his cheek along hers. Through a hint of perfume he drew in the clean odor of her hair. "Now come on, lass. Since we have to do things sequentially, let's concentrate on dancing."

She nodded. Though her movements continued deft, he felt no easing of the tension that had risen in her, and her fingers gripped his needlessly hard.

Therefore, at the end of the number he suggested, "Suppose we drink the next one out," and led her to an offside bar. When a champagne glass was in her hand, she said in turn, "I'd like to watch the sea for a while."

They found a private place by the outer rail. Vine-heavy trellises screened them from the dance floor and from any other pairs who might also have sought the peace that was here. Luna stood on the starboard quarter, casting a broad track and making the nearer wave crests sparkle; elsewhere the water was like fluid obsidian. Leaves shone wan among shadows. The deck underfoot carried a pulse of engines through feet and bones, as quiet as the pulse of blood in the heart, and a *hush-hush-hush* around the bows barely reached a keen hearing. A breeze carried the least touch of night chill.

Falkayn put forth his free hand to lift Coya's chin toward him. He smiled on the left side of his face. "Don't worry about me," he said. "You never did before."

"Oh, I did when I was a youngster," she answered. "I'd hear about the latest adventure of the fabulous *Muddlin' Through* team and go icy at the thought of what might have happened to you."

"I didn't notice you fretting after you'd joined us; and we hit a few turbulences then."

"That's it. I was there. Either we had nothing to fear or we were too busy to be frightened. I didn't have to stay home wondering if I'd ever see you again."

Her gaze went from his, skyward, until it reached the ghost-road

24

of the Milky Way and came to rest on a white star within. "Each night I'll look at Deneb and wonder," she said.

"May I remind you," he answered as genially as he was able, "in that general neighborhood, besides Babur and Mirkheim, is Hermes? If I came from there once, I'll surely repeat."

"But if war does break out—"

"Why, my citizenship is still Hermetian, not Commonwealth. And I'm on a straightforward mission of inquiry and unofficial diplomacy, nothing else. The Baburites may not be the most accommodating race in the universe, but they're rational. They won't want to make enemies needlessly."

"If your task is that simple and safe, why must *you* go?"

Falkayn sighed. "You know why. Experience. For over thirty years, I've been dealing with nonhumans; and Adzel, Chee, and I make a damned efficient unit." He grinned anew. "Modesty is the second most overrated virtue in the canon. The first is sincerity, in case you're interested. But I'm dead serious about this. Gunung Tuan was right when he asked us to go. We'll have a better chance than anybody else of accomplishing something useful, or at least of bringing back some definite information. And you know all this, darling. If you wanted to raise objections, why wait till our last evening?"

She bit her lip. "I'm sorry. I thought I could keep my fears from showing . . . till you were gone."

"Look, I was being honest, too, when I said bad words on getting the job precisely when you can't come. I really meant it when I wished aloud you could. Would I do that if I anticipated any risk worth fussing about? The biggest unknown in the equation is simply how long we may be gone."

She nodded slowly. They had both stopped space roving when their Juanita was born, because it meant indefinite absences from Earth. An older, more hedonistic, less settled generation than Coya's had bred enough neurotics that she felt, and made her husband feel, children needed and deserved a solid home. And now she had another on the way.

"I still don't see why it has to be you," she said in a last hint of mutiny. "After three years in the Solar System—"

25

"You're a bit rusty, yes," he finished for her. "But you only had five years of trade pioneering with us. I had more than twenty. The tricks of the trade are practically stamped on my genes. When the old man asked, I couldn't well refuse."

Not when it was the very world of Mirkheim which caused me to betray his trust in me, eighteen years ago, went through his mind. *I've been forgiven, I'm van Rijn's crown prince, but I've never quite forgiven myself, and here is a chance to make amends.*

Coya knew what he was thinking. She raised her head. "Aye, aye, sir. I apologize. If we do get a war, a lot of women will be much worse off than I am."

"Right," he replied soberly. "It's barely possible that my gang can contribute a smidgen toward keeping the peace."

"Meanwhile we have hours and hours left." She lifted her glass in the moonlight. Music rollicked forth afresh. "Our first duty is to this excellent champagne, wouldn't you say?"

"That's my girl talking." Falkayn smiled back at her. The rims clinked together.

When the two human members of the *Muddlin' Through* team retired, the two nonhumans went their separate ways. Chee Lan signed on as the xenobiologist of another trade pioneer crew. She didn't feel ready to settle down yet. Besides, she wanted to become indecently wealthy off her commissions, in order to indulge her every whim when at last she returned to that planet which astronomy designates as O_2 Eridani A II and the Anglic language calls Cynthia. She happened to be on Earth when the Mirkheim crisis developed, and this was probably what had crystallized Nicholas van Rijn's idea of reviving the threesome—though he must have consulted his company's registry first in hopes of learning that he could indeed contact her immediately.

"What?" she had spat when he phoned her at her lodge. "Me? To spy and wheedle—No, shut up, I realize you'll call it 'gathering intelligence' and 'attempting negotiations.' You waste syllables like a drunken lexicographer." She arched her back. "Do you seriously propose sending us to Babur . . . in the middle of a possible war?

Those barrels of butter you eat every day must have gone to your head.''

Van Rijn's image in the screen rolled eyes piously in the general direction of heaven. "Do not get excited, little fluffcat," urged his most unctuous voice. "Think on traveling once more with your closest friends. Think on helping prevent or stop trouble what gets people killed and maybe cuts into profits. Think on the glory you can win by a daring exploitation, to smear off on your children. Think—''

''I'll think on what good hard cash you offer,'' Chee interrupted. ''Name a figure.''

Van Rijn spread his hands in a gesture of horror. "You speak so crass in this terrible matter? What are you, anyways?''

''We know what I am. Now let's decide my price.'' Chee made herself comfortable on a cushion. In lieu of alcoholic refreshment, which did not affect her nervous system, she put a mildly narcotic cigarette in an interminable ivory holder and kindled it. This was going to take a while.

With lamentation by him and scorn by her and much enjoyment on both sides, the fee was haggled out for a service which might be dangerous and certainly would not yield a monetary return. She insisted that Adzel be paid the same. Left to himself, the Wodenite was too diffident, and looking out for the big bumbler's interests could count as her good deed for the month. Van Rijn admitted what she had suspected, that Adzel had been recruited by a shameless appeal to his sense of duty.

He was still in the Andes Mountains, and did not intend to leave until the eve of departure. When that time came, Chee found from an update of the registry that he had taken a room in a cheap hotel in Terraport. She recognized its name from former days; it was the kind which had no facilities for approximating the home environment of a nonhuman. Well, she thought, Adzel didn't actually need two and a half standard gravities, thick hot air, the blinding light of an F5 sun, and whatever other delights existed on the world men knew as Woden. He had managed without during the years aboard *Muddlin' Through*, not to speak of the Buddhist monastery where he had spent

27

the past three as a lay brother. *No doubt he figures to give the money he's saving to the poor, or some cause similarly grubby,* she guessed, then caught a cab to the nearest airport and the next transoceanic flight from there.

En route, she drew stares. An extraterrestrial fellow passenger was still rather a rarity on Earth—even from Cynthia, whose most advanced culture was well into the spacefaring stage. She was used to that, and content to let people learn what a truly graceful species looked like. They saw a small being, ninety centimeters in length plus a bushy tail which added half again as much. Her legs were long in proportion, ending in five prehensile toes on each foot; her arms were equally long, the hands six-fingered. Her round head bore huge emerald eyes, pointed ears, a short muzzle with a broad nose, a delicate mouth with exceedingly sharp teeth framed in wiry whiskers. Silky fur covered her body save for the bare gray skin of hands and feet; it was pure white except where it formed a blue-gray mask around her eyes. She had once heard herself compared to a cross between an Angora cat, a monkey, a squirrel, and a raccoon, and idly wondered which of these were supposed to be on what side of the family. The speculation was natural, since she came of a bisexual, viviparous race like Adzel—homeothermic like his, too, though neither of them was strictly a mammal.

A little boy cried, "Ooh, kitty!" and wanted to pet her. She glanced from her printout of the London *Times* and said sweetly to the mother, "Why don't you eat your young?" Thereafter she was left in peace.

Arriving, she hailed another cab and gave it the hotel's address. The time here was after sundown and Adzel should be in. She hoped he wasn't meditating too deeply to notice a buzz at his door. Hearing the dry rustle of scales across scales, she knew he was uncoiling and about to admit her. Good. She'd be glad to see the old oaf again, she supposed.

The door opened. She looked up, and up. Adzel's head was more than two meters off the floor, on the top of a thick, serpentine neck and a horse-bulky torso which sprouted two correspondingly powerful arms with four-fingered hands. Rearward, his centauroid body stretched four and a half meters, including the crocodilian tail. His

28

head was likewise faintly suggestive of a reptile: long snout, rubbery-lipped mouth, omnivore's teeth that had among them some alarming fangs, large amber-colored eyes protected by jutting brow ridges, bony ears. A serration of triangular plates ran from the top of his skull and down his spine to its end. One behind the torso had been surgically removed in order that comrades might safely ride on him. Scales shimmered over the whole frame, dark green above shading to gold on the belly.

"Chee Lan!" he boomed in Anglic. "What a splendid surprise. Come in, my dear, come in." Four cloven hoofs carrying a ton of mass made a drum-thunder as he moved aside for her. "I did not expect to greet you before we meet at the ship tomorrow," he went on. "I thought it best if I—"

"We shouldn't need much preliminary checkout, we three and Muddlehead," she agreed.

"—if I attempted—"

"Still, I figured we'd do well to compare notes in advance. You couldn't get Davy loose from his family with a crowbar before rendezvous time, but you and I don't have any current infatuations."

"I am attempting to—"

"Do you?"

"What? I am attempting to brief myself on the current situation." Adzel gestured at the room's video. A man was speaking:

"—review the background of the crisis. It goes back well beyond the discovery of Mirkheim this past year. In fact, that was a rediscovery. For about fifteen years before, the Supermetals consortium were in possession of the planet, mining its riches without ever letting it be known where the treasure they had to sell came from. They tried to give the impression that their source was a secret manufacturing process, beyond the reach of any known technology. This trick succeeded to a degree. But eventually various scientists concluded it was far more likely that the supermetals had been produced and concentrated by nature—"

"You've heard that!" Chee jerked her tail at the screen.

"Yes, of course, but I have hopes he will give me a comprehensive précis of current events," Adzel said. "Remember, for three years I have heard no newscast, read no secular literature besides planetological journals.'' Chee was glad to learn that he had not neglected his profession. It probably wouldn't be needed on this trip; but you were never sure, and in any event, his keeping abreast of scientific developments showed that he had not been completely spun off the wheel of his particular karma. ''We got occasional visitors,'' the dragon continued, ''but I avoided them as much as possible, fearing that my appearance might distract them from the serenity of the surroundings.''

''Seeing your version of the lotus position certainly would,'' Chee snapped. ''Listen, I can brief you better and faster than that klong.''

''Would you like a spot of tea?'' Adzel asked, pointing to a five-liter thermos. ''I had it brewed at the place where I got supper. Here, this ashtray is clean.'' He set it on the floor and poured it full for Chee to lap. He himself hoisted the container to his mouth.

Meanwhile the lecturer skimmed over basic physics.

From the actinide series onward, the periodic table of the elements holds nothing but radioactives. In the biggest atoms, the mutual repulsion of protons is bound to overcome attractive forces within the nucleus. Beyond uranium, the rates of disintegration become great enough that early researchers on Earth found no such materials in nature. They had to produce neptunium and plutonium artificially. Later it was shown that micro-micro amounts of these two do occur in the rocks. But their presence is a mere technicality. Virtually all that there was in the beginning has vanished, broken down into simpler nuclei. And beyond plutonium, half-lives are generally so short that the most powerful and elaborate apparatus can barely make a quantity sufficient to register on ultrasensitive instruments; then the product is gone.

Yet theory indicated that an ''island of stability'' should exist, beginning at atomic number 114 and ending at 122: nine elements, most of whose isotopes are only weakly radioactive. To manufacture infinitesimal amounts of these was a laboratory triumph. Gigantic energy was required to fuse that many particles. Theory went on to hint at physical and chemical properties, whether of the materials themselves or of solid compounds of those that were volatile in isolation. These were an engineer's dream, in catalysts, conductors, components of alloys with supreme strength. Nobody saw any road to the realization of that dream . . . until a sudden thought occurred.

(It came first to David Falkayn, eighteen years ago. But the speaker was unaware of that. He simply recited the reasoning of later thinkers.)

We believe all matter began as a chaos of hydrogen, the smallest atom. Some of it was fused in the primordial fireball to form helium; more of this process happened later, in the enormous heat and pressure at the hearts of stars which condensed from that gas. And there the higher elements were built, step by step as atoms interacted. Scattering mass in their solar winds, or as dying red giants, or as novae and supernovae, the early generations of stars enriched with such nuclei the interstellar medium from which later generations of suns and planets would form. The carbon in our proteins, the calcium in our bones, the oxygen we breathe were forged in those ancient furnaces.

Had no extremely big stars ever formed, the series would have ended with iron. It is at the bottom of the energy curve; to join together still more protons and neutrons lies beyond the power of any steadily burning sun. But the monster stars do not die peacefully. They become supernovae, briefly shining on a scale comparable to an entire galaxy. In that moment of unimaginable violence, reactions otherwise impossible take place; and copper, gold, uranium, every element above iron comes into being, and is blown into space to enter the stuff of new stars, new worlds.

Among the substances thus created are the supermetals of the island of stability. Being as hard to make as they are, they occur only in a tiny proportion, so tiny that at first none were found in nature, not even after man broke free of the Solar System and began exploring his corner of the galaxy. Yet they should be there. The problem was to locate a measurable concentration of them.

Suppose a giant star had a giant planet, sufficiently massive that its core would survive the explosion. That was not impossible, though theory said it was improbable. The bursting sun would cast a torrent of elements across the core. Those with low volatility should condense, or even plate out. True, they would be a minute fraction of the total which the supernova vomited into space; but that fraction should equal billions of tons of valuable metals, and a lesser amount of immensely more precious supermetals. Given their comparatively slight radioactivity, a worthwhile proportion of the supermetals ought to last for several million years. . . .

"—evidently its first discoverers had run a mathematical analysis on a computer of the highest capabilities," the speaker said. "By using available data on present star distributions and orbits in this galactic vicinity, plus similar data for interstellar gas and dust, magnetic fields, et cetera, a sophisticated program could calculate the probability of there having been a supernova with a superjovian companion within the appropriate span of time and space, and show roughly where its remnants ought to be in this epoch. More accurately, the program computed out a space-time distribution of probabilities, which in turn yielded an optimal search pattern. The odds looked best in the general direction of Deneb, in a region at about half its distance.

"If scientists a year or two ago could make this deduction, then it was reasonable to believe that the Supermetals combine had made it earlier. Hence the treasure hoard *must* exist. Energetic seeking must eventually find it. Ships went eagerly forth.

"Captain Leonardo Rigassi of the European Exploratory Foundation succeeded.

"The secret was out. The beings who spoke for Supermetals now told quite openly how they had been working the planet, which they called Mirkheim. They had tried to get legal ownership. Immediately a stinging swarm of questions arose. First and fiercest is the question of who has jurisdiction, what government can rightly rule. The Supermetals operators have no government behind them, they are loners, and—"

"Will you shut that blatbox off?" Chee Lan demanded. "You can't help already knowing everything it can conceivably say."

"Forgive me, but that is a rather unhumble attitude," Adzel reproached her. Nevertheless he reached over and tapped the switchplate. For a moment, silence filled the shabby room.

Likewise did his bulk. In a gesture familiar of old, he settled down on the floor and curled the end of his tail to make a comfortable rest for Chee. She accepted it, taking her ashtray of tea along.

"For example," he said, "I was relieved to find that we—you, Davy, and I—have not yet been publicly identified as the original discoverers of Mirkheim, indeed, the bestowers of the name. Notoriety would be most distressing, would it not?"

"Oh, I've toyed with notions for cashing in on it, should that happen," Chee replied. "But with matters as crazily half-balanced as they are—yeh, no doubt it's just as well the Supermetals people have kept faith. I don't know how much longer they will. They've no obvious reason left to preserve our anonymity. I suppose they're doing it out of habit—not to give anything, not even a reminiscence, to the slimespawn who want to pluck them of their treasure."

"And their hopes," Adzel said low. "Do you think they can get a fair compensation?"

"From whichever government makes its claim stick, the Commonwealth or Babur? Ho, ho, ho. Commonwealth control means control by corporations out for nothing but a bonanza, and by politicians and bureaucrats who hate the Supermetals Company because it never truckled to them. Baburite possession means—who knows? Except that I can't imagine Babur giving two toots on a flute for the rights of a few oxygen breathers."

"Do you seriously believe Babur might get Mirkheim? The basis of its claim, the 'sphere of interest' principle, sounds preposterous."

"No more absurd than the Commonwealth's 'right of discovery.' I daresay a good brisk war will decide."

"Would they actually fight over a . . . a wretched lump of alloy?" Adzel asked, appalled.

"My friend, they'll have trouble avoiding a war, unless Babur is bluffing, which I doubt." Chee drew breath. It smelled of tea and of the Wodenite's warm, slightly acrid body odor. "You do understand why van Rijn is sending us there, don't you? Mainly for information—any information whatever, so he can plan what to do. Right now, everything is a-rattle. The Commonwealth government is blundering blind the same as everyone else, not knowing what to expect of creatures as alien as the Baburites. But also, if we possibly can, we

33

should try to make, or at least suggest, a bargain. They're in a position to harm quite a chunk of Solar Spice & Liquors' holdings, its trade; and they do have a grudge against us in particular."

"Why?"

"You don't know? Well, about thirty years back, they tried to muscle in on a business that Solar had in a stuff called bluejack, on a planet in their neighborhood. For them, it was more lucrative than for us. Still, our factor there didn't see why we should tamely accept what amounted to straight robbery. He euchred them out of their gains by a clever trick, and made sure they could get no benefit from returning. That was the first aggressive move Babur made in space. They seem to think they're ready for the real action now. And cosmos knows the Commonwealth is ill-prepared."

"And so we fare forth again, we three and our ship, like our young days come back," Adzel sighed, "except that this time our mission is not into the hopeful yonder."

II

Still below the horizon, Maia, sun of Hermes, made the tops of steeples and towers in Starfall shine as if gilded. When it rose out of Daybreak Bay, its light struck westward over the Palomino River and straight along Olympic Avenue to Pilgrim Hill. There the brightness lost itself among trees, gardens, and buildings, the gray stone mass of the Old Keep, the fluid lines and many-paned walls of the New Keep, the austere erectness of Signal Station. A beam went past an upper balcony on the New Keep, through the French doors beyond, and across the bed of Sandra Tamarin-Asmundsen.

She woke from dreams. "Pete, darling," she whispered, reaching for him. Her eyes opened and she remembered she was alone. For an instant, emptiness possessed her.

But the accident that claimed Peter Asmundsen (big, boisterous, strong but fundamentally gentle man) lay more than four years in the past. Time had eased pain, time and the work of being Grand Duchess, head of a planet whereon dwelt fifty million willful people. She sat up and made herself take pleasure in cool air and soft light.

As usual, her alarm was not quite ready for her. She turned it off, rose, and strode out onto the balcony. A breeze from the dew and flowerbeds below caressed her bare skin. Nobody else seemed to be about, though her vision swept from the hilltop, down across the city to the bay and the Auroral Ocean beyond. A nidifex flew past, flutter of colorful wings and trill of song.

After a minute Sandra went back inside, switched her phone to television reception, and commenced her daily half hour of exercises. She had more faith in them than in antisenescence, though in her mid-fifties she was duly taking those treatments. Her big body had changed little since youth. On the broad, high-cheekboned face were

35

not many wrinkles, those mostly crow's feet around the dark-browed green eyes. But her blond hair had gone silvery.

Automatically moving, she escaped boredom by holding her attention on an early newscast. The Mirkheim crisis came first.

"Rumors were widespread that Babur has issued a new declaration, a copy of which has reached Hermes. Spokesmen for the throne would neither confirm nor deny this, but promised a public statement soon.

"The basis of the rumor was the landing at Williams Field yesterday of a navy speedster known to have been stationed at Valya. I'll just give review to that situation. The Baburites have delivered their last three Anglic-language pronunciamentos to the primitive planet Valya, by a ship which has gone into orbit and radioed the message to the scientific outpost there, with a request that the content be distributed as widely as possible. So several governments, including ours, are keeping boats on the scene, and by agreement aren't allowing news services to do likewise. 'Tis the closest thing to contact that anybody has with that nonhuman race, and officials say they fear possible bad results of premature disclosures.''

The rumors were true, though the reality wasn't worth overmuch excitement. "The Autarchy of United Babur,'' whatever that meant, had simply reiterated its claim. Because Mirkheim was located so near, as interstellar distances went, and because the supermetals were of incalculable strategic importance, Babur could not and would not tolerate possession of that globe by any power which had demonstrated hostility to Babur's legitimate activity in space. The sole novelty was that this time these powers were bluntly identified, the Solar Commonwealth and the Polesotechnic League. At the urging of her advisors, Sandra had withheld publication of the note until a committee of xenologists could have examined it for new implications. She doubted they'd find any.

"Yesterday also we received a tape of an address by Prime Minister Lapierre of the Solar Commonwealth at a convention of the Justice Party. He maintained that his government is willing to negotiate, but that Babur thus far has made none of the normal preliminary moves, such as arranging for exchange of ambassadors. At the same time, he said, the Commonwealth will under no circumstances yield to what he called 'naked aggression.' Somberly, he admitted that Babur does appear to have great naval strength. He recalled the concentration of warcraft which human officers were invited to observe, shortly after a Baburite ship, with stunning insolence, radioed that first claim to Mirkheim from orbit around Earth. He said that, while information is far from complete, the signs are that Babur has somehow—unnoticed over a long period—built a fleet still larger than what it revealed. Nevertheless, Lapierre insisted, the Commonwealth will stand firm, and if necessary will take, quote, 'forceful measures.' ''

Sandra muttered an oath. This was ancient. The fastest hyperdrive vessel took worse than two weeks, Terrestrial calendar, to go from Earth's sun to Babur's, Mirkheim's, or Hermes'. Between any two of those systems out in this sector, travel time must still be reckoned in days. Societies could put themselves on collision courses for sheer lack of data. She wished bitterly that some faster-than-light equivalent of radio existed.

Although you could argue that because of isolation, the early colonists of Hermes had been free to develop a new kind of civilization which, on the whole, she found good. . . .

Not everybody did. The program gave a report, with visuals, of the latest Liberation Front rally. It had been held last night at a resort on the Longstrands. The intemperance of the orators and the size and enthusiasm of the crowd were worrying. If that many Travers would meet on a chilly seashore in person, how many more watched and cheered in their homes?

Items of less importance soon drove her to switch over to those memoranda which her staff had recorded for her while she slept. At once she slammed to full attention. Calisthenics forgotten, she crouched on the floor and stared at the image of her executive secretary.

"About midnight, a ship belonging to the Supermetals Company landed at Williams Field," his voice said. "The captain identified himself to the port authorities and got through to me at home. He urgently asked for a private interview with you, madame. I considered having you roused, but trust I did right in scheduling him for 0930, subject to your approval. Meanwhile, as a precaution, I had his crew ordered to stay on board their vessel.

"The commander's a Wodenite hight Nadi." Visuals showed the great shape striding among humans. "He heads the small defensive force which Supermetals maintains around Mirkheim. You'll belike recall how, having captured the ship of Leonardo Rigassi, the recent rediscoverer, Nadi soon ordered her released, because the secret was out and keeping prisoners would only brew ill will without much delaying the inevitable.

"Instead, he says, the outfit has decided to appeal to Hermes, that we establish a protectorate over Mirkheim. This is what he wants to discuss with you."

Sandra stiffened. *Isn't that a red-hot rivet dropped into my palm!* She forced herself to continue her gymnastics. They brought a measure of calm to which a cold shower added. She likewise took her time about braiding her hair and dressing. Her garments she made more formal than ordinarily, a gown whereon the only bright colors belonged to the Tamarin family shoulder patch. With leisured strides, she sought her breakfast room.

Her two younger children, the ones whom Pete had given her, were still abed. Eric was at the table, emptying his coffee cup in fierce draughts. The chamber was fragrant with cooking in the kitchen. The west wall was a vitryl pane whose view swept down that side of Pilgrim Hill, over the last buildings in Starfall, and on across intensely green farmland. Pale above the horizon floated the snow-peak of Cloudhelm.

Eric stood up at Sandra's entrance, as men did for women on Hermes. He was clad in crisp tunic and breeks, but looked as if he hadn't slept. Had he been out carousing? Her oldest son and probable heir was a steady enough fellow as a rule, but sometimes the blood of his father rose in him. *No*, she decided after scanning his features, *not this time*.

"Good morning, Mother," he blurted. "Listen, I heard about Nadi, I've been out and talked to him and his crew. . . . Will we grab the chance? It's going by almighty fast."

Sandra seated herself and tilted the coffeepot. "Come back down from the stratosphere," she advised.

"But we can *do* it!" Eric paced before her. His soles clacked on the parquet. "Babur, the Commonwealth, the League, they're

38

dithering despite their brags, not? Each fears to commit itself. A single decisive move—''

The waiter appeared with laden trays. ''Sit down and eat,'' Sandra said.

''But—look you, Mother, you know I hold no roots-in-air notion of us as an imperial power. We could never stand against any of the others. If we're there at Mirkheim, though, in possession, firmly allied with the original discoverers, who do own the clearest moral right, would the rest of them not hold back?''

''I can't tell. Moral rights seem of scant account these days. Do sit down. Your food will cool.''

Eric obeyed. His right hand jerked through gestures while his left lay in a fist. ''We're the natural arbiters. None need be afraid of us. We could see to it that everybody gets a fair share.'' Behind his homely visage was fire. ''Only, damnation, first we've need to assert ourselves! Fast!''

''The Polesotechnic League has been suggested for the same role,'' Sandra reminded him.

''Them?'' He chopped the air in contempt. ''When they're too divided, too corrupt to control their own members according to the ethical rules in their own covenant— You jest, not?''

''I don't know,'' Sandra said heavily. ''When I was young, the League was a force for peace because in the long run peace is more profitable than war. Now . . . sometimes I shudder. And sometimes I daydream that it can be reformed in time.''

By men like Nicholas van Rijn, your father, Eric? she wondered. *Not that he would ever feel called on to carry out a holy mission. He'd simply want to preserve his independence, by whatever means will also shake more money out of the universe.*

Is it too late for that?

Through her mind passed a swift review of history, as familiar as her own life but skimmed over once again in the dim hope of finding some hope.

Given abundant nuclear energy, comparatively cheap and easily operated hyperdrive spacecraft, and related technological developments, interstellar trade was bound to burgeon. Theoretically, any habitable planet should be self-sufficient, able to synthesize whatever did not occur naturally. In practice, it was often more economical to import goods, especially in view of restrictions on industry to preserve the environment. Besides, the wealthier Technic civilization grew, the more it dealt in luxuries, arts, services, and other commodities which could not be duplicated at home.

Private enterprise, ranging over greater reaches of space than any government, frequently where no effective government whatsoever existed, and soon becoming richer than any state, took over most of the Technic economy. The companies formed the Polesotechnic League as an association for mutual help and, to a degree, mutual discipline. The Pax Mercatoria spread among the stars.

When did it go bad? Did it succumb to the vices of its very virtues?

Often having to serve as their own magistrates, legislators, naval commanders, and being in any case usually rambunctious, acquisitive individualists with gigantic egos, the great merchants of the League began more and more to live like ancient kings. Abuses grew ever more common: coercion, venality, reckless exploitation. The sheer scale of operations and overwhelming rate of information flow made it apparently impossible to cope with much of this.

No, wait. The League might have brought itself back under control just the same—had not the attempt at control created two mighty factions which as the years went on grew ever more unlike.

There were the Home Companies, whose businesses were principally within the Solar System: Global Cybernetics, General Atomistics, Unity Communications, Terran Synthetics, Planetary Biologicals. Their relationship with the dominant unions—United Technicians, Service Industries Workers, the Commonwealth Scientific Association—grew steadily closer.

And there were the Seven In Space: Galactic Developments, XT Systems, Interstar Transport, Sanchez Engineering, Stellar Metals, Timebinders Insurance, Abdallah Enterprises—the corporate titans among the other suns.

The rest, such as Solar Spice & Liquors, remained precariously unallied, openly competitive. Most were essentially one-man or one-family fiefs. *Does any future lie in them? Aren't they mere fossils of an earlier, freer age? Oh, Nick, my poor devil. . . .*

"Let be the brattling philosophy, and let's get a Hermetian presence at Mirkheim," Eric said. "If naught else, think you what a bargaining lever that gives us against the Seven. Long enough have they been jacking us up. We needn't fear the Commonwealth making war on us. Public opinion wouldn't stand for humans fighting humans while Babur gloats in the background."

"I'm unsure of that. Nor am I sure Babur will sit passive. Frankly, that realm frightens me."

"Bluff."

"Count not on it. Everybody always supposed oxygen breathers and hydrogen breathers would never have any serious conflict because they want not the same real estate, and they're mutually too alien for strife over ideologies. That's why so little attention has been paid to Babur, why it's still so mysterious. But . . . what intelligence I can get shows me the Imperial Band of Sisema as a powerful aggressor that's taken over the whole planet and isn't sated yet. And Mirkheim is real estate that everybody wants."

Not simply out of greed, Sandra's mind went on. *Already the supermetals begin to revolutionize technology, in electronics, alloys, nuclear processes, I know not what else. Did Babur get a hold on the sole source, Babur could deny the stuff to mankind.*

"I agree we humans had best put our feuds aside for a spell," she said. "Maybe Hermes should cooperate with the Commonwealth."

"Maybe. But see you not, Mother, if we take charge first, we can set conditions for handing Mirkheim over and—Well, elsewise, if we stay put, we must needs take whatever somebody else chooses to dole out."

Not his spark of idealism but his angry impatience to act reminded Sandra of his father.

A Wodenite was not exactly inconspicuous among humans, and larynxes must be buzzing throughout Starfall. However, nobody else would listen to what she and Nadi said this morning.

The room where they met was intended for confidential conferences: long, darkly wood-paneled, its windows open on a lawn where a mastiff kept watch. She had made it her own with souvenirs of her

41

youthful offplanet travels: pictures of exotic scenes, odd little bits of art, weapons intended for nonhuman hands racked on the wall. Entering some minutes in advance of appointment time, she found her eye falling on a battle-ax from Diomedes. Her spirit followed, back through years, to Nicholas van Rijn.

She had never loved the merchant. In many ways, even at that unfastidious stage of her life, she found him almost unendurably primitive. But that same raw vigor had saved both their lives on Diomedes. And she was looking for a man who would be a partner, neither domineering nor subservient toward her who was the likeliest successor to the throne of Hermes. (Duke Robert was then old and childless. His niece Sandra was a natural choice for the electors, since not much else could be said for any of the other possible Tamarins.) Nobody she had met on Hermes had greatly stirred her, which was one reason why she went touring. Whatever his flaws, van Rijn was not a man she could be casual about. No previous affair of hers had been as full of thunderstorms and earthquakes—nor of memories to laugh or exult at afterward. When a year had passed, she knew he wouldn't consider marriage, or anything else she might want that he didn't. Eric was in her womb, because at the time she had been an ardent eugenicist. Regardless, she left. Van Rijn made no effort to stop her.

Their parting was not altogether acrimonious, and they had exchanged a few business communications afterward whose tone was not unfriendly. As the years passed, she came to remember him in a more kindly fashion than at first—when she thought of him at all, which was seldom after she met Peter Asmundsen.

He was Hermetian, not of the Kindred but of respectable Follower family; he had organized and personally led enterprises on sister planets of the Maian System; various deeds had made him a popular hero. When ! married Sandra Tamarin and legally adopted Eric, the scandal that had surrounded her return home was laid to rest. Not that it had been much of a scandal. Under the influence of League and Commonwealth, the Hermetian aristocracy had acquired an easygoing attitude toward personal matters. Nevertheless, probably her consort had had a great deal to do with her election to the throne after

Duke Robert's death. And when Pete died—she didn't imagine she would ever want anybody else.

Then why am I thinking about Nick, when I should be thinking about what to do with Nadi?

Because of Eric, I suppose. Eric will inherit this world as I have helped shape it, for weal or woe. So will Joan and Sigurd, of course; but Eric may be saddled with the leadership of it.

If aught is left to lead.

She took a restless turn around the chamber, stopped at the ax and let her fingers curl around its haft. How she wished she could be out in this beautiful day, hunting, steeplechasing, skiing, sailing, driving her hovercycle at speeds which horrified her well-wishing subjects. Or she might visit the theatrical troupe she patronized; her fascination with drama was lifelong. Or—

The door opened. "Madame, Captain Nadi of the Supermetals Company," said the guard, and closed it when the huge body had passed through.

Sandra had never met a Wodenite before. Most of the dwellers on that planet were at a savage stage of technology, though they had apparently developed several intricate, subtle cultures. A few, in contact with Polesotechnic trading centers, had won scholarships or otherwise earned their way into space. Nadi gravely offered his hand, which engulfed Sandra's. The warmth of it surprised her; she had unconsciously expected a scaly being to be cool, as they were on Hermes or Earth.

"Welcome," she said a trifle uncertainly.

"Thank you, my lady." The Anglic was fluent, comprehensible though indescribably accented by the nonhuman conformation of the vocal tract. "I will endeavor not to take unduly much of your time. Yet I feel that what I have to relate is of the highest importance to your people also."

"Belike true. Ah . . . I'm sorry we've no suitable furniture here. Please make yourself comfortable as best you can."

"I can quite well stand indefinitely in this low gravity." The pull of Hermes was ninety-seven percent that of Earth. "I realize you humans sit by choice."

43

"I will. First, though, care you for a smoke? Not? Mind you if I light up? Good." Sandra took a cigar from a humidor, struck fire to it, and lowered herself into an heirloom armchair. Its carven massiveness was somehow reassuring. The tobacco soothed her palate.

"I will go directly to the point," Nadi rumbled. "Do you know how and why I departed from Mirkheim?"

Sandra nodded. She had spent an hour after breakfast getting informed. "You propose that we of Hermes act unilaterally, making ours the government in possession."

"By the express wish of the original discoverers and rightful owners, my lady. Naturally, we understand you will have to grant access to others. But you can regulate this so that each group will get a proper share, including ours."

"If the great powers will let us."

"They may be happy to have you present them with such a formula. Please believe me, this is not a sudden counsel of desperation on our part. We knew from the beginning that our monopoly would be short-lived, and studied possible tactics to use after the news was out. David Falkayn himself suggested Hermes as the eventual caretaker. True, he was only thinking of the Commonwealth versus the League as rivals for Mirkheim. He did not foresee Babur's entry. However, we have decided his idea remains the best we have."

"David—the hero of the Shenna affair? Said you his name?"

"You do not know? I took for granted the story would be widespread by now." Nadi stood a while silent. It was almost as if Sandra could see gears turning ponderously in his head. At length:

"Well, I will no longer be betraying a trust if I tell you, and it may be that you will understand our position better if you know of its origins."

She settled back in her chair. He was right. If nothing else, a background explanation would give her nerves time to ease, her brain time to rally. "Go on," she invited.

"Eighteen standard years ago," Nadi said, "David Falkayn, as you doubtless recall, was still a trade pioneer of the Solar Spice & Liquors Company. Together with his partners, he went in secret, deliberately seeking a world like Mirkheim. Analysis of astronomical

44

data showed him that possibly one existed, and approximately where it would be if it did. He found it, too.

"Instead of notifying his employer, as a trade pioneer is supposed to do whenever he finds a promising new territory, Falkayn went elsewhere. He went to well-chosen leaders among the backward peoples, the poor peoples, the humble peoples whose neglect and abuse by the League had roused his indignation. He it was who got them to form a consortium for the purpose of mining and selling the wealth of Mirkheim, that the gain might go to their folk."

Sandra nodded. Since Rigassi's expedition, spokesmen for Supermetals had pleaded their cause in those terms. She remembered one man who had addressed an audience in Starfall:

". . . How will planets like Woden, Ikraлanka, Ivanhoe, Vanessa—how will the inhabitants of planets like these reach the stars? How will they come to share in the technology that eases labor, preserves health, prevents famine, educates, gives mastery over an indifferent nature? They have hardly anything to market—a spice, a fur, a style of artwork, possibly a few natural resources like oils or easily available minerals. They cannot earn enough thus to buy spaceships, power plants, automatons, research laboratories, schools. The League has no interest in subsidizing them. Public and private charities already face more demands than they can handle. Must whole races then spend millennia full of preventable anguish, in order to develop for themselves everything that has long existed elsewhere?

"And what of colonies planted by humans or Cynthians or other spacefaring species? Not the prosperous, successful colonies like Hermes; the gaunt ones, the outlying ones, whose settlers have little except the pride of independence. They can modify their harsh environments if they can buy the means. Else they risk final extinction.

"The Supermetals Company was organized by trustworthy dwellers on such worlds. The profit to be won on a comparatively minor capital investment was fantastic. But would the magnates of the League respect their property rights? Would governments leave them in sovereign peace? The prize was too great for that—"

"Ah . . . my lady?" came Nadi's voice.

She started back out of her recollection. "I beg your pardon," she said. "My mind wandered."

"I fear I have bored you."

"Not, not. Far from it. In fact, later I'd like to hear details of the tricks you used to keep your holdings hidden. Evasive maneuvers when scouts trailed your ships, precautions against bribery, kidnap, extortion— 'Tis amazing you lasted as long as you did."

"We saw the end was near when Falkayn's employer, Nicholas van Rijn, deduced that the supermetals must come from a world of Mirkheim's type, and used the same method of search to find it. . . . Did I distress you?"

"No. You, you surprised me. Van Rijn? When?"

"Ten standard years ago. Falkayn and Falkayn's future wife persuaded him to maintain silence. In fact, he very kindly helped our agents keep the issue confused, to delay the eventual rediscovery."

"Mmm, yes, Nick would have gotten fun out of doing that." Sandra leaned forward. "Well. This is fascinating, but 'tis past. As you remarked, I knew most of it beforehand, and we can fill in the details later. If you and I stay in touch. I sympathize with you, but you realize my first duty is to Hermes.' What can our people gain at Mirkheim that's worth the cost and hazard?"

The giant being looked helpless and alone. "We beg for your assistance. In return for keeping us in business, you will become sharers in the wealth."

"And targets for everybody who wants that same share, or more." Sandra drew hard on her cigar. "Maybe you're not aware, Captain Nadi, I am no absolute ruler. The Grand Duke or Duchess is elected from the Tamarin family, which may not belong to any domain, by the presidents of the domains of Hermes. My powers are strictly limited."

"I understand, my lady. But I am told you can call a legislative assembly, electronically, on an hour's notice. I am told that your leaders, living on a world which still has a frontier of wilderness, are used to making quick decisions.

"My lady, your intervention could prevent whole armadas from clashing. But very little time remains for you to take action. If you do not move soon, then best you never move."

46

Sandra's pulse accelerated. *By cosmos, he's right as far as he goes,* she thought amidst the bloodbeat, *he and Eric and . . . no few others, I'm sure. The gamble isn't too much if we're careful, if we keep a line of retreat open. I'll need more information, more opinions, of course, before I can even raise the presidents and lay a recommendation before them. But at this moment I think we have a chance.*

Yes, we! I've been soberly hard-working too bloody damn long; and I am commander-in-chief of the navy. If Hermes sends an expedition, I'm going to lead it.

III

The Council of the Polesotechnic League met in Lunograd to consider the Mirkheim situation. Hastily convened, it did not include a representative of every member. Several heads of independent businesses could not be reached in time or could not leave their work on notice that short. However, between them the Home Companies and the Seven In Space almost made up a quorum, and speakers for enough of the unallied organizations arrived, or were already on hand, to complete it.

After the first twenty-four hours of deadlock, Nicholas van Rijn invited two delegates to his suite in the Hotel Universe. They accepted, which they would scarcely have done for any other independent. Van Rijn's enterprise was sufficiently large and spread its tentacles sufficiently wide to make him powerful. Many observers found it hard to believe that, even with modern data and logic systems, one man could stay on top of it without having to incorporate like the giants. He was the natural leader of those outfits which had entered into no close-knitting agreements such as bound together the Seven In Space or the five Home Companies.

For their parts, Bayard Story seemed to be the guiding genius of the first group and Hanny Lennart of the second.

It was close to Lunar midnight. From the main room of the suite, the view through a transparency was awesome. Buildings stood well apart and were not high. They must stay below the forcefields which kept air in this bubble and the ozone layer beneath. But between them were parks wherein the low gravity let trees soar and arch like the fountains, amidst fiercely colored great blossoms. Lamps, on posts formed to resemble vines, glowed everywhere. They did not haze view of the stark crater floor beyond the fields, of Plato's ringwall

48

shouldering in cliffs and steeps over the near horizon, or of the sky. Against infinite darkness, stars shone in their myriads, keen, jewel-hued, unwinking; the Milky Way was a quicksilver river; Earth's heart-snaring loveliness hung blue and white in the south. Confronting that sight, the opulence of the chamber seemed tawdry.

Lennart and Story arrived together. Van Rijn skipped across the floor to let them in. He had left unused the unit that could have supplied Terrestrial weight. "Ho, ho, you been confabulating before you come here, *nie*?" he bawled as the door opened. "No, don't deny, don't tell lies to a poor old lonely fat man who got one foot in the gravy. Come drink his liquor instead."

Story swept a glance across him and said genially, "For as far back as I've heard about you, Freeman van Rijn, and that's farther than I could wish, people tell how you've been lamenting your age and feebleness. I'd give long odds that you still have twenty years or more of devilment left."

"*Ja,* I look healthy, me, built like a brick wedding cake. But low gee helps more than you think, you two what could be my son and daughter except I always had better taste in women. How I long for to retire, forsake the bumps and inanities of this wicked world, wash my soul clean of sin till it squeaks."

"In order to make room for new and bigger sins?"

"Please stop that nonsense," Lennart interrupted. "This is supposed to be a serious discussion."

"If you insist, Freelady," Story said. "Myself, I feel ready for a little fun. Might as well take it, too. The Council is an exercise in futility. I wonder why I bothered to come."

The others regarded him narrowly for a moment, as if they also wondered. They had never met him before this occasion; they had only known—as a result of routine information gathering—that for the past ten years his name had been on the list of directors of Galactic Developments, in that corporation's headquarters on Germania. Evidently he was so rich and influential that he could kill publicity about himself and operate almost invisibly.

He was a rather handsome man, medium-sized, slender, his features regular in a tanned rectangular face, eyes blue-gray, hair and mustache smooth brown with a sprinkling of white. An elastic gait indicated that he used his muscles a good deal, perhaps under intermittently severe conditions. His soft speech held a trace of non-Terrestrial accent, though it was too far eroded by time to be identifiable. An expensive slacksuit in subdued greens fitted him as if grown from his body. Beside him, dark-clad Lennart looked dowdy and haggard. Beside either of them, van Rijn was outrageous in his favorite clothes of snuff-stained ruffled blouse and a sarong wrapped around his Jovian equator.

"Eat, drink, smoke," the host urged, waving at a well-stocked portable bar, trays of intricate canapés, boxes of cigars and cigarettes. He himself held a churchwarden pipe which had seen years of service and grown fouler for each day of them. "I wanted we should talk here, not on a circuit with seals, so we could relax, act honest, not have to resent what anybody maybe says."

Story nodded and took Scotch whisky in the civilized manner, neat with a water chaser. Van Rijn refilled a tumbler of Genever gin, adding a dash of what he called *angst en onrust* bitters. They settled down in loungers. Lennart sat upright on a sofa opposite, accepting nothing.

"Well," she said. "What do you have in mind?"

"We should see if we can compromise, or if not that, map out our areas of disagreement. Right?" Story supplied.

"Also horse-trade information," van Rijn said.

"That can be a mighty valuable commodity, especially when it's in short supply," Story observed.

"I hope you realize neither of us can make promises, Freeman van Rijn." Lennart clipped off each word. "We are simply executives of our corporations." She herself was a vice president of Global Cybernetics. "And in fact, neither the Home Companies nor the Seven form a monolith. They are only tied together by certain business agreements."

The recital of what a schoolboy should know did not insult van Rijn. "Plus interlocking directorates," he added blandly, taking up a tiny sandwich of smoked eel upon cold scrambled egg. "Besides, each of you got more voice in things than you let on, *ja*, you can bellow like wounded blast furnaces any time you want. And those business agreements, what they mean is the Seven is one cartel and the Home Companies another, and got plenty of political flunkies in high places."

"Not us in the Commonwealth," Story said. "That's become your plutocracy, Freelady Lennart, not ours."

Her thin cheeks flushed. "You can say that truly of your poor little puppet states on their poor little planets," she retorted. "As for the Commonwealth, we've now had fifty years of progressive reforms to strengthen democracy."

"By damn," van Rijn muttered, "maybe you really believe that."

"I hope we aren't here to rehearse stale partisan politics," Story said.

"Me too," van Rijn answered. "That is what it will amount to, what the Council we do if we leave it to itself. Members will take their positions and then not be able to get off because they have spread so much manure around. They will quarrel till plaster falls from the sky. And nothing else will happen . . . unless a few leaders agree to let it happen. That is what I want us to wowpow about."

"The issues are simple," Lennart declared. She repeated what she had said more than once at the conference table. "Mirkheim is too valuable, too strategic a resource, to be allowed to fall into the claws of beings that have demonstrated their hostility. I include certain human beings. The Commonwealth has a just title to sovereignty over it, inasmuch as the original discoverers represented no government whereas the Rigassi expedition was composed of our citizens. The Commonwealth likewise has a duty to mankind, to civilization itself, to safeguard that planet. The Home Companies support this. It's a patriotic obligation, and I am frankly surprised that persons of your education don't recognize it."

"My education was in the school of hard knockers," van Rijn replied. "Yours too, I suspect, Freeman Story, ha? You and me should understand each other."

"*I* understand why you change the subject," Lennart flung forth. "A discussion of morals would embarrass you."

"Well, speaking of morals, and immorals too," van Rijn said,

51

"what about those original discoverers of Mirkheim, ha? What rights you think they have?"

"That can be decided in the courts, after Mirkheim is secured."

"*Ja, ja*, in courts whose judges you buy and sell like shares of stock. I hear a background noise already, you whetting your lawyers. That was why the Supermetals Company worked in secret."

Story raised his brows. "Do you expect us to believe, Freeman, that you aided and abetted them for a decade out of an abstract sense of justice?"

"What makes you suppose I was in any plot, a plain old peddler of belly comfort like me?"

"It's not been made public, but Rigassi learned from the workers at Mirkheim that a member of the Polesotechnic League had been helping in their cover-up, ever since he tracked the planet down. They didn't say who he was; they were simply, rather pathetically, trying to seem stronger than they are—"

Lennart drew a sharp breath. "How do you know that?" she exclaimed.

Story grinned. He was not about to reveal whatever espionage system his bloc maintained. He continued addressing van Rijn: "In retrospect, the man has to have been you. And a gorgeous job you did. Especially those hints you let drop, those clues you let be found, indicating an entire civilization more advanced than ours was producing the supermetals. Expeditions going solemnly out in search . . . Surely the most magnificent hoax in history." After a moment: "Do you mind telling us why you did it?"

"Well, you would call me a liar if I said I thought it was the right thing, and could be I would myself." Van Rijn swallowed a confection of Limburger cheese and onion on pumpernickel, tamped his pipe with a horny forefinger, and drank smoke. "I admit, partly I got talked into it by somebody I care about," he went on, between blowing rings. "And partly, for independents like me, is best if supermetals be on a free market. I don't want either of your cartels having the power that a Mirkheim monopoly in your hands would give. The original outfit, it is more reasonable."

That was what he had argued for at the Council: that the Polesotechnic League exert the might it had when it was united, in an effort to have Mirkheim declared a stateless planet under the protection of the League, which Supermetals would join. He knew perfectly well that there was no chance of the resolution being adopted unless a lot of hard minds got changed. The Home Companies insisted that they would support the Commonwealth's cause; the Seven were for the entire League holding clear of any struggle, strictly neutral and prepared to negotiate with whatever party won.

He now pursued the matter. "Story, it does not make sense we should sit by and piddle on our thumbs. Freelady Lennart has right as far as she goes: if Babur takes Mirkheim, is the worst outcome for all of us. And Babur is perhaply better armed than the Commonwealth. It for sure has shorter lines of communication."

"Who brought affairs to this pass?" Lennart's tone grew shrill. "Who first began trading with the Baburites, sold them the technology that got them into space, for a filthy profit? The Seven!"

"We had dealings, yes," Story said mildly. "At the time, that kind of transaction was standard practice, you recall. Nobody objected. Subsequently—well, I admit our companies let trade fall to almost nothing because it was no longer paying very well, not because we foresaw Babur's arming. We didn't. Nobody did. Who would have? Just the research and development necessary— incredible they could do it in so few years.

"But." He made a lecturer's gesture. "But from our earlier experience, we know we can do business with the Baburites. The possibility that we'll have to buy our supermetals from them is no more frightening than the possibility we'll have to buy them from the Home Companies, which is what a Commonwealth takeover would amount to. We'll still have things to exchange that Babur needs."

"Would you not prefer buying at a cheaper price from the present owners, and from other companies that will also work Mirkheim and sell on the open market?" van Rijn asked.

"They won't necessarily be cheaper," Story said. "Oxygen breathers are too apt to be in direct competition with us." He bridged his fingers and looked across them first at Lennart, then at van Rijn. "To be blunt, I think most of the fear of Babur is nothing but a child's fear of the unfamiliar. You never took the trouble to learn about it, when it seemed to be only one more obscure planet off in the fringes of known space. But I happen to be a former xenologist, who specialized in subjovians. I've studied all records the Seven have of their dealings with it. I've been there myself in the past and talked with its leaders. So I tell you—and I'm here to tell the entire Council —Babur's no den of ogres. It's the home of a species as reasonable by their lights as we are by ours.''

"Exactly," van Rijn growled. "God help reason, if we and they is the best it can do. But I had a little brush-up with the Baburites myself once. I also have lately been scanning what data on them can be got here in the Solar System. Their lights is very flickery.''

"Their claim to Mirkheim is ridiculous," Lennart put in. "Nothing but a slogan for territorial aggression.''

"Not in terms of their own dominant culture," Story said.

"Then it isn't a culture we can afford to let become strong. It makes no bones about intending to establish an empire. If that meant only Babur-type worlds, perhaps we could live with it. But as I read their statements and actions to date, they plan to seize hegemony over that entire volume of space. That cannot be tolerated.''

"How will you stop it?"

"For a start, by taking appropriate action at Mirkheim. Quickly, decisively. Our intelligence indicates Babur will back down from a *fait accompli*.''

" 'Our' intelligence?" Story murmured. "How good are your connections to the Ministry of Defense?''

Van Rijn jetted thick blue clouds. "I think you just answered something I wasn't so sure about, Lennart," he said.

She stared. Apprehension crossed her features. "I didn't—I am only advocating, personally, you realize—''

"I got connections of my own. Not to nothing secret, like you seem to. But so simple a datum as clearances of civilian craft for deep space—suddenly for a while a lot of them got to wait—that kind of thing—*ja*, drop by drop by drop of fact I collect, till I got a full jigsaw puddle. Your way of talking, after these many years I have known you, Lennart, that says much too.''

Van Rijn stood up, lightly in the low weight, like a rising moon which eclipsed the radiance of Earth. "Story," he said, "it will not be announced right away, but I bet you rubies to rhubarb the Commonwealth government has already dispatched a task force to Mirkheim. And I am not the least bit sure Babur will take that meekly-weakly." He turned to a little Martian sandroot statuette of St. Dismas that stood on the bar, his traveling companion of a lifetime. "Better get busy and pray for us," he told it.

IV

Under full hyperdrive, spaceship *Muddlin' Through* fared from the Solar System toward the sun that men had named Mogul. Pulsed Schrödinger waves drove her at a pseudovelocity equivalent to thousands of times the true speed of radiation; and in galactic terms those stars were near neighbors. Yet her clocks would have registered two and a half weeks when she reached her destination. So big is the universe. Sentient beings speak lightly of crossing light-years because they cannot comprehend what they are doing.

David Falkayn, Chee Lan, Adzel, and Muddlehead were in the saloon playing poker. Rather, the first three were. The computer was represented by an audiovisual sensor and a pair of metal arms. It was an advanced model, functioning at consciousness level, very little of its capability needed en route to maintain the systems of the ship. The live travelers had even less to do.

"I'll bet a credit," said Chee. A blue chip clattered to the middle of the table.

"Dear me." Adzel laid down his hand. "Can I fetch more refreshment for anyone?"

"Thanks." Falkayn held out an empty beer mug. "I'll raise." He doubled the bet. After half a minute during which the faint purr of engines and ventilators came through silence: "Hey, Muddlehead, what's keeping you?"

"The probabilities for and against me are calculable as being exactly balanced," said the flat artificial voice. Electronic brooding continued for a few seconds. "Very well," it decided, and matched Falkayn.

"*Ki-yao?*" wondered Chee. Her whiskers dithered, her tail switched the stool on which she sat. "Well, if you insist." She raised back.

Inwardly, the human jubilated. He had a full house. Outwardly, he pretended to ponder before he raised again. Muddlehead saw him. "Are you sure you don't need some readjustment somewhere?" Falkayn asked it.

"Whom the gods would destroy," said Chee smugly. Again she raised back. Meanwhile Adzel, his hoofs thudding on the carpet, returned with Falkayn's beer. The Wodenite himself refrained from drinking it on a voyage—no ship could have carried enough—and instead sipped a martini in a one-liter chillglass.

Falkayn raised another credit. Muddlehead saw. Chee and Falkayn peered its way, as if they could read an expression in the vitryl lens. Slowly, Chee added two chips to the pot. Falkayn suppressed a grin and raised once more. Muddlehead raised back. Chee's fur stood on end. "Damn your mendacious transistors to hell!" she screamed, and threw down her hand.

Falkayn hesitated. Muddlehead *had* implied its cards were mediocre, but— He called. His opponent revealed four queens.

"What the jumping blue blazes?" Falkayn half rose. "You said the probabilities—"

"I referred to the odds in favor of suckering you," explained Muddlehead, and raked in the pot.

"It appears that after our long hiatus, we will have to learn each other's styles of play *ab initio*," Adzel remarked.

"Well, listen." Chee shuffled the deck. "I'm growing tired of nothing but straight poker. Dealer's choice, right? I say seven card stud, low hole wild."

Falkayn grimaced. "That's a nasty thing to say."

"The odds in wild card games are precisely as determinable as those in the standard versions," declared Muddlehead.

"Yes, but you're a computer," Falkayn grumbled.

"You want to cut?" Chee asked Adzel.

"What?" The dragon blinked. "Oh—oh, my apologies. I was taking the opportunity to meditate." With astonishing delicacy, an enormous hand split the pack.

The beating he took in that round did not seem to disturb his feelings. But when the deal came to him, he announced placidly, "This will be baseball."

"Oh, no!" Falkayn groaned. "What's happened to you two in the past three years?" He soon folded and sat grimly drinking and thinking.

His turn arrived. "I'll show you bastards," he said. "This will be Number One. You know it? Seven card stud, high-low, kings and tens wild for low, sevens and deuces wild for high."

"Om mani padme hum," whispered Adzel shakenly.

Chee arched her back and spat. Settling down again on her cushion, she protested, "Muddlehead could blow a fuse."

"The problem is less complex than computing an entry orbit," the ship reassured her, "though rather more ridiculous."

The game went on, in a weird fashion. Falkayn took the whole pot, largely by default. "I hope we've all learned our lesson," he said. "Your deal, Muddlehead."

"I believe I am also permitted to call an unorthodox game," replied the machine.

Falkayn winced, Chee Lan bottled her tail, but Adzel proposed, "Fair is fair. However, let us thereafter confine ourselves to straight draw and stud."

"My assessment is that this one will confirm you in that desire," Muddlehead told them, shuffling. "It is played like draw except that there is no point in drawing. Players pick up their cards with the backs toward them, so that each can see the hand of everybody but himself."

After a shocked silence, Chee demanded: "What kind of perverts were they that gave you your last overhaul?"

"I am self-programming within the limits of the types of task for which I am built," the computer reminded her. "Thus whenever I am activated but idle, I endeavor to make that idleness creative."

"I think the Manichaean heresy just scored a point," said Adzel. Van Rijn would have understood the reference, but it went by Falkayn, though he was reasonably well-read.

At least play was mercifully short. At its end, the man rose. "Deal me out," he said. "I want to check on dinner." Gourmet cooking was among the hobbies with which he passed the time on voyages, as painting and sculpture were for Chee, music and the study of Terrestrial history for Adzel.

Having basted the roast, he did not immediately return to the saloon but lit his pipe and sought the bridge. His footfalls sounded loud. This was during the period of several hours per twenty-four when the ship's gravity generator was set at fifty-five percent above Earth's pull, to accustom the crew to what they would undergo on Babur if they landed there. An added forty-five kilos of weight did not unduly tire him. It was uniformly distributed over a body in good condition. What he and his mates had to adapt was chiefly their cardiovascular systems. Nonetheless he felt the heaviness in his bones.

On the bridge, optical compensators projected an exact simulacrum of whichever half of the sky they were set to show. Falkayn stopped at the control board. Beyond the glowing instruments, darkness roofed him in, housing a wilderness of stars. They gleamed at him from every side, sword-sharp swarms, the Milky Way an argent cataract, the Magellanic Clouds and the Andromeda galaxy made small and strange by distances he would never see overleaped. As if he felt the elemental cold between them, he cradled the bowl of his pipe in one fist, his campfire symbol. Beneath the susurrus of the ship lay an infinite stillness.

And yet, he thought, yonder suns were not quiet. They were appallingly aflame; and the spaces roiled with matter, seethed with energy, travailed with the birth of new suns and new worlds. Nor was the universe eternal; it had its strange destiny. To look into it was to know the sorrow and glory of being alive.

More than once Coya had gotten her wish that they make love here.

Falkayn's eyes sought in the direction of Sol, though it had long since dwindled from sight. His trained gaze could still find its way among constellations that had changed, some beyond recognition, and were nearly drowned in the number of stars that shone through airlessness. *How are you doing now, darling?* he wondered, knowing full well that "now" was a noise without meaning when cried across the interstellar reaches. *I didn't expect to feel homesick on this trip. I forgot that home is where you are.*

He recognized his regret as being partly guilt. He had not been frank with her. In his judgment, this journey held more dangers than he had admitted. (But then, she had tried to hide from him that she thought the same.) Regardless, when van Rijn broached the idea, the blood had leaped in him, after three staid years. Some lines passed through his head, from the archaic poetry which was a special interest of his:

> *"I am a part of all that I have met;*
> *Yet all experience is an arch wherethro'*
> *Gleams that untravell'd world, whose margin fades*
> *For ever and for ever when I move.*
> *How dull it is to pause, to make an end,*
> *To rust unburnish'd, not to shine in use!*
> *As though to breathe were life. . . ."*

Consoling himself with smoke, he decided he might as well admit that he had a hopeless case of go-fever. Coya and, yes, the kids could come a-roving with him later. Meanwhile

> *"My mariners,*
> *Souls that have toil'd, and wrought, and thought with me—*
> *That ever with a frolic welcome took*
> *The thunder and the sunshine, and opposed*
> *Free hearts, free foreheads—"*

A chuckle interrupted. Neither Adzel nor Chee Lan would take kindly to the idea of manning oars in a Grecian galley. Not but what they hadn't done equally curious things from time to time, and might again. He'd better get back to the game. After dinner, if their mood suited, he'd break out his fiddle and play for them. The sight of those two dancing a jig together never wearied him.

V

The sun of Babur was more than twice as bright as Sol; but the planet was more than six times as far from its luminary as Earth. Thus Mogul stood in the spatial sky as a tiny disc of unbearable brilliance. A moon of Babur's four was close enough to show craters; the rest were like small sharp sickles. The world itself was a tawny globe partly shaded by night, partly veiled by bands and swirls of cloud, white tinged with gold, brown, or pale red. The majesty of the sight gave Falkayn to understand why its human discoverer had named it for a conqueror who went down in the memory of India as the Tiger. *He didn't know how well he chose*, he thought.

The bridge where he sat felt profoundly silent, only a breath from the ventilators to be heard. Hyperdrive was off and *Muddlin' Through* maneuvering on gravs at a true speed of a few kilometers per second. Chee was in the weapons control turret, Adzel in the engine room: their trouble stations. On Falkayn rested the burden of deciding when danger grew so great as to require fight or flight. He doubted that either would be possible here. The two warcraft that had challenged the ship as she approached and escorted her in now flanked and paced her arrowhead hull like wolves herding along a prey. Distance made them tiny until Falkayn magnified their sections of the view; then he saw them the size of a Technic destroyer but much more heavily armed, flying arsenals.

When Muddlehead spoke, he started, fetching up short against the safety web that held him in his seat. "I have commenced analysis of data obtained from neutrino and mass detectors, radar, gravity and hyperdrive pulse registers, and the local interplanetary field. Subject to correction, approximately fifty vessels are in wide orbit around Babur. Only one is of a size to be a possible dreadnought or equivalent thereof. Many of the rest appear to be noncombatant, perhaps groundable transports. More detailed information should be available presently."

"Fifty? Huh?" Falkayn exclaimed. "But we know—Babur put on that show near Valya—we know its fleet is at least equal to the Commonwealth's. Where are the majority?"

His companions had been listening on the intercom. Adzel's slow basso rolled forth: "It is fruitless to speculate. We lack facts about Babur's plans, or even about the society whose masters have hatched those plans."

Nobody paid attention until too late, Falkayn thought. *Not to hydrogen breathers, who are alien, who can offer us oxygen breathers very little in the way of markets or resources, and by the same token should find nothing to quarrel with us about. There were too many planets which did lure us with treasure, with homesteads, with native beings not hopelessly unlike ourselves. We scarcely remembered that Babur existed—a whole world, as old and many-faced and full of marvels as ever Earth was.*

"I think I know where their missing ships are," Chee said. "They were never intended to orbit idle."

Falkayn's mind paced a rutted track: *How did Babur do it—how build up so great a strength in a mere twenty or thirty years? They couldn't simply put armament on copies of the few merchant vessels they'd produced. Nor could they simply work from plans of human men-of-war. Everything had to be adapted to the peculiar conditions of Babur, the peculiar requirements of its life forms.*

He recalled the shapes of the ships escorting his, bulge-bellied as if pregnant (with what sort of birth to come?). The extra volume housed cryogenic tanks. Air recycling alone was not adequate for hydrogen breathers, whose atmosphere leaked slowly out between the atoms of a hull and must be replenished from liquid gases. A thin plating of a particular supermetal alloy could cure that—but no Baburite knew there was a Mirkheim when the decision was made to found a navy. And the leakage problem was only the most easy and obvious of those the engineers had met.

The research and development effort before manufacture could begin must have been extraordinarily sophisticated. How could the

Baburites complete it in the time it had actually taken, they who had never gotten off their home world when men first found them?

Could they have hired outside experts? If so, whose, and how could they pay them?

His repetition of questions which been raised since the menace first manifested itself, to no avail, was broken off. Muddlehead was making one of its rare contributions to talk: "Conceivably the Baburites have been anticipating fights with other hydrogen breathers."

"No," Adzel replied. "There aren't any with comparable technology, anywhere in known space, except the Ymirites; and they are as different from the Baburites as they are from us."

"I suggest you write me a program in political science," the computer said.

"Will you two klooshmakers stop snakkering?" Falkayn barked. "The fact is they've got far fewer ships here than we know they own. And I share Chee's foul notion of where the rest of those ships have gone. If we—"

His outercom chimed. He switched it on, and the screen filled with the image of a Baburite.

Around the eldritch caterpillar-centaur-lobster shape, which did not really look like any of those animals, shadowy figures flitted through gloom. Four tiny eyes behind a spongy snout could not make true contact with his. The being hummed its League Latin, noises which a vocalizer transposed into the proper phonemes. "We have notified the Imperial Band of Sisema and you are about to receive your instructions. Stand by." The statement was neither polite nor rude; it announced how things were.

Then the image faded out. For a minute Falkayn sat alone with his thoughts. Again they ran back over what little he knew.

"Sisema" was nothing but the vocalizer's rendition of a sound that in the original was a thin droning. "Imperial Band" was a Baburite attempt, probably suggested by earlier human visitors, to translate a concept that had no counterpart on Earth. Seemingly in Acarro—as the vocalizer called one region on the planet—the unit of society was not individual, family, clan, or tribe. It was an association of beings, tied together by bonds more powerful and pervasive than any that men could experience, involving some mutuality or complementarity of their sexual cycles but extending from this to every aspect of life. Each Band had its own personality, which differed more from that of its fellow Bands than members of any did from each other. Yet informants had told xenologists that every single member was unique, with a special contribution to make; the merging together was not subordination, it was communication (communion?) on a level deeper than consciousness. Telepathy? It was hard to know what such a word might mean on this world, and the informants had been unwilling or unable to speak further. A Baburite did radiate variably at radio frequencies, strongly enough to be detected by a sensitive instrument in the neighborhood. If that was due to neurochemistry (?), perhaps another nervous system (?) could act as a receiver. Perhaps in this way a part of tradition was not oral or written but directly perceived.

Potentially immortal, a Band recruited itself by adoption as much as by reproduction. Cross-adoptions linked various groups as cross-marriages had once allied human families. The Imperial Band seemed to have first choice in such cases, and to that extent was dominant, providing a leadership that had finally brought the entire planet under its sway. Yet it was not a true monarchy or dictatorship. Self-regulating, not given to conflict with their own kind, the Bands needed little government in the Terrestrial sense.

Which made their sudden aggressiveness all the less comprehensible, Falkayn thought. They'd tried some sharp business in this sector thirty years ago, and been worsted by the Solar Spice & Liquors factor—but sunblaze, that was a trivial incident, no cause for them lately to start trumpeting about their "right to control ambient space." Nor did the idea of dividing the stars up into spheres of interest seem like a safe one. The League could not tolerate that, if the League wanted to survive as a set of free-market entrepreneurs. The Commonwealth might accept the principle . . . but not if that involved loss of Mirkheim, the exact explosive issue Babur had chosen for precipitating the crisis.

I suppose even the agents of those companies of the Seven that formerly traded here have been baffled to foresee what minds so strange to us will do next—Hoy!

Again the screen gave him the picture of a Baburite. Though Falkayn was well schooled in noting individual differences between nonhumans, he identified this one as new only by the color and cut of robe. The outlandishness of the whole simply drowned every detail in his perception. "You are Captain Ah-kyeh?" the being demanded without preamble. It had not heard his name well enough to hum an accurate equivalent. "This member speaks to you for the Imperial Band of Sisema. You have told our sentinels your purpose in coming. Redescribe it, in exact detail."

The muscles tightened around Falkayn's belly and between his shoulderblades. For an instant he was more conscious of stars, planet, moons, sun in the hemisphere above him than he was of the image he confronted. To go down in death, losing all that splendor, losing Coya and Juanita and the child unborn . . . But those warcraft hemming him in would not wantonly open fire. Would they? The habit of courage took charge of him and he answered steadily:

"Forgive me if I leave off a greeting or similar courtesy. I've been told your people don't employ such phrases, at least not with a foreign species." *Sensible. What rituals could we possibly have in common?* "My partners and I are here not on behalf of any government, but as representatives of a company in the Polesotechnic League, Solar Spice & Liquors. We know you had a dispute with us on the planet we call Suleiman, somewhat more than two of your years ago. We hope this won't prevent you from listening to us now."

He employed a vocalizer himself, not because he knew anything of the other sophont's language, but in order that it might convert his words into sounds that the latter could readily hear. He wondered how badly his meaning got distorted. If the Siseman speech had been tonal like Chinese, little but gibberish would have gotten through. The Baburite was wise to require reiteration.

"We listen," it said.

"I'm afraid I haven't any precise plan to describe. The conflict over Mirkheim disturbs us greatly. By 'us' I mean, here, the company for which my companions and I work. And of course the leaders of associated firms feel the same way. A war would be as disastrous to trade as to everything else. Besides, uh, economic motives, common decency demands we do whatever we can to help prevent it. You doubtless know the Polesotechnic League is not a government, but commands comparable power. It will gladly lend its good offices toward reaching a peaceful agreement.''

"You do not speak for the entire League. It no longer has a single voice."

Touché! thought Falkayn, and felt indeed as if a blade had pierced him. *How in cosmos do the Baburites know that? They ought to be as ignorant of the ins and outs of Technic politics as we are of theirs.*

True, if they've been preparing for a long time to fight us, they'd investigate us carefully beforehand. But when did they, and how? A Baburite traveling around among us and asking questions would be too conspicuous for van Rijn not to have heard about. And surely they couldn't rely on occasional traders from the Seven for such information, especially after that trade became practically extinct.

The fact that they are this well-informed is a flamingly important datum all by itself. Van Rijn needs to know.

He had reached his conclusion in a nearly intuitive leap. Best not to let the officer (?) guess how dismayed he was. "We will be glad to discuss that with you, and anything else," he temporized. "If we can give some understanding, and gain some for ourselves, that will make our journey a success. I'd like to emphasize that we don't represent the Commonwealth in any way. In fact, none of us three is a citizen of it. No matter who gets Mirkheim in the end, companies of the League will be dealing with them," *unless Babur gets it and then keeps the supermetals exclusively for itself.* "I hope you will regard us as ambassadors of a sort," *who double in espionage if they get the chance.* "We're experienced in dealing with different races, so maybe we have more chance than average of exchanging information and ideas."

The Baburite fired several disconcertingly shrewd queries, which Falkayn answered as evasively as he dared. Since the being knew the League was divided against itself, he strove to give the impression of a less serious breach than was the case. At last his interrogator said, "You will be conducted to a landing place on Babur. Earth-conditioned quarters will be provided."

66

"Oh, we can quite well stay in our ship, in orbit, and communicate by screen," Falkayn said.

"No. We cannot allow an armed vessel, surely equipped with surveillance devices, to remain loose in local space."

"I can see that, but, um . . . we could set down on a moon."

"No. It will be necessary to study you at length, and you may not have access to your ship. Else you might try to break away from us if the process takes an inconvenient turn. A guide vessel is on its way. Do as its chieftain commands you." The screen blanked.

Falkayn sat still for a while, hearing Chee swear. "Well," he said at last, "if nothing else, we'll get a close look at the ground. Keep those surveillance devices busy, Muddlehead."

"They are," the computer assured him. "Data analysis is also proceeding. It has become evident that most of the ships around Babur belong to oxygen breathers."

"Huh?"

"Infrared radiation shows their internal temperatures are too high for denizens of this planet."

"Yes, yes, obviously," Chee's voice came. "But what are the crews? Mercenaries? How in the name of Nick van Rijn's hairy navel did the Baburites contact them, let alone recruit them?"

"I suspect those are questions we are better off not asking," Adzel said. "To be sure, we must try to find the answers."

The guide came in sight, larger than *Muddlin' Through* but with similar streamlining proving that she was groundable. The part of her armament that showed was by itself more than the League ship carried. Falkayn did not propose making a dash for freedom.

Having received his travel orders and turned them over to Muddlehead to execute, he gave his attention to the viewscreen hemisphere. From time to time he rotated the scene or enlarged a part of it. He wanted to see everything he could, and not merely because an item might prove useful. This was a new, utterly strange world on which he was about to tread. A *world*. After all his years of roving, and even today when he fared under guard, the old thrill tingled through him.

Babur swelled in his sight as the ships accelerated inward. The approach curve took him around the globe, and he saw the tiny, fiery sun set in gold and rise in scarlet over an ocean of subtly tinted clouds. Then he was braking heavily and the planet was no longer before him or beside him, it was below. A thin scream of split atmosphere reached his ears. The stars of space vanished in a sky gone purple. Lightning flared across a storm far under this hurtling hull.

The surface came in view. Mountains glimmered blue-white, either sheathed in ice or purely glacial. Here water was a solid mineral. The liquid that took its place was ammonia. Air was hydrogen and helium, with traces of ammonia vapor, methane, and more complex organic compounds. Certain materials had gone on to become alive.

A sea heaved gray beneath rosy clouds. It was small for a body with twelve and a third times the mass of Earth, two and four-fifths times the diameter. Ammonia is less plentiful than water. The interiors of the enormous continents were arid; there the black vegetation grew sparsely, glittering dust scudded across the horizon's vast circle, and never a trace of habitation showed.

A volcano blew flame and smoke on high. It did not erupt like one on Earth; it was melting itself, streams raging forth and congealing into mirror-bright veins and sheets. The very structure of Babur was unearthly, a metallic core overlaid with ice and rocky strata, water in the depths compressed into a hot solid ever ready to expand explosively when that pressure happened to ease. Here there were true Atlantises, lands that sank beneath the waves in a year or less; new countries were upheaved as fast. Falkayn glimpsed such a place, hardly touched as yet by life, raw ranges and plains still ashudder with quakes.

On their downward slant, the ships passed above a second desert and then a fertile seaboard. A forest was squat trees on which long black streamers of leaves were fluttering. Aerial creatures breasted a gale on stubby wings. A leviathan beast wallowed blue in a gray lake beneath a lash of ammonia rain. Wilderness yielded to farms, darkling fields laid out in hexagons, houses built of gleaming ice and anchored with cables against storms. By magnification, Falkayn spied workers and their draft animals. He could barely tell the species

68

apart. Would a Baburite see as little distinction between a man and a horse?

A city appeared on the shore. Because it could not grow tall, it spread wide, kilometers of domes, cubes, pyramids in murky colors. In what seemed to be a new section, buildings were aerodynamically designed to withstand winds stronger than would ever blow across Earth. Wheeled and tracked vehicles passed among them, aircraft above—but remarkably little traffic for a community this size.

The city went below the curve of the world. "Make for that field," directed the guide. Falkayn saw a stretch of pavement, studded with great circular coamings that were mostly covered by hinged metal discs. A few stood open, revealing hollow cylinders beneath, sunk deep into the ground. It had been explained to him that for safety's sake, spacecraft which landed here were housed in such silos. The guide told him which to take, and Muddlehead eased its hull down.

"Here we are," Falkayn said unnecessarily. The words came dull and loud, now that his view was only of fluoro-lit blankness. "Let's get our suits on pronto. Our hosts might not like to be kept waiting. . . . Muddlehead, hold all systems ready for action. Don't let anybody or anything in except one of us. In case of arguments about that, refer the arguer to us."

"We might want a countersign," came Adzel's voice.

"Good thinking," Falkayn said. "Hm . . . does everybody know this?" He whistled a few bars. "Somehow I doubt the Baburites have ever heard 'One-Ball Riley.' " Beneath his cheerfulness, he thought, *What does it matter? We're totally at their mercy.* And then: *Not necessarily, by God!*

At the main personnel lock, he, Adzel, and Chee donned their spacesuits. They took time for a complete checkout. The walk ahead of them was short, but the least failure would be lethal. "Fare you well, Muddlehead," said Adzel before he closed his faceplate.

"Provided you don't sit here inventing new distortions of poker," Chee added.

"Would backgammon variations interest you?" asked the computer.

"Come on, let's move along, for Job's sake," Falkayn said.

Having completed their preparations, they took each a ready-packed personal kit and cycled through the lock. A platform elevator in a recess in the silo wall, with an up-and-down lever control, bore them to the top. Adzel was forced to use it alone, and at that most of him hung over the edge. Nevertheless, the fact that it could carry him was suggestive. It was meant solely for passengers; elsewhere on the field Falkayn had seen support cradles for ships that were to be loaded or unloaded, and cargo handling equipment. So the Baburites had visitors bigger than themselves often enough to justify a machine like this, did they?

As he emerged, Falkayn paid attention also to the controls of the hatch cover. A wheel steered a small motor which ran the hydraulic system moving the heavy piece of metal up or down.

Heavy . . . Unrelieved by his vessel's interior gee field, weight smote him. Without optical amplification, his eyes saw the world as twilit. Mogul glared low above buildings on his left, near the end of Babur's short day. Clouds hung amber in purple heaven; beneath them blew a ruddy wrack. With three and a third Terrestrial atmospheres of pressure behind it, the wind made motion through it feel like wading a river. Its sound was shrill, as was every noise borne by this air.

Several Baburites met him. They carried energy weapons. Pointing the way to go, they led the newcomers trudging across the expanse. A complex occupied an entire side of it. When close, able to make out details through the dusk, Falkayn recognized the structure. No workshop or warehouse of ice such as shimmered elsewhere, this was a man-made environmental unit, a block fashioned of alloys and plastics chosen for durability, thick-walled, triple-insulated. Light from some of the reinforced windows glowed yellow. Inside, he knew, the air was warm and recycled. As part of that cycle, the hydrogen that seeped through was catalytically treated to make water. The helium that entered took the place of a corresponding amount of nitrogen. A fifth of the gas was oxygen. A grav generator kept weight at Terrestrial standard.

"Our home away from home," he muttered.

Chee's astonishment sounded in his radio earphones: "This large a facility? How many do they house at a time? And why?"

A member of the escort thrummed into a communicator beside an airlock. Evidently it summoned assistance from within, for after a couple of minutes the outer valve swung back. The three from Sol entered the chamber in response to gestures. There was barely room for them. Pumps roared, sucking out Babur's air. Gas from the interior gushed through a nozzle. The inner valve opened.

Beyond was an entryroom, empty save for a spacesuit locker. Two beings waited. They were lightly clad, but they carried sidearms. One was a Merseian, a biped whose face was roughly manlike but whose green-skinned body, leaning stance, and ponderous tail were not. The other was a human male.

Falkayn stepped out, almost losing his balance as the pull on him dropped. He unlatched his faceplate. "Hello," he heard. "Welcome to the monastery."

"Thanks," he mumbled.

"A word of warning first," the man said. "Don't try making trouble, no matter how husky your Wodenite friend is. The Baburites have armed watchers everywhere. Cooperate with me, and I'll help you settle in. You'll be here for quite a spell."

"Why?"

"You can't expect they'll let you go till the war is over, can you? Or don't you know? The main fleet of Babur is off to grab Mirkheim. And scoutboats have reported human ships on their way there."

VI

The man, large, heavy-featured, thick-mustached, introduced himself as Sheldon Wyler. "Sure, I'm working for the Baburites," he said almost coolly. "What's the Commonwealth or the League to me? And no, don't bother asking for details, because you won't get them."

He did, though, name his sullenly mute companion, Blyndwyr of the Vach Ruethen. "A fair number of Merseians are enlisted in the navy," he volunteered. "Mostly they belong to the aristocratic party at home and have no love for the League, considering how it shunted their kind aside and dealt instead with the Gethfennu group. You know, not many League people seem to understand what a cosmos of enemies it's made for itself over the years."

After the newcomers had unsuited, he squeezed past Adzel to a phone set in the wall. When he had punched, the screen lit with the likeness of a Baburite. "They're here," he reported in Anglic, and went on to describe the three from *Muddlin' Through*. "We're about to show them their quarters."

"Have you examined their effects for weapons?" asked the vocalizer voice.

"Why, no. What good—Well, all right. Hold on." To the prisoners: "You heard. We've got to check your gear."

"Proceed," Adzel said dully. "*We* are not so foolish as to use firearms inside an environmental unit; so we have brought none."

Wyler laughed. "Blyndwyr and I are good enough shots to blast you without putting a hole anywhere else." He went quickly through the luggage. The Merseian kept hand on gun butt. Chee's whiskers quivered with rage, her fur stood on end, her eyes had gone ice-green. A sickness gripped Falkayn by the throat.

Having verified the bags contained nothing more dangerous than compact tool kits, Wyler blanked the phone and led the way down a corridor. A room opening on it held four bunks and a window rapidly filling with night. "Bath and cleanup yonder," he pointed. "You can cook for yourselves; the kitchen's well stocked. Blyndwyr and me, we don't live here just now, but you'll be seeing a good deal of us, I'll bet. Behave yourselves and you won't be hurt. That includes telling us whatever we want to know."

Adzel brought his forelimbs through the door and the room grew crowded. "Uh, I guess you'd better sleep in the hall, fellow," Wyler said. "Tell you what, we'll go straight on to the mess, where there's space for all of us, and talk."

Falkayn gripped his spirit as if it were a wrestler trying to throw him. As he walked, his neck ached from its own stiffness. *Lead him on,* he thought. *Collect information, no matter how unlikely it is you'll ever bring it to anybody who can use it.* "What's this building for?" he got out in what he attempted to make a level tone.

"Engineering teams used to need it," Wyler said. "Later it housed officers of oxygen-breathing auxiliary forces while they got their indoctrination."

"You speak too freely," Blyndwyr reproved him.

Wyler bit his lip. "Well, I didn't sign on to be a goddamn interrogator—" He relaxed a little. "What the muck, my answer was pretty obvious, wasn't it? And they aren't going anywhere with it, either. . . . Here we are."

The messroom was broad and echoing. Furniture had been stacked against the walls and the air smelled musty, as if no one had adjusted the recyclers for some time. Adzel went motionless, like a statue of an elemental demon. Chee poised at his feet, her tail whipping her flanks and the floor. Falkayn and Wyler drew out a couple of chairs and sat. Blyndwyr stood well aside, ever watchful.

"Suppose you start by telling me exactly who sent you and why," Wyler said. "You've been goddamn vague so far."

Our assignment itself was vague, Falkayn thought. *Van Rijn trusted we'd be able to improvise as we went, as we learned. Instead, we've been captured as casually as fish in a net. And as hopelessly?*

73

Aloud, he dared be defiant: "We might both be more interested in what you're doing. How can you claim it's not treason to your species?"

Wyler scowled. "Are you going to spout a sermon at me, Captain? I don't have to take that." He considered. "But okay, okay, I will explain. What's so evil about the Baburites? Without a navy, they'd never stand a chance. The Commonwealth would grab Mirkheim and the whole goddamn industrial revolution that Mirkheim means, with crumbs for anybody else. Or the League would. The Baburites think differently. To them, this is no question of profit or loss on a balance tape. No, it's an opportunity for the race. With it, they can buy their way into the front rank—buy ships, mount expeditions, plant colonies, not to speak of all they might do at home—immediately!"

"But Mirkheim was not foreseeable," Falkayn argued. "Before that, why was Babur arming? Why did it plan to fight . . . and whom?"

"The Commonwealth has a navy, doesn't it? And the League companies keep warships too. They've seen use. We never know what we may come up against tomorrow. You of all people should remember the Shenna. Babur has a right of self-defense."

"You talk like a convert."

"You do not talk like a businessman, Captain Falkayn," Wyler said in anger. "I think you're stalling me. And I'm not going to stand for that, you hear? Maybe you imagine being famous will protect you. Well, forget that. You're a long ways off into a territory that doesn't care a good goddamn about your reputation. They don't feel obliged here to send you back undamaged, or send you back at all. If we have to, we'll pump you full of babble juice. And if that doesn't seem to be working so well, we'll go on from there."

He stopped, swallowed, smoothed countenance and tone: "But hey, let's not quarrel. I'm sure you're a reasonable osco. And you say one of your aims is to see what you can dicker out for your employer. Well, I might be able to help you there, if you help me first. Let's brew some coffee and talk sense."

Chee Lan rattled a string of syllables. "What?" Wyler asked.

She spat out words like bullets: "I was making remarks about those refrigerated centipedes of yours that you wouldn't want to translate for them.''

Falkayn sat very quiet. His blood made a cataract noise in his ears. Chee had used the Haijakatan language, which they three knew and surely no one else within many light-years. *"If we don't escape, we'll die here sooner or later. And even what little we've learned is important to bring home. I think we can take these two, and get Davy back to the ship in disguise."*

"Her comments are, however, quite apposite," the Wodenite put in. "I myself might go so far as to say—" He switched to Haijakatan. *"If you can begin on the greenskin, Chee, I can handle the man."*

"True and triple true." The Cynthian did not pace, she bounded, back and forth like a cat at play but with her tail bottled to twice its normal size.

Wyler's hand slipped down toward his gun. Blyndwyr drew a hissing breath and backed off, gripping his own blaster in its holster. Falkayn held himself altogether still, believing he saw what his comrades intended but not quite sure, ready only to trust them.

Start by distracting attention. "You can't blame my friends for getting excited," he said. "They're not Commonwealth citizens. Neither am I. And we haven't come on behalf of the League, just of a single company. Nevertheless we're to be interned indefinitely and quizzed under threats, possibly under drugs or torture. The best thing you can do, Wyler, is make the higher-ups of Babur listen to us. They should put away this blind hostility of theirs to the League. Its independent members want it to be in charge of Mirkheim. That'd guarantee everybody access to the supermetals."

"Would it?" Wyler snorted. "The League's split in pieces. And the Baburites know that."

"How? When we're as ignorant about them as we are, how did they get so close an impression of us? Who told them? And what makes them ready to stake their whole future on the word of those persons?"

"I don't know everything," Wyler admitted. "Goddamn, this planet's got eight times the surface of Earth, most of it land surface. Why shouldn't the Imperial Band feel confident?" He thrust out his jaw. "And that will be the last question you get to ask, Falkayn. I'm starting now."

Chee's restlessness had brought her near the Merseian. His alertness had focused itself back on the seated humans. Abruptly she made a final leap, sidewise but straight at him. Landing halfway up his belly, she gripped fast to his garment with her toes while both arms wrapped around his gun hand. He yelled and tried to draw regardless. She was too strong; she clung. He hammered at her with his free fist. Her teeth raked blood from it.

Adzel had taken a single stride. It brought him in reach of Wyler, whom he plucked from the chair, lowered, and bowled backward across the floor. His tail slapped down over the man's midriff to hold him pinioned. Meanwhile Adzel kept moving. He got to Blyndwyr, picked him up by the neck, shook him carefully, and set him down in a stunned condition. Chee hauled the blaster loose and scampered aside. Wyler was struggling to get at his gun. Falkayn arrived and took the weapon from its holster.

Adzel released Wyler and stepped back with his comrades. Wyler lurched to his feet; Blyndwyr sat gasping. "Are you crazy?" the human chattered. "What is this nonsense, you can't—can't—"

"Maybe we can." Glee surged through Falkayn. He knew he should have been more cautious, vetoed the attack, stayed meek lest he get himself killed. *But if none of us three is an Earthling, Coya is; and on the whole, Earth has been good to us too. Besides, ours is Old Nick's single ship in these parts. He sent us mainly to gather information, that he might not have to grope totally blind. And his welfare is also the welfare of thousands of his workers, millions among the planetary peoples who trade with him. . . . To Satan with that. What counts is breaking free!* The fire in his flesh roared too loudly for him to hear any fright.

At the same time, the logical part of him was starkly conscious. "Stay where you are, both of you," he told Wyler and Blyndwyr. "Adzel, Chee, your idea is that I can go out dressed as him, right?"

"Of course." The Cynthian settled down on her haunches and began to groom herself. "One human must look like another to a Baburite."

Adzel cocked his head and rubbed his snout with a loud sandpa-

76

pering sound. "Perhaps not entirely. Freeman Wyler does have dark hair and a mustache. We must do something about that."

"Meanwhile, Wyler, off with your clothes," Chee ordered. The Merseian, half recovered, made as if to rise. She swung the blaster in his direction. "You stay put," she said in his native Eriau. "I'm not a bad marksman either."

Bloodless in the cheeks, Wyler cried, "You're on collision orbit, I tell you, you can't get away, you'll die for goddamn nothing!"

"Undress, I told you," Chee replied. "Or must Adzel do it?"

Looking at the muzzle of her weapon and the implacable eyes behind, Wyler started to remove his garments. "Falkayn, haven't you any sense?" he pleaded.

The response he got was a thoughtful "Yes. I'm planning how we can take you along to quiz."

Chee lifted her ears. " 'We,' Davy?" she asked. "How are Adzel and I going to get out? No, you can ransom us later."

"You two most certainly are coming," Falkayn said. "We don't know how revengeful Baburites are, or their human and Merseian chums."

"But—"

"Besides, I'll need your help with Wyler, not to mention after we're spaceborne."

Adzel returned from the kitchen where he had been rummaging. "Here is the means to provide you with dark hair and mustache," he announced proudly. "A container of chocolate sauce."

It didn't seem like what a really dashing hero would use in a jailbreak, but it would have to do. While he stripped, put on Wyler's garb, and submitted to the anointing, Falkayn exchanged rapid-paced words with his companions. A scheme evolved, not much more precarious than the one which had gotten them this far.

Adzel ripped up Blyndwyr's clothes and tied him securely in place. He and Chee kept Wyler unbound, naked, under guard of her firearm. The Wodenite uttered a benediction, all the goodbye that Falkayn took time for. They three might never fare together again, he might never come back to Coya and Juanita, but he dared not stop to think about that, not now.

The hallway clattered to his footfalls. At the airlock, he punched the number he had seen and stood feeling as if he waited to be shot at in a duel. When the Baburite's four eyes peered out of the screen at him, he couldn't help passing his tongue over dry lips. A sweet taste reminded him of how crude his disguise was.

He spoke without preliminary, as Wyler had done before: "The prisoners seem to have lost morale. They asked me to fetch some medicines and comforts for them from their ship. I think that may make them cooperative."

He was gambling that human psychology would be as little known here as human bodies were.

A heartbeat and a heartbeat went by before the creature answered: "Very well. The guards will be told to expect you." Blankness.

Falkayn found Wyler's spacesuit and its undergarment in a locker. The suit was distinctively painted; probably every offplanet employee had an individual pattern for identification purposes. So he must adjust it to fit his somewhat taller frame. He could have used help, but didn't dare have anyone else in scanner range of the phone, lest the Baburite call him back.

Cycling through the lock, he emerged into bulldog jaws of gravitation. The field stretched bare before him, pockmarked with hatch covers. Here and there a caterpillar shape crossed it on some unguessable errand. Blue-white lights glared along the fronts of buildings till their ice shimmered like cold made visible. A wind whined and thrust. In darkness overhead, two moons shone dimly, but no stars. The walk was long to his destination.

It seemed impossible that no one challenged him while he opened the silo, stepped onto the elevator, and descended. By the time he had reached the personnel entrance of his ship, his helmet was chokeful of sweat-reek, he could barely whistle the countersign, and superstition rose from the grave of his childhood to croak, *This can't go on. You're overdue for bad luck*.

We've already had it, he defended. *We came too late—after the fleet had left*.

Do you think if it were still here, you would have been this lightly guarded?

The valve turned. Waiting in the chamber for air exchange, Falkayn invoked some of Adzel's Buddhist techniques and regained a measure of calm. "There should be no bow, no arrow, no archer: only the firing."

He left his space armor on inside, though frost was instantly white upon it. A flick of a switch in the heater controls cleared his faceplate, and he hurried to the bridge. Working his awkward bulk into his shockseat, he said via radio, "Muddlehead, we have to break Adzel and Chee loose. I'll steer, because you haven't seen where they are. We'll land in front of an entry lock. Blast it instantly—they won't have time to go through in the regular way—and have the outer valve of the number-two belly entrance open for them. The moment they're aboard, lift for space, taking such evasive maneuvers as your instruments suggest are best. Go into hyperdrive as soon as we're far enough out, and I mean as soon; forget about safety margins. Is this clear?"

"As clear as usual," said the computer.

The power plant came to full, murmurous life. Negafield generators thrust against that fabric of physical relationships which we call space. The ship glided upward.

"Yonder!" Falkayn yelled uselessly. Dancing over the manual pilot console, his fingers were handicapped by their gloves. But if the hull should be seriously holed by an enemy shot, an unprotected oxygen breather would be dead. Air roared outside. He had left the acceleration compensator off, in order that he might have that extra sensory input for this tricky task, and forces yanked at him, threw him against the safety web and then back into the seat. Hai-ah!

The building was straight ahead. He dropped, he hovered. A gun in its turret flung forth a shaped-charge shell. Flame erupted, the outer portal crumpled in wreckage. With surgical delicacy, an energy cannon sent its beam lancing at the inner valve. Metal turned white hot and flowed.

The caterpillar figures dashed about on the field. Had they no ground defenses? Well, who could have anticipated this kind of attack? Wait—above—forms in the moonglow, suddenly diving, aircraft—

The barrier went down. A frost-cloud boiled as Baburite and

Terrestrial gases met. Falkayn was fleetingly glad that automatic doors would close off the module where Blyndwyr lay. Doubly gigantic in his spacesuit, Adzel stormed forth. Was he carrying Chee and Wyler? A firebolt spat from above. The spaceship swung her cannon about and threw lightning back. Adzel was out of sight, below the curve of the hull. What had happened, in God's name, what had happened?

"They are aboard," Muddlehead reported, and sent the vessel leaping.

Acceleration jammed Falkayn deep into his chair. "Compensators," he ordered hoarsely. A steady one gee underfoot returned. Split atmosphere raved and the first stars came in sight. Falkayn unlocked his faceplate and reached shakily for the intercom button. "Are you all right?" he called.

A shell exploded close by, flash of light, buffet of noise, trembling of deck. *Muddlin' Through* drove on outward.

Adzel's tones rumbled through the fury round about. "Essentially we are well, Chee and I. Unfortunately, a shot from an aircraft struck our prisoner, who was under my right arm, penetrated his suit, and killed him instantly. I left the body behind."

There's our bad luck, raged within Falkayn. *I would've put him under narco and maybe learned—Damn, oh, damn!*

"My own suit was damaged, but not too badly for the self-sealing to work, and I suffered no more than a scorched scale," Adzel went on. "Chee was safe on my left side. . . . I would like to say a prayer for Sheldon Wyler."

Steadiness took over in Falkayn. "Later. First we've got to escape. We've surprise and speed on our side, but the alarm must be in space by now. Take battle stations, you two."

He knew as well as they that in a close encounter with any fighter heavier than a corvette, they were done for. They might ward off missiles for a time; but so would the enemy, and meanwhile its energy beams, powered by generators more massive than *Muddlin' Through* could carry, would gnaw through plating much thinner than its own.

The chance of combat was small, however. Probably no Baburite had such a position and velocity at this moment that its grav drive was capable of equalizing vectors, at the same point in space, with the furiously accelerating Solar craft. Nearly all slug-it-out contests took place because opponents had deliberately sought each other.

Target-seeking torpedoes, whose mass was small enough to permit enormous changes in speed and direction, were something else. So were rays that traveled at the speed of light.

The sky of Babur had fallen well aft, the globe was still huge in heaven but dwindling. Stars burned manyfold, some among them the color of blood.

"When can we go hyper, Muddlehead?" Falkayn asked. It shouldn't be long. They were already high in the gravity well of Mogul and climbing upward fast in Babur's. Soon the metric of space would be too flat to interfere unduly with fine-tuned oscillators; and once they were moving at their top faster-than-light pseudovelocity, practically nothing ever built had legs to match theirs.

"One-point-one-six-hour, given our present vector," said the computer. "But I propose to add several minutes to that time by applying transverse thrust to bring us near the satellite called Ayisha. My instruments show a possible anomalous radiation pattern there."

Falkayn hesitated a second. If heavy ground installations were on the moon . . . Decision: "Very well. Carry on."

Time crawled. Twice Chee yelled savagely, when her guns destroyed a missile on its intercept course. Falkayn could only sit and think. Mostly he remembered, in jumbled oddments—wingsailing with Coya at Lunograd, a red sun forever above a desert on Ikrananka, his father's sternness about *noblesse oblige*, fear that he might drop newborn Juanita when she was laid in his arms, *The Flyting of Dunbar and Kennedie*, his first night with Coya and his last, youthful beer hall arguments about God and girls, Rodin's *Burghers of Calais*, a double moonglade on the Auroral Ocean, a firefall between two stars, Coya beside him beholding the crooked towers of a city on a planet which did not yet have a human-bestowed name, his mother using a prism to show him what made the rainbow, Coya and he laughing like children as they had a snowball fight at an Antarctic resort, the splendor of an Ythrian on the wing, Coya bringing him sandwiches and coffee when he sat far into a nightwatch studying the data readouts on a new world the ship was circling, Coya—

The scarred moon-disc grew big in the viewscreen. Falkayn magnified, searched, suddenly found it: a sprawling complex of domes, turrets, ship housings, spacefield, test stands. . . . "Record!" he ordered automatically.

Did Muddlehead sound hurt? Impossible. "Of course. Infrared signs are of beings thermodynamically similar to or identical with humans."

"You mean that stuff's not meant for Baburites? Why, then—"

"*A-yu!*" Chee Lan screamed; and incandescence flared momentarily. "Close, friends, close!"

"I suggest we do not dawdle," Adzel said.

The colony, or whatever it was, reeled out of sight behind a mountain range as the ship sped past Ayisha. "According to my instruments," Muddlehead reported, "if we persevere as at present, surrounding conditions will grow progressively less unsalubrious for us."

That means we're going to get away, Falkayn thought. *We're clear.* The pains and tingles of tension spread upward through his body to the brain.

"Where are we bound, then?" he heard Chee ask.

He forced himself to say, "Mirkheim. We just might arrive ahead of the Baburites, in time to warn those approaching humans, whoever they are, and the workers there."

"I doubt that," the Cynthian replied. "The enemy probably has too big a jump on us. And should we take the risk? Isn't it more important to bring home the information we've collected, that somehow Babur's acquired a substantial corps of military and technical oxygen breathers? A courier torp might not get through."

"No, we must attempt to warn," Adzel said. "It could forestall a battle. One violent death is too much."

Falkayn nodded wearily. His gaze sought back to the uncaring stars. *Poor Wyler,* he thought. *Poor everybody.*

VII

An intercom presented the captain of *Alpha Cygni*. "Madame,"
he said, "Navigation reports we are one light-year from destination."

"Oh—" Sandra gathered in her wits. So soon? Then how had the
trip from Hermes taken so long? *A light-year,* raced through her. *The
extreme distance at which the space-pulses from our hyperdrives are
detectable. Instantaneously. Now they'll know at the planet that
we're coming. And "they" could be an enemy.* "Order all units to
prepare for action."

"Yellow alert throughout. Aye, madame." The image disap-
peared.

Sandra stared about her. Save where viewscreens showed heaven,
the admiral's bridge was a narrow and cheerless cave. It throbbed
slightly with engine beat; the air blew warm, smelling faintly of oil
and chemicals. Abruptly it felt unreal, her naval uniform a costume,
the whole proceeding a ridiculous piece of playacting.

Clad in a similar two-toned coverall, which could at need be the
underpadding in a spacesuit, Eric gave her a wry look. "Buck
fever?" he murmured. "Me too." He could speak candidly, since he
was the only other person there.

"I suppose that's what it is." Sandra tried to shape a smile and
failed.

"I'm surprised. When you're one of the few people along who
have any combat experience."

"Diomedes wasn't like this. That was hand-to-hand warfare.
And . . . and anyway, nobody expected me to issue commands."

*Why didn't I hire mercenaries, years ago, to form the nucleus of a
proper-sized officer corps?*

Because it didn't seem that the peace we had always known on

Hermes would ever be threatened. Brushfire clashes happened around stars too far off for us to really notice: nothing worse. We were warned of aliens getting into space; but surely they were not too dangerous—not even the Shenna, whom, after all, the League put down before any great harm was done. Double and triple surely, Technic civilization would never know wars among its own member peoples. That was something man had left behind him, like purdah, tyranny, and cannibalism. We kept a few warcraft with minimum crews to act as a police and rescue corps, and as insurance against a contingency we didn't really believe was possible. (Inadequate insurance, I see today.) Their practice with heavy weapons we considered rather a joke, except when taxpayer organizations complained.

"Damn me for letting you come!" she blurted. "You should have stayed behind, in charge of the reserves—"

"We've been over that ground often enough, think you not, Mother?" Eric answered. "No better man than Mike Falkayn could be holding the reins there. What I wish is that I'd had sense to ask for an assignment that'd hold me busy here. Being your executive officer sounded big, but it turns out to be sheer comic opera."

"Well, I'm scant more than a passenger myself till we start negotiating. Pray God I can do that. In history, comic operas have had a way of turning into tragedies."

If only Nadi were along. His company quiets me. But she had sent the chief of the Supermetals patrol on ahead, to ready the entire outfit for cooperation with hers.

About three hours till arrival, at their top pseudospeed . . . She drew several deep breaths. Never mind about a battle. If that came, let her leave it in the hands of her captains, with the skipper of this flagship the coordinator, as had been agreed at the outset. Their purpose then would almost certainly be just to fight free and escape. They had no great strength. Besides *Alpha Cygni*, a light battleship, it was two cruisers, four destroyers, and a carrier for ten Meteor-class pursuers. At that, they had not left much behind to guard their home.

Her job was to prevent a clash, to establish Hermes as an impartial agent intervening to see justice done and order restored. And she did know something about handling people. She settled into her shockseat, lit a cigar, and began consciously relaxing, muscle by muscle. Eric paced.

"Madame!" The words came harsh and not quite even. "Hyperdrives detected."

Sandra made herself remain seated. "Coming to meet us?"

"No, madame. They're in our fourth quadrant. As near as can be extrapolated, we and they have the same destination."

She twisted her head about, eyes seeking from screen to screen. Darkness still held the sun of Mirkheim. They would have to come almost on top of that dim remnant to see it. The fourth quadrant—She could not identify what she sought there. It was only a small spark at its remove, lost among thousands. But in the fourth quadrant lay Mogul.

Eric smacked fist into palm. "The Baburites!"

"A moment, please, sir," said the captain. "I'm getting a preliminary data analysis. . . . 'Tis a huge force. No details computable yet; but in numbers, at least, 'tis overwhelming."

For a moment Sandra gulped nausea, as if she had been kicked in the gut. Then her mind went into emergency operation. Self-doubt fell away. Decisions snapped forth. "This changes things," she said. "Best we try for a parley. From this ship, since I'm aboard her. Prepare an intercept course for us. The rest of ours—they can reach Mirkheim well ahead of the newcomers, not? . . . Good. Let them continue yonways under leadership of *Achilles*, rendezvous with Nadi, and hold themselves combat ready. But in case of doubt—'fore all, if something appears to have happened to us on *Alpha*—they are to return home at once."

"Aye, madame." In a corner of herself, Sandra felt sorry for the captain. He was a young man, really, striving to be cool and efficient in the face of ruin. He repeated her instructions and his image vanished.

"Oh, no," Eric groaned. "What can we do?"

"Very little, I'm afraid," Sandra admitted. "Let me be, please. I have to think." She leaned back and closed her eyes.

An hour passed. From time to time, relayed information hauled her mind briefly out of the circle around which it struggled. The Babu-

85

rites were holding course at moderate pseudospeed. Their complacency was almost an insult. Finally one ship left formation and angled off to meet the oncoming Hermetian. A while later, signals began to go back and forth, modulations imposed on hyperdrive oscillations: *We wish to communicate—We will communicate.* The calls were stereotyped, an on-off code, the rate of conveyance of meaning tormentingly slow: for the uncertainty principle is quick to make chaos of space-pulses. Not until vessels are within a few thousand kilometers of each other is there enough coherence for voice transmission. Pictures require more proximity than that.

Which is why we can't send messages directly between the stars, crossed Sandra's head, relic of a lesson in physics when she was young. *Nobody could position that many relay stations. Nor would they stay positioned. So we must use couriers, and hell can come to a boil someplace before we know aught has gone wrong.*

Instruments accumulated ever better data, computers analyzed, until it was clear that the strange craft was approximately the size of *Alpha*, surely as well armed. At last the captain's face reappeared. He was pale. "Madame, we've received a vocal communication. It goes . . . goes . . . quote, 'You will come no nearer, but will match hypervelocity to ours and stand by for orders.' Close quote. That's how it goes."

Eric reddened. Sandra peeled lips back from teeth and said, "We'll go along. However, phrase your acknowledgment, hm, 'We will do as you request.' "

"Thank you, Your Grace!" The captain's whole being registered an appreciation that should spread through the crew . . . though doubtless the Anglic nuance would quite go by the Baburites.

Still the viewscreens held only stars. Sandra could imagine the foreign ship, a spheroid like hers, never meant to land on a planet, studded with gun emplacements, missile launchers, energy projectors, armored in forcefields and steel, magazines bearing the death of half a continent. She would not see it in reality. Even if they fought, she probably never would. The flesh aboard it and the flesh aboard *Alpha* would not touch, would not witness each other's perishing nor hear the anguish of the wounded. The abstractness was nightmarish. Peter Asmundsen, Nicholas van Rijn, she herself had ever been in the middle of their own doings: a danger dared, a blow struck or taken, a word spoken, a hand clasped, all in the living presence of the doers. *Is our time past? Is the whole wild, happy age of the pioneers? Are we today crossing the threshold of the future?*

Preliminaries must have taken place before the captain announced, "Lady Sandra Tamarin-Asmundsen, Grand Duchess of Hermes; the delegate of the Imperial Siseman Naval Command."

The sound of the vocalizer was emotionless and blurred by irregularities in the carrier wave. Yet did a roughness come through? "Greeting, Grand Duchess. Why are you here?"

She dismissed her despair and cast back, "Greeting, Admiral, or whatever you want to be called. We're naturally curious about your purpose, too. You're no nearer home than we are."

"Our mission is to take possession of Mirkheim for the Autarchy of United Babur."

A part of her wished that the ships were close enough together for picture transmission. Somehow it would have helped to look into four little eyes in an unhuman visage. It would have felt less like contending with a ghost.

But the determination is as solid as yonder invisible sun, she thought, *and so are the weapons which back it.* She said with care, "Is't not obvious why we Hermetians have come? Our objective is simply to . . . to take charge, to act as caretakers, while a settlement is worked out. Being neither Commonwealth nor Babur nor League, we hoped we could make all sides stay their hands, think twice, and avoid a war. Admiral, 'tis not too late for that."

"It is," said the artificial voice. When it added its stunning news, was there the least hint of sardonicism? "We do not refer to the fact that the Imperial Band does not desire your interference, but to the fact, established by scouts of ours, that the Commonwealth already has a fleet at Mirkheim. We are coming to oust it. Hermetians will be well advised to withdraw before combat begins."

"Son of a bitch—" she heard Eric gasp, and herself whisper, "Merciful Jesus!"

"Rejoin your flotilla and take it home," said the Baburite. "Once action has commenced, we will attack every human vessel we encounter."

"No, wait, wait!" Sandra cried, half rising. No response came. After a minute her captain told her: "The alien is moving off, madame, back toward its companion units."

"Battle stations," Sandra directed. "Full speed on a course to intercept ours."

Stars streamed across viewscreens as *Alpha* swung about. The pulse of the engines strengthened.

"Was that crawler lying?" Eric roared.

As if in reply, the captain described readings, numerous hyperdrives activated in the neighborhood of the planet. Obviously somebody was present who had now detected the newest invaders. Who could that be but a Solar task force?

"Curse the cosmos, what a kloodge of amateurs we are." Pain stretched Eric's mouth wide as he spoke. "The Baburites kept watch on Mirkheim. They knew when the Earthlings arrived. We, we plowed ahead like a bull with a fever."

"No, remember, we relied on Nadi's patrol to come give us warning of aught untoward," Sandra reminded him mechanically. "No doubt the Earthlings captured them—he had nothing particularly fast or powerful—captured them with some idea of preserving surprise. But meanwhile the Baburites had high-speed observers in the vicinity." She grimaced. "It seems the worst amateurs are in the Commonwealth Admiralty."

They've never had to fight a war. Skills, doctrine, the military style of thinking evaporated generations ago.

Such things must needs be relearned in the time that is upon us.

Tidings continued to arrive. The fleet ahead was leaving Mirkheim, deploying in what looked like combat formation. It was considerably inferior to the armada from Babur. The sensible act would have been to cut and run. But no doubt its commander had his orders from the politicians back home: "Don't give up easily. We're sure those bugs will just attempt a bluff. They can't be serious about fighting *us*."

They sure can be, Sandra thought. *They are.*

Eric stopped in his tracks. It was as if a flame kindled in him, though he spoke low. "Mother . . . Mother, if we joined the Commonwealthers—our fellow humans, after all—"

She shook her head. "Not. 'Twould make slim difference, save to get Hermetians killed and ships wrecked that we'll want for home defense. I'm about to tell all other units of ours to sheer off and start back immediately."

He divined her intention. "We, though? *Alpha Cygni*?"

"We'll continue to Mirkheim. Belike the whole Solar strength will be gone by the time we get there, off to meet the Baburites. In any event, this is too formidable a craft for anybody to tangle with casually. We do have a duty to help Nadi's folk get free if possible. They're our allies, after a fashion. Including technicians on the ground." Sandra achieved a smile of sorts. "And since the news first broke about it, I've been curious to see Mirkheim."

No guard was at the planet. The Supermetals patrol vessels orbited empty. A quick radio exchange confirmed that their crews had been ferried down to the mining base, as deep an oubliette as ever was. The battleship took a circling station of her own. Boats sprang from her sides to evacuate the personnel below. Sandra left a protesting Eric behind, nominally in charge, and herself rode in one of the auxiliaries.

Mirkheim loomed monstrous ahead. The wanly glowing ashes of its sun were unseeable at its distance, and it might almost have been a rogue world which had never belonged to any star, drifting eternally among winter-bright constellations. Almost, not quite. No snows of frozen atmosphere decked it from pole to pole; its gleam was of metal, hard, in places nearly mirrorlike. Mountains and chasms made rough shadows. Regions of dark iron sketched a troll's face.

Soon the boat neared the surface and leveled off. Behind Sandra stretched a plain, on and on to a horizon so far off that a dread of being alone in limitless emptiness awoke in the soul of the onlooker. The ground was not cratered and dust-covered like that of a normal airless body; it was blank, dimly shining, here and there corrugated in fantastic ridges where moltenness had congealed. Its darkness cut sharply across the Milky Way. To right and left, the plain was pocked by digging. Incredibly—no, understandably—work went on; a robot tractor was hauling a train of ore cars. Ahead bulked a scarp, upthrown by some ancient convulsion through the crust of metals left by the supernova, a black wall beneath which the domes and cubes and towers of the compound huddled as if crushed, on whose heights a radio mast seemed to have been spun by spiders.

The scene tilted and appeared to leap upward as the boat descended. Landing jacks made a contact that vibrated through hull and crew. Engine purr died away. Silence pressed inward.

Sandra broke it. "I'm bound out," she said, leaving her seat.

"Madame?" her pilot protested. "But the drag's more than five gees!"

"I'm reasonably strong."

"We—you know, you ordered yourself—we'll simply take them directly aboard and scramble."

"I doubt not we'll hit complications even in that. I want to be on the spot to help cope, not at the end of a phone beam." *And I can hardly say it aloud, but I feel a need to . . . to experience, however briefly, this thing for which so many sacrifices have been made, for which so much blood may soon be spilled. I need for Mirkheim to become real to me.*

A pair of crewmen accompanied her, checking out her spacesuit with more than usual care and flanking her when she cycled through the airlock and stepped forth. That was well. Caught by the gravitation as she left the boat's interior field, she would have crashed to a bone-breaking fall had the men not supported her. The three of them hastily activated their impellers to hold them up, as if suspended in a harness. That let them shuffle forward across the steely soil, forcing leaden ribs to draw air in and out of them, staring past sagging lids with eyeballs whose weight sent blurs and blotches floating across vision. Unseen, unfelt, radioactive emanation sleeted through them, enough to kill in a matter of weeks.

And workers have been coming here for eighteen years, Sandra remembered. *Do I love my own kind that much?*

They were emerging from a dome. Despite their variegated suits, she recognized their races from past contact or from reading and pictures. Nadi the Wodenite led them, of course. Near him came two raven-featured Ikranankans, a four-armed shaggy-headed Gorzuni, a leonine Ivanhoan, a faintly saurian-looking Vanessan, two Cynthians (from societies less advanced than the spacefaring one, which had

90

shown no desire to help them progress), and four humans (from colony planets where existence could become much easier if an adequate capital investment be made; but Technic capital was attracted to more lucrative things). In the middle of barrenness, they were like grotesque symbols of life; Vigeland might have sculptured them.

It was not surprising that they were so few. Environment made short the periods during which any sophont could work here, and forced him to stay mostly indoors. Flesh and blood were present chiefly to perform certain maintenance and communication tasks, and to make decisions which were not routine. Otherwise, machines dwelt on Mirkheim. They prospected, mined, transported, refined, loaded, did the brute labor and most of the delicate. Some were slaved to others which had self-programming computers, while the central computer at the base was of consciousness level. The entire operation was a miracle of technological ingenuity—and still more, Sandra thought, of *sisu, esprit*, indomitability, selflessness.

A man toiled ahead of the rest. The visage behind the vitryl of his helmet was battered and worn. "My lady from Hermes?" he began in accented Anglic. "I'm Henry Kittredge from Vixen, superintendent of this particular gang."

"I'm . . . happy to meet you. . . ." she replied between breaths.

His smile was bleak. "I dunno 'bout that, lady. These aren't exactly happy circumstances, are they? But, uh, I do want to say how grateful we are. We've already overstayed our time, should've been relieved many days ago. If we'd had to stay much longer, working outdoors as often as usual, we'd've gotten a dangerous dosage. After a while, we'd've died."

"Couldn't you have kept indoors?"

"Maybe the Earthlings would've let us. I doubt the Baburites would. Why should they care? And we'd've been wanted to show them how to run these digs."

Sandra nodded, though it was an effort to pull her head back up again. "You've had years of accumulated experience, sometimes at the cost of lives, not?" she said. "That's a good strategic reason for evacuating you. Without your help, anybody else will be a long, expensive time about resuming exploitation. You—you and your coworkers, wherever they live, you might just prove to be a valuable bargaining counter."

"Yes, we've talked about that 'mong ourselves. Listen." Eagerness awoke in the tired voice. "Let's take some of the key equipment with us. Or if you don't want to delay that long, let's sabotage it. Huh?"

Sandra hesitated. She hadn't considered that possibility, and now the choice was thrust upon her. Dared she linger for extra hours?

She did. The fleets would not likely end their strife soon. "We'll remove the stuff," she said, and wondered if she was being wise or merely spiteful.

VIII

"We're too late."

The words seemed to hang for a moment in the murmurous quiet of the bridge. Any of three, Adzel, Chee Lan, David Falkayn, might have spoken them, out of shared pain and anger. All of three stared emptily forth into darkness and uncaring suns. There fire had blossomed, tiny at its remove but still a dreadful glory.

Another spark winked, and another. Nuclear warheads were exploding throughout the space near Mirkheim.

Chee reached for the hyperwave receiver controls. As she turned them past different settings, the speaker buzzed, chattered, crackled, gobbled: coded messages from ship to ship, across distances that light would take hours to bridge. The frontrunners of either fleet had begun engagement—gone into normal state, moving at true speeds of kilometers per second and true accelerations of a few gravities, reaching for each other with missiles, energy beams, shells, Meteor boats.

Adzel studied instruments, held a soft colloquy with Muddlehead, and announced: "The battle cannot be very old as yet. Else we would observe more traces of fusion bursts, more complicated neutrino patterns left by engines, than we do. We have missed a beforehand arrival by an ironically small margin."

"I wonder if our warning would have made much difference," Falkayn sighed. "Judging by these data"—he swept his hand across a row of meters.—"the Commonwealth fleet came first, defied the Baburites in hopes they'd back down, found that wasn't the case, and will be fighting for bare survival."

"Why doesn't it simply flee?"

Falkayn shrugged, as if the fact were not gall in his throat. "Orders, no doubt—to inflict maximum damage if combat should erupt—orders issued by politicians safe at home, who've always held the theory and practice of war is too wicked a subject for civilized men to study.''

Fighting could go on for days before the Commonwealth admiral decides he must retreat, he thought. *Ships will accelerate, decelerate, orbit freely over millions of kilometers, seeking an opponent, meeting him, firing in an orgasm of violence, then both of them drawn apart by their velocities till they can come about for a new encounter, probably each with a new foe.*

"We had to try, of course," he went on dully. "The question is what we try next."

They had ransacked their minds for plans, contingency after contingency, while *Muddlin' Through* sped from Babur toward Mirkheim. "Not contact," Adzel said. They might rendezvous with a Solar vessel and, through her, get in touch with the admiral. But they had nothing left to offer him, and the risk involved was considerable.

"Hang around?" Chee asked—wait with power systems throttled down, nearly undetectable, on the fringes of war, till they had seen what happened. But surely survivors would bring that news to Earth.

Yet it was no longer certain, as it once had been, that the Commonwealth government would be frank with the people; and van Rijn needed a full account.

It was not even sure that he would receive the dispatch they had sent him in a courier torpedo after their escape. When the thing entered the Solar System and broadcast its signal, the Space Service that retrieved it might not forward the written contents. Falkayn doubted the cipher could be broken in reasonable time; still, van Rijn would remain in the dark.

Thus the safety of this crew was a prime criterion—not to speak of Coya, Juanita, and the child unborn. Nevertheless, here sentient beings were dead, dying, mutilated, in mortal peril; and the horror would go on. To skulk in the deeps before slinking home had a foul taste.

And— "We haven't accomplished such an everlovin' lot so far, have we?" Falkayn muttered. "Blundered into captivity and out again, getting a man killed in the process."

"Do not feel guilty about that, Davy," Adzel counseled. "It was tragic, true, but Wyler was collaborating with the enemy."

"The uselessness of it, though!" Knuckles stood white on the human's fists.

"You both ought to discipline those consciences of yours," Chee said. "They squeam at you too much." Her carnivore instincts awakened, she bounded onto the console and stood white against blackness, stars, the distant firebursts where ships perished. "We can do active, not passive intelligence collection," she declared eagerly. "Why are we dithering? Let's make for Mirkheim."

"Is there any point in our landing?" Adzel replied. They had talked about the rescue of Supermetals personnel stranded on the planet; but they could only take a few without overloading their life support system.

"Probably not," Chee said. "However, that course will bring us near the thick of action. Who knows what might turn up? Come *on!*"

Inward bound, they received a laser-borne message. That meant it was directed specifically at them; they had been detected. The code was Commonwealth. Falkayn knew this from having compared different signals they acquired. He could not read it, but the meaning was plain: *Identify yourself or we attack.*

Muddlehead reeled off data analysis. The other craft was most likely a Continent-class destroyer. Her position, velocity, and acceleration were more definite. She could not draw near enough on this pass ever to show to the unaided eye as a black blade drawn over the Milky Way. But her weapons could span the gap. And both were too close to the dead sun to enter hyperdrive.

"Evade," Falkayn ordered. He sent back a voice transmission in Anglic: "We are not your enemy, we happen to be here from Earth."

A minute later, Muddlehead reported a missile launched toward him. He was not surprised. The men in yonder hull must be dazed with weariness and strangled terror, stress had worn them down till they were nothing but duty machines, and if he failed to reply in code then he must be a Baburite attempting a ruse.

At such a distance, a ray would be too attenuated to do harm. A ship as small as his could not carry a forcefield generator sufficiently strong to ward off a hard-driven warhead. Nor, despite her low mass, should she have the potential of running from a killer that homed on her engine output.

But *Muddlin' Through* had power for twice her size and spent none of it on energy screens. The heavens wheeled crazily around Falkayn's head as her computer sent her through an arc that would have torn the guts out of an ordinary vessel. Sliding clear of the torpedo, she opened fire on it. It blew apart in a rain of flames and incandescent gobbets. She swung about again and resumed her original course. The Terrestrial ship receded without making a second assault.

Briefly before Falkayn stood the idea of a man aboard that destroyer. He came from—where?—Japan, say, and always in him dwelt a memory of those beautiful islands, old high-curved roofs, cherry trees in bloom under the pure steeps of Fuji, a garden where gardener and bonsai worked together through a lifetime's love, temple bells cool at evening when he walked forth with a certain girl at his side. This day he sat webbed in place before the idiot faces of instruments while engines droned through his bones; thirst thickened his tongue, he had sweated too much in his tension, his garments stank, salt stung his eyes and lay bitter on his lips. Hour crept by hour, the waiting, the waiting, the waiting, until reality shrank to this and home was a half-forgotten fever dream: then alarms yammered, creatures that he had never seen even in his nightmares were somewhere on the far side of a bulkhead, or so the instruments said, and he ordered the launch parameters computed for a missile, sent it forth, sat waiting once more to know if he had slain or they would slay him, hoped wildly that his death would be quick and clean, not a shrieking with his skin seared off and his eyeballs melted, and perhaps through him there flitted a wondering whether those monsters he fired at also remembered a beautiful home.

Where had Sheldon Wyler come from?

Falkayn spoke harshly at the intercom pickup: "We seem to've gone free this time."

The incident would have sent most crews scuttling immediately toward safety. Instead, it hatched a goblin of an idea in Chee. Adzel

96

heard her out, pondered, and agreed the possible gain was worth the hazard. Falkayn argued for a while, then assented, the part of him that was Coya's husband outvoted by a part he had imagined lay buried with his youth.

Not that they had any chance to pull off a swift, gleeful exploit. Time drained away while the ship moved cautiously about, detectors straining, Muddlehead sifting and discarding. Falkayn puffed on his pipe till his raw tongue could not taste the food he made himself swallow. Chee worked on a statuette, attacking the clay as if it threatened her life. Adzel meditated and slept.

Endlessness finally had an end. "A Solar vessel has demolished a Baburite," the computer announced, and recited coordinates.

Falkayn jerked out of half a doze where he sat. "Are you sure?" He sprang to his feet.

"The characteristic flash of a detonation has been followed by a cessation of neutrino emission from one of two sources. The other source is departing, and would be unable to return at any available acceleration for a period of more than a standard day."

"Not that she'll want to—"

"We can lie alongside the wreck in a period I calculate to be three-point-seven hours plus or minus approximately forty minutes."

It thrilled in Falkayn. "And I suppose we've a fifty-fifty chance she'll be Baburite."

"No, that is positive. I have conducted statistical studies of emission patterns from thermonuclear reactors in both fleets. This ship that was defeated showed a distinctly Baburite spectrum."

Falkayn nodded. Fusion engines built to operate under subjovian conditions would not radiate quite like those which worked for oxygen breathers. He'd been aware of that, but had not been aware enough data would come in to make the mathematics reliable. "Bully for you, Muddlehead," he said. "You keep surprising me, the amount of initiative you show."

"I have also invented three new wild card games," the computer told him . . . hopefully?

"Never mind," Chee snapped. "You make for that cockering wreck!"

Drive pulses intensified. "We fared more happily the first time we cruised this part of space," Adzel mused. "But then, we were younger, eighteen Earth-years ago." Was he being tactful? The span was not so great a part of his life expectancy as it was of a human's or a Cynthian's.

"We were proud," Falkayn said. "*Our* discovery, that was going to give a dozen races the chance they needed. Now—" His voice died away.

Adzel laid a hand on his shoulder. He must consciously stiffen himself against the gee-field to support such a weight. "Feel no blame that this is being fought over, Davy," the Wodenite urged. "What we gave was good. It may be yet again."

"We knew the secret couldn't last," Chee added. "It was sheer luck that the first person to repeat our reasoning was Old Nick, and we could talk him into keeping quiet. Sooner or later, a nasty scramble was bound to happen."

"Sure, sure," Falkayn answered. "But war—I'd thought civilization had evolved beyond war."

"The Shenna hadn't, the Baburites haven't," Chee snorted. "You needn't accuse the Technic societies because outsiders have bad manners. That notion of symmetrical sinfulness is a strange tendency in your species."

"Somehow I can't see the cases as being parallel," Falkayn argued. "Damnation, it made a contorted kind of sense for the Shenna to plot an assault on us. But the Baburites—why should they arm as they did, never foreseeing a Mirkheim to fight over? And why should they ever fight, anyway? If they could buy the tools and technology they needed to build the kind of navy they have, why, they could buy all the supermetals they'd require for a fraction of the cost. I have this gnawing notion that something in us, in Technic culture, is responsible."

"Wyler might have given us a hint or three if he'd lived. I wish you'd stop moping about him, Davy. He wasn't a nice man."

"Who can afford to be, these days? . . . Oh, to hell with this." Falkayn flung himself back into his chair.

"Agreed. To hell by express. Me, I'm going to do some more modeling." Chee left the bridge.

"Perhaps I, at least, could play cards with you, Muddlehead, if you want diversion," Adzel offered. "We have little else to occupy us until we arrive."

Except sit and wish nothing we can't handle will home on us, Falkayn thought.

"—Fear and trembling Hope,
Silence and Foresight; Death the Skeleton
And Time the Shadow. . . ."

Spacesuited, he gave himself a touch of impeller thrust and drifted across a hundred meters of void between his own craft and the ruin.

Stars and stillness enfolded him. Here he saw no trace of the battle; all that agony was lost in the hollow reaches of space, save for a twisted shape that tumbled before him among lesser metal shards. He dared not think how many lives were gone—surely Baburites rejoiced to see their sun, even as he did his—but bent his attention wholly, dryly, to the task ahead.

The ship had been more or less cruiser size. A missile had gotten past her defenses and shattered her. Without a surrounding atmosphere, concussion had been insufficient to blow her entirely to fragments. Survivors, if any, had found an undamaged lifeboat, in a section built to break away upon impact, and fled. The largest remnant of the hull was bigger than *Muddlin' Through* and ought to contain plenty of apparatus, not too badly damaged for study. A gauge on his wrist told him that the level of radioactivity was tolerable.

He felt and heard the thud as his bootsoles touched plates and gripped fast. Chee poised nearby; Adzel was a gigantic silhouette farther off against heaven. "You two stay put while I take a look around," he directed them, and plodded off. It felt a little like walking upside down, for he was weightless and the dead vessel was slowly spinning. Constellations streamed by, blacknesses flickered around the shapes of turrets and housings. His breath sounded loud in his ears.

When he reached an edge where the hull had been torn apart, he picked his way cautiously through a tangle of projecting, knotted girders. A body was caught between two of them. He stood for a minute gazing at it by the light of his flashlamp. Undiffused in

99

airlessness, a wan puddle of luminance draped itself over a form that was too alien to seem hideous, as human corpses usually did after a violent death; the Baburite looked pitifully small and frail. *I'm wasting time, which I still have though he no longer does,* Falkayn realized, and went onward, around the verge, into the cavity of the derelict.

Star-gleam and his flash picked out surrealistically intricate masses half submerged in darkness. A bleak pleasure jumped in him. *Good luck for us! This seems to've been the main drive room. Which means control units, too, if their craft are laid out along roughly the same lines as ours.*

It could be the fulfillment of the hope which had led to his and his companions' search. So little was known about the race which built the invading armada. Who could tell what clues might lie in their engineering?

Would the Commonwealth admiral get the same thought, and order a salvage operation for intelligence purposes? Probably not. His fleet was too hard pressed. Besides, its entire management bespoke idiocy—well, be charitable and say ignorance—at the highest levels of government.

And assuming that relics nevertheless did get back to Earth, the government would scarcely share them with van Rijn. Falkayn was not simply being loyal to his patron; he feared that the old man was the last competent thinker left in the Solar System. Van Rijn might be able to make something of a bit of evidence that was meaningless to everybody else.

Not that we can do any serious work here, Falkayn knew. *We haven't the facilities. Also, it's too bloody dangerous to linger very long. But we can spend a few hours investigating, and we can carry off selected items for closer examination. Maybe we'll make a marginally useful discovery. Maybe.*

Move! He crept toward the nearest of the forms which towered before him.

IX

The evening before he left, Bayard Story invited Nicholas van Rijn to join him for dinner. The Council of the League had dissolved in dissonance, and the delegates must now see to their own affairs as best they could.

The Saturn Room of the Hotel Universe was nearly full, though thanks to widely spaced tables and discreet lighting it did not seem so. Perhaps, when rumors of war hissed everywhere about them, friends and lovers were seizing whatever enjoyment they might while the chance lasted; or perhaps not. The Solar System had been without direct experience of armed conflict for so long that it was hard to guess how anybody would behave. Couples held each other close while they moved about on the dance floor. Was there really a wistful note in the music of the live orchestra? Overhead lifted the vast half-circles of the rings, tinted more subtly than rainbows in a violet sky where four moons were presently visible. Sparks of light flickered in the streaming arcs and meteors clove the heavens. Where a tiny sun was setting, dimmed by thick air, clouds lay tawny and rosy.

"The place is more suitable for romance than for a pair of tired businessmen," Story remarked with a slight smile.

"Well, any notion we can agree is plenty romantic," grunted van Rijn from the depths of the menu. His free hand brought to his mouth alternate slurps of akvavit and gulps of beer. Story sipped a champagne and rum. "Let me see—*dood en ondergang*, please to let me see, this place is dim like a bureaucrat's brain!—I begin with a dozen Limfjord oysters, Limfjord, mind you, waiter, the chilled crab legs and asparagus tips, and fifty grams of Strasbourg paté. Then while I eat my appetizer you can fill me a nice bowl of onion soup à la Ansa. You do not want to miss that, Story, it uses spices we maybe do not

101

get any more if comes something as stupid as a war. For a wine with the soup—'' He went on for several minutes.

"Oh, bring me the tournedos on the regular dinner, medium rare,'' Story laughed. "And, all right, I will have the onion soup, since it's recommended."

"You should pay better attention to what you eat, boy," van Rijn said.

Story shrugged. "I don't make a god of my stomach."

"You think I do, ha? No, by damn, I make my stomach work for me, like a slave it works. My palate, that is what I pay attention to. And what is wrong with that? Who is harmed? The very first miracle Our Lord did was turning water into wine, and a select vintage it was, too." Van Rijn shook his head; the ringlets swirled across his brocade jacket. "The troublemakers, they are those what are not contented with God's gifts of good food, drink, music, women, profit. No, they bring on misery because they must play at being God themselves, they will be our Saviors with a capital ass."

Story grew grave. "Are you sure you're not the self-righteous one? What you were advocating at the Council could have, almost certainly would have gotten the League into war."

Van Rijn's hedge of eyebrows twisted together in a scowl. "I think not. League and Commonwealth together would be too much for Babur. It would retreat."

"Maybe—if the Commonwealth were willing to go along with putting Mirkheim under League administration. But you know the Home Companies would never agree to that. Commonwealth—government—trusteeship will mean that *they* dispose of the supermetals. It'll be their entry into space on a scale of operations grand enough to threaten the Seven and the independents with being driven to the wall."

"So by keeping us deadlocked, you pest-bespattered Seven guaranteed the united League does nothing, does not even exist."

"The League will stay neutral, you mean. Do you actually want an open, irrevocable breach in it? As is, the Seven keeping on reasonably good terms with Babur, whichever side wins, the League as a whole will have a voice. In fact, when I'm back in my headquarters, I'm going to see if the Seven can lend their good offices toward a settlement." Story lifted a finger. "That's why I wanted to see you tonight, Freeman van Rijn. A last appeal. If you'd cooperate with us, and try to get the independents to join you—"

"Cooperate?" Van Rijn took out his snuffbox and brought a pinch to his nose. "What would that amount to? Doing whatever you tell? (*Hrrromp!*)"

"Well, of course we'd have to have a central strategy. It would involve an embargo, declared or undeclared, on trade with either side. We could plead hazard, to be diplomatic about it. Both would soon start hurting for materials, including military materials, and be more ready to accept League mediation."

"Not the League's," van Rijn said. "Not the whole League's. How would the Home Companies fit in? They and the Commonwealth government is two sides of the same counterfeit coin, by damn. They been that way more and more for—how long?—ever since the Council of Hiawatha, I think."

"I'm not saying anything I haven't often before," Story pursued. "I simply have a—well, I won't call it a prospect of making you see reason. Let's say I feel it my duty to keep trying to persuade you till the last minute."

"My duty is not that I listen. I told you and told you, me, if the independents join up with the Seven, or with the Home Companies either, that is truly the end of the League, because we independents is the last properly spiritous members of it." Van Rijn leaned back, glass to lips, and gazed at the mighty simulacrum above him. Night had fallen on the scene, the moons hung in frost halos and Saturn's shadow began to creep across the rings. No stars had appeared. He sighed. "We was born too late, though. If I had been at the Council of Hiawatha, what I could have warned them!!"

"They made a perfectly logical decision," Story said.

Van Rijn nodded. "*Ja*. That was the deadly part of it."

Not until long afterward would historians appreciate the irony of the meeting having gathered where it did. At the time, if there was any conscious symbolism in the choice of site, it expressed optimism. After all, the O'Neill colonies had not only given man his first dwellings in space, the burgeoning of wholly new industries within them had been of primary importance in a revival of free enterprise. So thoroughgoing did that revival become, in ways of thinking and living as well as in economics, that, together with the alloying of formerly disparate Terrestrial societies, a whole civilization can be thought to have come freshly into existence—the Technic. After the development of the hyperdrive, man's explosive expansion away from Sol made the artificial worldlets obsolete. Yet they continued faithfully orbiting around their Lagrangian points, in Luna's path but sixty degrees ahead or behind, and were not abandoned overnight. In particular, Hiawatha and its companion Minnehaha still housed substantial working populations when the Polesotechnic League called the most fateful of its executive sessions.

The problem it faced was manifold. Quite naturally, most governments resented it. Although its constitution made it simply a mutual-help association, it wielded more strength than any single state. It hampered as well as humiliated governments when it gave them no part in decisions which deeply affected domestic trade; when its hard credit displaced their fiat money; when their attempts at regulation were covertly subverted or openly scorned. Nor was this a mere matter of officialdom hankering for power. Many grudges were genuine. No system that mortals devise is perfect; all break their share of lives. A poor boy or girl or nonhuman might rise to living like a god and controlling forces that would have been beyond the imagination of mythmakers. Efficient underlings could do very well for themselves. But those would always exist who did not have the special abilities or the plain luck. Most were not too unhappy at becoming routineers; some were poisonously embittered. More important, perhaps, was that large percentage of mankind which never really wanted to be free. Of this, a majority yearned for security, which political candidates promised to get for them. A more active minority wanted solidarity behind exciting causes, and thought that everybody else should desire the same thing.

The League had its own troubles. Sheer scale and diversity of undertakings, the overwhelming rate of information flow, were undermining administration of the larger companies. The concept of free contract was being increasingly abused, as in the establishment of indentures. Reckless exploitation of societies and natural resources was waxing. Ominous was the introduction of modern technologies to backward races without careful prior consideration—irresponsibly, for a quick credit, regardless of whether it was desirable to have such cultures loose with things like spaceships and nuclear weapons.

A parliament was finally elected in the Commonwealth that was pledged to thoroughgoing reforms; and its jurisdiction was still the League's greatest market and source of manpower. In the "thousand days" it passed an astonishing number of radical new laws and, what counted, began enforcing them as well as a good many old ones.

Therefore the Polesotechnic League called a Grand Council at Hiawatha to discuss what to do.

It enacted several resolutions which founded more humane and farsighted policies than hitherto. Where it unknowingly came to grief was in the question raised by the measures in the Commonwealth. These included a central banking commission, floors and ceilings on interest rates, income tax, an antitrust rule, compulsory arbitration of certain kinds of disputes, loans by the state to distressed enterprises, subsidies to industries deemed critical, production quotas, and much else.

A few hotheads among the delegates talked about resorting to arms, but were shouted down. While members of the League had occasionally overturned difficult local governments, the League itself was not in the business of government. The decision to be made was: Should it boycott the Commonwealth until the recent legislation was repealed, or should it acquiesce within the Solar System?

Acquiescence won. A boycott would be immensely expensive, would ruin several members if they weren't underwritten and badly hurt the rest. It would also create an unpleasant image of sabertoothed greed versus the altruistic statesman. In vain did some speakers argue that in the long run it is best to stand firm by one's principles, and that the principle which gave the League its sole meaning and justification was liberty. Opponents retorted that liberty demands frequent compromises and, on a less exalted plane, so does common sense; the laws were not totally bad, they actually had various features desirable from a mercantile point of view; and in any case, by remaining on the scene the League companies would stay influential and could work for modifications.

And indeed this proved to be true. Regulatory commissions soon turned into creatures of the industries they regulated—and discouraged (at first) or stifled (later) all new competition. This was much aided by a tax structure heavily weighted against the middle class. After a while, the great bankers were not just handling money, they were creating it, with a vested interest in inflation. Union leaders, with enormous funds to invest, fitted cozily into the system; if you did not enroll, you did not work, and the leaders and the managers between them set the conditions under which you must work. Antitrust actions penalized efficient management to the satisfaction of the less enterprising. Likewise did quotas, tariffs, wage and price limits, preferential contract policies. A set of ineffective but self-perpetuating welfare programs helped produce the votes useful for maintaining the corporate state.

For that is what the Commonwealth became. No longer distinct from politicians or bureaucrats, the magnates of the Home Companies gained a powerful say in decisions about matters far removed from finance or engineering. Their natural allies became the heads of various other constituencies—geographical, cultural, professional —which were thus brought under ever closer governmental control.

Meanwhile, companies which did not have an originally strong position in the Commonwealth found themselves being more and more squeezed out. Accordingly, they concentrated on developing markets beyond its borders. They were involved in the declarations of independence of several colony planets, some of whose politics they then gradually took over. Certain of them began to make cooperative agreements, limiting competition among themselves, to the exclusion of the rest of the League. Thus, by slow stages, were born the Seven In Space.

Lesser companies, fearful of being engulfed, avoided joining either side, and formed no organization of their own. They were the independents.

By no means did the Council of Hiawatha produce these results overnight. In fact, the period which came immediately after seemed, if anything, more dominated by capitalists than before. It was the most expansive, most brilliant time which Technic civilization would ever know. At home, remedies applied to the body politic took hold quite gradually, and their side effects were still slower to become obvious. On the stellar frontier, discovery followed discovery, triumph followed triumph; each year told of an evil conquered, a fortune made; if strife ran high, likewise did hope. The tree was growing, ever leafing, though a snake gnawed its roots. Thus was it often before on Earth, in the age of the Chun-Chiu, the age of the Delian alliance, the age of the Renaissance.

But when a century had passed—

"Well, never mind stale history," Story said. "We're alive now, not then. Will you join the Seven in making a peace effort?"

"Join." Van Rijn tugged his goatee. "You mean take orders from you and not ask rude questions."

"We'll try to consult, of course. But with communications as slow as they are, compared to the speed with which a crisis can build up, we must have a clear chain of command."

Van Rijn shook his head. "No, always I am too hungry for feedback."

Story made a chopping gesture. "Do you want to cut yourself off entirely from whatever congress makes the peace?"

"It is not sure there will be a congress, and double not sure what tune it will dance to. . . . Ah, here comes my appetizers. You will be surprised, Freeman, at how much I can bite all by myself."

X

Sandra Tamarin-Asmundsen was in the Arcadian Hills, hunting, when word reached her. Though she had felt guilty about leaving Starfall at a time of crisis—domestic as well as foreign, with more and more of the Traver class in an uproar—a brief escape from its atmosphere was like spring water going through a dried-out throat.

Her hounds had gotten on the track of a cyanops. Their baying resounded down forest vaults, a savage plainsong in green cathedral dimness. She bounded in pursuit of the noise. Her hands parted branches and scanty underbrush, her feet overleaped fallen trees, her lungs drank breath after sweet-scented breath, her eyes beheld high boles, overarching branches rich with leaves, sunflecks in shadow, the brilliant wings of a nidiflex, her body rejoiced. After her bounded half a dozen men from the ancestral estate at Windy Rim. Otherwise the wilderness was hers alone.

She sped up a slope and came out onto a meadow along the top of a cliff. The light of Maia was almost blinding on the low lobate yerb, studded with tiny white wildflowers, that covered this open ground. Beyond, she saw further hills, rank upon arrogant rank, and in the distance the solitary peak of Cloudhelm, its snows veiled in mist. The dogs had the cyanops cornered at the edge. A rangy, heavy-jawed, dun-coated breed raised by folk in these parts, they knew better than to attack iron-gray scales and raking claws. But since they could, together, pull the big herpetoid down if they must, it had lumbered from them. Now it stood its ground and hissed defiance.

"Oh, good!" Sandra exulted. She unslung her rifle and approached with care. A hasty shot might hit a dog or merely madden the beast. It was hard to kill except by a bullet straight through one of those eerily innocent-looking blue eyes.

The portable phone at her belt buzzed.

She stopped dead. The clamor of hounds and men dropped out of her awareness. Via relay satellite, the phone leashed her to the New Keep and nowhere else. It buzzed again. She unclipped the small flat box and brought it near her face. "Yes?"

A voice rattled forth: "Andrew Baird, Your Grace"—her appointed vice executive whom she had left in charge during her absence. "We have received word from Admiral Michael"— Michael Falkayn, her second in command of the little Hermetian navy. "They've detected a substantial fleet bound this way under hyperdrive, apparently from the general direction of Mogul. Distance is still too great for anything but simple code signals. The strangers have sent none so far, nor responded to any of ours."

It was as if a machine spoke for Sandra, free of the dread that shocked through her: "Get every unit into space that isn't already, and have them report to him for duty. Alert every police and rescue corps. Keep me informed of developments as they occur. 'Twill take me . . . about ninety minutes to reach my car, and another hour to fly to you." Not pausing to hear his goodbye, she put the phone back on her belt and swung about. Her men stood in a bunch; their gaze upon her was troubled. As if sensing something, the hounds grew less noisy.

"I must return immediately." She rinsed her mouth from her canteen before she started down into the forest at a long, energy-conserving lope. Two hunters tarried to call off the pack. The cyanops stared after them, not understanding the fortune which had saved its life.

Sandra's eastbound flight kept her near the Palomino River, which shone like a saber drawn across the lowlands. They were an agrarian property of the Runeberg domain. At the present season, the summer green of pastures was fading; but even from her altitude, the herds that grazed them were majestic. Opulent grainfields mingled with orchards and groves. Houses belonging to Follower families in charge of various sections stood snug beneath their red tiles, amidst their gardens. Afar she glimpsed the mansion of the Runebergs themselves. She had visited there and remembered well its gracious rooms, ancestral portraits, immensity of tradition, and children's laughter for a sign that new life was ever bubbling up from beneath these things.

Not for the first time, a moment's wistfulness touched her. To be born into the Kindred, the thousand families who headed the domains . . . Her descent went back as far as theirs; her forebears had also been among the first passengers from Earth. It was almost an accident that the early Tamarins had not founded a corporation to tame a particular part of this world. Instead, they had mostly been scientists, technicians, consultants, explorers, teachers: free lances.

Too late to change, she thought. When the constitution of an independent Hermes was written, it specified that the chief executives would be of Tamarin birth but that the Tamarins should have no domain: a lonely glory.

I could have refused election, she recalled. *Why didn't I? Well, pride, and . . . and Pete was there, my consort, to help me. But supposing he'd not been . . . well, had I refused, I'd have become like any other Tamarin who's not made Grand Duke or Duchess, I'd have had my living to earn as best I could—a Traver in all but name and, yes, in having a vote.* Defensively, as if an accuser from that class confronted her in yet another public debate: *And what's so bad about Traver status? Comes the word not simply from* travailleur, *worker, descendant of latecomers, a hireling or an unaffiliated businessman?*

I might have joined a family of the Kindred by marrying into it. That would have been best. She could have gotten the in-between degree of Follower in the same way, merging her bloodline with one that held entailed shares making it a junior partner in a domain. But she would always have been embarrassed to address with certain courtesies the high-ranking people who had been her childhood playmates. To be of the Kindred, though—not necessarily serene on a landed estate; quite likely in some other of the industrial, scientific, cultural, or public service undertakings of a corporation—yes, thus she could strike roots deep into her planet, and know how securely her children would belong.

The car phone projected Eric's image. "Mother!" he cried. "You've heard . . . Listen, I just have, and—"

"Get off the circuit," she interrupted. "Baird may be calling me at any minute." Because he was betrothed and she hoped for grandchildren, she took time to add: "You might make sure Lorna gets to a safe place. I daresay you'll insist on being at the Keep."

"Right. I . . . I'll stand by in the Sapphire Office." His countenance vanished.

The wind of her speed roared around the car's canopy. Sandra straightened in her seat. No use wishing she were different from what she was. And did she really wish it, anyway? Somebody had to hold the reins of the state. If only because of experience, she could probably do so better than anyone else. *Hang on,* she thought ahead of her. *I'm coming.*

Starfall appeared on the horizon, at first a darkness along the bright sheet of Daybreak Bay; then as she slipped downward it became the buildings, streets, parks, quays, monuments she had loved of old. Yonder stood the Mayory in red brick dignity, nearby lifted the slim spire of St. Carl's Church, the Hotel Zeus soared above Phoenix Boulevard, flowers flaunted themselves like banners around Elvander's statue in Riverside Common, traffic was dense and terrace cafés busy at Constitution Square, she actually identified Jackboot Lane where stood the Ranger's Roost tavern that had seen her drink and talk and sing in her youth like generations before her. . . . Pilgrim Hill stood ahead. A police car hung above Signal Station. Sandra flashed it her name and made for the ducal parking roof. The thought that all this might go out in a burst of radioactive flame was unendurable.

The Insignia Room was large and austere, ornamented only with the devices of the Kindred on its walls. They were colorful, but a thousand of them crowded together soon became featureless in the mind. On this high floor, windows gave on sky, long evening light, a glimpse of ocean, an ornithoid winging by. Yet as Sandra sat behind her desk, the chamber felt small, warm, dear, against the darkness at its far end.

A three-dimensional comscreen occupied half that wall. It was as if cold radiated from the scene it held, deep into human marrow. The Baburite whose outlines posed before her did not seem dwarfish or bizarre—rather, the eidolon of something gigantic and triumphant. The picture showed a bit of a compartment aboard its ship, which hung in synchronous orbit above the city and sent down a tight beam. The fittings and furnishings were too alien for her fully to see. Behind and around the being loomed reddish dusk wherein dim shapes stirred.

"Hear us well," a vocalizer said for it. "We represent the Imperial Band of Sisema and the united race.

"War is inevitable between the Autarchy of Babur and the Solar Commonwealth. We have intelligence that the Commonwealth will seek to occupy the Maian System. Your resources would obviously be of extreme value to a navy campaigning far from home: especially the terrestroid planet Hermes. There bases are easy to build, repairs and munitions to make, accumulated toxins to flush out of the life support systems of ships; personnel can get rest and hospital care, recruits can possibly be found among the populace. The Imperial Band cannot permit this."

"We're neutral!" Sandra's hands strained together. Their palms were damp, their fingers chill.

"Your neutrality would not be respected," said the Baburite. "It is necessary that the Imperial Band forestall the Commonwealth and establish a protectorate. Hear us well. A fleet detachment, which your admiral will have told you is considerably your superior in strength, is waiting at the outer limits of your planetary system. Its mission is to prevent Commonwealth forces from entering.

"You will cooperate with it. A majority of the crews are oxygen breathers who will be based on Hermes. Their correct behavior is guaranteed; but hostile actions directed at them will be severely punished. You will deal with them, as well as with the Baburite command, through our military authority.

"Conduct yourselves properly, and you need have no fears. The Maian System contains no planet which Baburites could colonize. Their ways and yours are so mutually foreign that interference of one with another is unlikely in the extreme. You should instead fear Commonwealth imperialism, against which you will be shielded."

Sandra half rose. "But we don't want your shielding—" She choked down more words like *you filthy worm*.

"It is necessary that you accept," said the emotionless voice. "Resistance would cost the Imperial Band casualties, but you your

112

entire armed service. Thereafter, Hermes would lie exposed to bombardment from space. Consider the welfare of your people."

Sandra sank back. "When would you come?" she whispered.

"We will move as soon as this conference is over."

"No, wait. You realize not—I can't issue orders to a whole world, I've not dictatorial powers—"

"You will have time to persuade. The ships of the Imperial Band will need it to deploy, since they cannot use hyperdrive within the inner parts of the system. You can be granted as much as four of your planetary rotations before the surrender of your navy and the landing of the first occupation units must be accepted."

There was more: hot protest and frosty demand, plea and refusal, bargaining over detail after detail, wrath and despair met by calm immovability; but the time was far shorter than it would have been between two humans. The Baburite was simply not concerned about honorific formulas, face savings, alternatives, compromises. Conceivably it might have been, had the gulf between the races been less unbridgeably wide. Sandra remembered the cyanops on the cliff edge, hounds and hunters before it.

When at last the screen blanked, she covered her eyes for a little before she summoned her cabinet to come witness the playback and give her what counsel it could.

Up and down Eric Tamarin-Asmundsen paced, from end to end of the living room in his mother's apartment. She had set the lights low and left open the French doors to the balcony, for it was a beautiful night, both moons aloft and nearly full, dew aglimmer on lawns and the crowns of trees, cool air full of the odor of daleflower and the trills of a tilirra. Beyond the garden wall, a modest sky-glow from the city picked out a few steeples. The lamps of cars flitting overhead were like many-colored glowflies.

Eric's boots thudded savagely on the carpet. "We *can't* just give in," he said for the dozenth frantic time. "We'd be slaves forever."

"We're promised internal self-government," Sandra reminded him from the chair where she sat.

"How much is that promise worth?"

She drew heavily on her cigar. The smoke tasted harsh; she'd had too many in the past several hours. "I know not," she admitted in a flat tone. "Still, I can't imagine any interest the Baburites might take in our local politics."

"Intend you to wait with folded hands and find out?"

"We can't fight. Michael sent me his considered opinion that our forces are grossly outnumbered. Why kill and be killed to no good end?"

"We can organize guerrillas."

"They'd spend nigh their whole time surviving." At the present epoch, Hermes had a single continent, Greatland, so enormous that most of its interior was a desert of blazing summers and bitter winters. "Worse, they'd invite reprisals on everybody else. And never could they defeat well-equipped troops on the ground, missile-throwing ships in orbit."

"Oh, we can't free ourselves alone." Eric's arm slashed the air. "But see you not, if we lie down to be walked on—if we actually add our fleet to theirs, let our factories work for them—why should the Commonwealth care what happens to us? It might leave us under Babur as part of a bargain. Whereas if we're its allies, no matter how minor—"

Sandra nodded. "Believe me, the Council and I discussed this at length. I dare not tell Michael to lead our ships off. He'd be intercepted by a squadron of theirs, have to fight his way past them."

Eric stopped in midstride. "Hermes isn't responsible if he and his men disobey your orders, is it?"

Sandra locked her glance with his, for seconds. "The admiral and I have our understanding," she said at last.

"What?" It blazed in Eric.

"No untoward sentence passed between us. I'd better not say more, even to you."

"And you're going, too!" he shouted. "A government in exile, by the whole Trinity, yes!"

"My duty is here."

"No."

Sandra slumped. "Eric, dear, I'm wrung dry. Plague me not. You should go join Lorna."

He gazed at the big woman, who had turned her face outward to the night, until he said, "All right. I see. For your part, will you help Lorna forgive me?"

She nodded wearily. "I expected you'd go, and I'll not plead," she replied low. "You are my son."

"And my father's."

She shook her head. The ghost of a smile crossed her lips. "He'd not hare off to be a dashing warrior. He'd stay put and brew trouble till the Baburites wished they'd never stirred from their planet." Her calm broke. "Oh, Eric!" She dropped her cigar and rose, arms outspread. They embraced hard. Nothing remained to say in words. After a while, he kissed her and departed.

He did not take the ducal space-yacht, but his personal runabout. It barely overhauled the Hermetian ships. They were already accelerating out of the system. Admiral Falkayn did not summon him aboard *Alpha Cygni*, but assigned him to the destroyer *North Atlantis*. That proved to be sound thinking.

Soon afterward, as had been easily predictable, they encountered those units of the Baburite task force which were near enough to intercept them. As yet, they were too deep in Maia's gravitational well to go safely into hyperdrive. "Hold vectors steady," Falkayn ordered them. "We'll not have more than this engagement. Fire at will."

The captain of *North Atlantis* had allowed Eric on the bridge as a courtesy, provided the heir apparent keep absolutely quiet. That was a command more stern than chains. Presently he felt the scourge, as the hostile forces closed.

Around his eyes blazed the stars in their thousands, the Milky Way foamed across the girth of heaven, a nebula shone distance-dimmed bearing new suns and worlds in its womb, the Magellanic Clouds and the Andromeda galaxy glimmered in their mystery. That was one part of reality. The opposite part was the hardness which enclosed him, faint beat of driving energies and mumble of ventilators, men who stood thralls of instruments and controls, the wetness and reek of his own sweat . . . and a muttered "First shot theirs. Must've been a missile from *Caduceus* that stopped it," as flame winked briefly afar.

The kinetic velocities of both groups were too high to match in a single pass. They intermingled, exchanging fire, for minutes; then they were moving out of effective range. Eric saw a ghastly rose unfold, where a weapon from his vessel had tracked down another from the foe. Otherwise the explosions were remote, hundreds of kilometers off, and registered as glints; an energy beam striking a target did not register at all.

Seated like a statue, the destroyer's captain heard the combat analysis officer report in a cracking voice: "Sir, practically every strike of theirs is concentrated on *Alpha Cygni*. They must hope to saturate her defenses."

"I was afraid of that," the captain said dully. "The only capital ship we've got. The Baburites are more interested in stopping her than buzzbugs like this."

"If we accelerated in her direction, sir, we might be able to catch a few of their missiles."

"Our orders are to maintain our vectors." The captain's features remained visor-blank; but he glanced across at Eric. "The important thing is that *some* of us escape."

The officer swallowed. "Aye, sir."

A few minutes later, the information arrived: *Alpha Cygni* had taken a warhead. No further word came from her—but flash after flash of fireball did, for her screens and interceptors were now gone, and even receding, the Baburites could pound her hulk into dust and slag.

The captain of *North Atlantis* looked straight at Eric. "I think you're our new commander, sir," he said.

"C-carry on." The son of the Duchess wrestled down a scream.

Battle faded out. Eventually the Hermetian flotilla dared enter hyperdrive. Detectors declared the enemy was not pursuing. Because they spent their main effort on the battleship, the invaders had taken losses of their own, making theirs temporarily the inferior force. Divisions of their armada elsewhere were too far-flung to have any hope of catching up. Besides, fighting at faster-than-light was a tricky business of drawing alongside and trying to match phase; a kill was too unlikely to make the attempt worthwhile, when Hermes had not yet been brought under the yoke.

Eric rose. Each muscle felt like a separate ache. "Proceed toward Sol at the highest feasible rate," he ordered. "Have everybody stand by for a message from me." His grin was acid. "I'd better give them a talk, not?"

In this wise died Michael Falkayn, older brother of David and, since their father's death a pair of years ago, head of the Falkayn domain.

XI

As swift as any vessel in that near-infinitesimal droplet of the galaxy which we have slightly explored, *Muddlin' Through* reached Earth almost simultaneously with the first messengers from the embattled Mirkheim expedition, whose survivors would not come limping in for two or more weeks. Traffic Control kept her hours in orbit. Her crew did manage to swap a few radioed words with Nicholas van Rijn. "I will meet you at Ronga," the merchant said—and little else, when communication was surely being monitored.

The likelihood of war had evidently thrown the bureaucrats in charge of space safety into a blue funk. But clearance finally came. Ship and pilot were licensed to set down anywhere on the planet that adequate facilities existed. Muddlehead got orders to make for a certain atoll in the South Pacific Ocean.

Approached from above, the scene was impossibly lovely. The waters shone in a thousand shades of blue and green, sunlight sparkling over their wrinkled vastness; breakers burst silvery on the coral necklace of the island, within whose arc a lagoon lay like an amethyst; tall clouds massed in the west, their purity shaded azure, while elsewhere heaven was a dome of light. *We have so few places like this left on Earth,* David Falkayn thought fleetingly. *Is that—not ambition, not adventure, no, the longing for a peace which only our genes remember—is that what really sends us out into the universe?*

Feather-softly, landing jacks touched the surface of a small paved field. The main personnel lock opened and its gangway extruded. Falkayn had been waiting there, but Chee Lan darted between his legs and reached ground first, bounced in the air, sped to the adjacent beach, and rolled on warm white sand. He followed more sedately, until he saw who came to meet him. Then he also ran.

"Davy, oh, Davy!" Coya flung herself at him and they kissed for an unbroken minute or better, while Adzel paraded discreetly by. Waves rushed and murmured, seabirds cried.

"I tried to call you right after the boss," Falkayn stammered. What a poor greeting words gave.

"He'd already contacted me, told me to come here," she said, leaning happily against him.

"How're Juanita and X?" He saw, as he had felt, the growth of the child within her during the weeks of his absence.

"Fat and sassy. Look over yonder. C'mon." She tugged his arm.

Van Rijn stood at the border of the field, holding his great-granddaughter by the hand. As the newcomers reached them, the girl released herself, flew to Daddy to be hugged, then from his embrace looked up at Adzel and chirped, "Ride?"

The dragon set her on his back and all started for the house. Palms soughed in a wind whose salt was sweetened by odors of jasmine; hibiscus and bougainvillea glowed ardent in arbors. "Welcome home, by damn," van Rijn boomed. "Was a poxy long wait, not knowing if you was chopped into cutlets or what."

Falkayn broke stride. A chill blew across his joy. "Then you didn't get our dispatch?" he said. "We sent a torp from the neighborhood of Mogul."

"No, nothings. Our data bank stayed bare as a mermaid's bottom."

Falkayn's grip tightened around Coya's waist. That time had surely been, for her, the frozen ninth circle of hell. "I was afraid you might not," he said slowly.

"You mean somebody snaffled it?" Coya asked.

"*Ja,*" van Rijn growled. "The Space Service, who elses? Plain to see, they got secret orders to take anything for me to somebody different."

"But that's illegal!" she protested.

"The Home Companies is behind it, of course, and in a case like this they don't give snot whether it's illegal or well eagle. I hope you used cipher, Davy."

"Yes, naturally," Falkayn said. "I don't think they can have broken it."

119

"No, but you see, they kept me from getting maybe an advantage in this diarrhea-fluid situation we got. I seven-point-three-tenths expected it. . . . Here we are." The party climbed the steps, crossed a verandah, and entered an airily furnished room where stood a table covered with drinks and snacks.

Chee soared to a chair, crouched on it, and chattered, "You've heard about a battle commencing at Mirkheim, I gather. We were there. Earlier, the *wan-yao jan-gwo chai reng pfs-s-st* Baburites jailed us—" Her native phrase gave a succinct description of their ancestors, morals, personal cleanliness, and fate if she could have her way.

"Oh, no," Coya breathed.

"Hold, hold," van Rijn commanded. "I decree first we snap some schnapps, with a little liter or so of beer in tow and maybe a few herring filets or such for ballast. You do not want your new baby should become an adrenalin addict, ha?"

"Nor this young lady," said Adzel, for Juanita's giggles had given place to a worried silence. He reached around, lifted her off his shoulders, and started juggling her from hand to enormous hand. She squealed in delight. Her parents didn't mind; she was safer with him than with anybody else they knew, including themselves.

"Well—" Falkayn could not quite yield to pleasure. "What's been happening at home?"

"Nothing, except the bomb going ticktacktoe," van Rijn said. "Bayard Story, he made one last try to get me in combination with the Seven, what meant putting me under their orders. I told him to paint it green, and he left the Solar System. Otherwise, only rumors, and news commentators who I would like to do a hysteria-ectomy on."

"Who's Bayard Story?" Chee inquired.

"A director of Galactic Developments, delegate to the meeting at Lunograd," van Rijn told her. "He was pretty much the spokesman for the Seven. In fact, I suspect he was the wheelsman."

"Mmm, yes, I remember now, I happened to see his arrival on a newscast," Falkayn put in. "I admired his skill in giving the reporter a brief, crisp, straightforward statement that didn't say a flinkin' thing." He turned to Coya. "No matter. Haven't you anything special to relate, darling?"

"Oh, I was offered a contract by Danstrup Cargo Carriers," she answered, referring to an independent within the League. Since she stopped trade pioneering, she had worked out of her home as a high-powered free-lance computer programmer. "They wanted an analysis of their best strategy in case of war. Everybody is terrified of war, nobody knows what the consequences would be, nobody wants it, but still we drift and drift. . . . It's horrible, Davy. Can you imagine how horrible?"

Falkayn brushed a kiss across her hair. "Did you take the job?"

"No. How could I, not being sure what had become of you? I've filled in the time with routine-type stuff. And—and I've played a lot of tennis, that sort of thing, to help me sleep." She shared his distrust of chemical consolations.

In a way, van Rijn did too. He used alcohol not as a crutch but as a pogo stick. "Drink, you slobberwits!" he roared. "Or do I have to give it to you with a hypochondriac needle? You got home safe, that's what matters first. So crow about it; then look at this nice table of goodies and raven."

Adzel set Juanita down. "Come," he said, "let us go off in a corner and have a tea party." She paused to pet Chee. The Cynthian submitted, merely switching her tail.

Yet it was impossible to pretend for long that no universe existed beyond the blue overhead. Soon the *Muddlin' Through* trio were relating their experiences. Van Rijn listened intently, interrupting less often than Coya with questions or exclamations.

At the end: "This equipment you salvaged from the warship, did you learn anything about it on your way home?" he asked.

"Very little." Falkayn rubbed the back of his neck. "And damned puzzling. Most of what we saw, as well as what we took away, is modeled on Technic designs, as you'd expect. But certain transistors—we can't figure out how they were manufactured in a hydrogen atmosphere. Hydrogen would poison the semiconductors."

"Maybe they're produced off Babur, like on a satellite," Coya suggested.

121

"Maybe," Falkayn said. "Though I can't see why. Alternative kinds of transistor exist which don't require going to that much trouble. Then there's a unit which we guess to be a containment field-strength regulator. It involves a rectifier operating at a high temperature. Okay. But this particular rectifier is cupric oxide. Hydrogen reduces that stuff when it's hot; you get copper and water. Oh, yes, the piece is inside an iron shell to protect it. But hydrogen leaks through iron. So what the Baburites have got is a part less reliable, more often in need of replacement, than necessary."

"Bad engineering as a result of haste," Coya offered with a quirked smile. "Not the first time in history."

"True," Falkayn said. "But— Look, the Baburites have had offplanet help. That much was admitted to us; and we identified an oxygen-breather colony on one of their moons, you recall; and there are those foreign mercenaries, also oxygen-breathing. Obviously they hired such outsiders to help them with research, development, and production of their military machine. Why didn't the outsiders do a better job?"

Van Rijn stumped about, worrying his goatee and crunching bites off a Spanish onion. "More interesting is how the Baburites found those people, and how paid them as well as the other costs," he opined. "Babur is not a rich world nor very populous, proportional to its size, even allowing for industrial backwardness. Too much of it is desert, for lack of liquid ammonia. What has it to pay *with*?"

"It did do some interstellar trade in the past," Falkayn reminded. "Possibly somebody made contact or—I don't know. You're right, it's tough to find an economic explanation for everything they've managed to accomplish."

"Or any kind of explanation for their actions, by billy damn. I never sent you off expecting the kind of gumblesnatch you got into. No, I thought sure the Baburites would talk at you, probably not tell you much but anyhows talking. The sensible thing from their viewpoint should be, if they going to butt heads with the Commonwealth, they stay friends with the League, or at least not make it also an activated enemy. *Nie*?"

"They seemed, from what microscopic contact we had with them, they seemed contemptuous of the League. They certainly know it's divided against itself."

"How can they be so cock-a-doodle sure of that? Do we savvy the ins and outs of their politics? And why not try to take advantage of our divisions? For instance, they might get the Seven and the independents bidding competitive for business with them . . . if they treat the representatives halfway decent."

"Could you simply have run into an overzealous official?" Coya wondered.

Falkayn shook his head. "From what smidgen we know of the Baburites, hardly," he replied. "They don't appear to be organized that way. They don't have hierarchies of individuals holding positions. In their dominant culture, if not in all, it's a matter of whole Bands overlapping. So-and-so many single beings may each be responsible for a fraction of a job, and confer about it with their mates; a given being can be on several different teams."

"That makes for fewer contradictions," Adzel added, "though likewise, I suspect, less imagination and a lower speed of reaction to developments."

"Which suggests it was a policy agreed on beforehand, that any strangers who arrived would promptly be thrown in the freezer," Chee said. "Oh, we three have had plenty of time to speculate."

"Have you speculated about companies of the Seven possibly maintaining quiet relationships with Babur?" Coya asked.

"Yes." Falkayn shrugged. "If so, under present circumstances you wouldn't expect them to advertise the fact, would you? They could easily have been kept in the dark for decades about the intentions of the Imperial Band."

"Are you positive, dear?"

"Well, what can such a relationship actually have amounted to? Occasional visits by one or a few agents to a strictly limited region of a planet with more than twenty-two times Earth's area—a much bigger proportion of it dry land, at that."

"Still," Chee murmured, "the section where significant action has been taking place isn't necessarily huge." A phone chimed.

"*Kai-yu!* Of every tyranny you humans have ever saddled your-selves with, that thing has got to be the most insolent."

"Nobody knows I am here but my top secretary," said van Rijn. His bare feet slap-slapped across the *tatami* to the instrument. When he pressed accept, it announced, "Edward Garver wishes to speak to you personally, sir. What shall I tell him?"

"What I would like you to tell him is not anatomically possible," van Rijn grunted. "Put him on. Uh, the rest of you stand back from the scanner. No sense handing out free information."

Square shoulders, bald head, and pugdog face sprang into simulac-rum. "You're on Ronga, I believe, where your snoopship is," said the Commonwealth's Minister of Security without preamble.

"You got told about her, ha?" van Rijn replied, quiet as the center of a hurricane.

"I issued standing orders the day I learned she'd left." Garver hunched forward, as if to thrust himself past the vitryl. "You've been a special interest of mine for an almighty long while."

Falkayn—still more, perhaps, Adzel, who had once been arrested after a certain incident—remembered. Since the years when he was chief law enforcement officer of the Lunar Federation, Garver had hated van Rijn. His terms in the Commonwealth Parliament had put a fresh edge on that. It was an oddly pure passion. Because of the particular encounters they chanced to have had, he saw the merchant as an archetype of everything he abominated about the Polesotechnic League.

"I want to know where the crew have been, what they've done, and why," he said. "I'm calling personally so you'll know I mean this . . . personally."

"Go ahead and want as much as you feel like." Van Rijn beamed. "Wallow in it. Scrub your tummy with it. Blow bubbles. Try dif-ferent flavors." Behind his back, he crooked a finger. Falkayn in turn gestured to Chee and Adzel, who went quickly out. The younger man stayed by Coya. His partners could remove the log and Baburite apparatus—to which the health inspector had paid no particular attention prior to their descent—from *Muddlin' Through* before a search party arrived with a warrant.

Another log would remain, which had been faked as a matter of routine. He'd better brief his wife and his grandfather-in-law fast.

"—no more of your apishness," Garver was rasping. "I presume you know about the Baburite attack on our ships. It means war, I guarantee. Parliament will meet, by multiway phone, inside the next hour. And I know what the vote will be."

I do too, Falkayn thought sadly, while silent tears started forth in Coya's eyes. *Not that we should do nothing about the killing of our men. But this haste—? Well, the Home Companies see a vital interest in Mirkheim. Let the Commonwealth possess it, and that will be their foothold in space, against the Seven.*

"And the war will purify us," Garver said.

It will give the government powers over free enterprise that it never had before. You can't consider the Home Companies free enterprises any longer. No, they're part of the power structure. He loathes us because we've never either joined or toadied to the coalition of cartels, politicians, and bureaucrats. To him, we represent Chaos.

Garver checked himself from orating. With iron joy, he went on: "Meanwhile, as of an hour back, the Premier has declared a state of emergency. Under it, my department takes authority over all spacecraft. We'll be commandeering, van Rijn; and no ship will move without our permission. I've called you like this in the faint hope that'll make you comprehend the gravity of the situation, and what'll happen to you if you don't cooperate."

"How sweet of you to tell me," the merchant replied expressionlessly. "Was there more? Hokay, pippity-pip." He switched off.

Turning to the rest, he said, "I would not give him the satisfaction." He jumped up and down. The floor thundered. He pummeled the air with his fists. *"Schijt, pis, en bederf !"* he bellowed. "God throw him in Satan's squatpot! His parents was brothers! May he *wish* to become decent! Make us a four-letter Angular-Saxon language just for him! *Ga-a-a-ah—"*

Adzel, reentering the house, dropped his load to cover Juanita's ears. Chee scuttled past him, carrying the log reel, in search of a good hiding place for it. Coya and Falkayn caught at each other. A whine rose outside as two Central Police vehicles came over the horizon and turned downward for a landing.

XII

Was this truly Earth?

Eric could sit still no longer. The program he watched was interesting—doubtless banal to a native, but exotic to him. However, he was too restless. He flung himself off the lounger, strode across his room, halted at a window.

Evening was stealing across Rio de Janeiro Integrate. From his high perch his gaze swept over the flowing lines and rich tints of skyscrapers, bold silhouettes of Sugarloaf and Corcovado, bay agleam as if burnished, Niterói bridge an ethereal tracing. Cars torrented along streets and elevated roads below him, wove an intricate dance through the flight lanes above. He touched a button to open the window and filled his lungs with unconditioned moist heat. No traffic noises actually reached him, but he had a sense of them, the unheard throb of a monster machine, almost like the pulse of a spaceship. The sheer existence of such a megalopolis came near being frightening, now that he stood brow to brow with it.

His right hand's grip on his left wrist tightened. *I am not nobody*, he defied the immensity. *I led a score of warcraft here*.

The door chimed. He spun on his heel, heart irrationally jumping. "Come in," he said. The door swung itself wide.

A man, small and dark as most Brazilians apparently were, stood there in a fanciful uniform, holding a package. "This came for you, sir," he announced in accented Anglic. The Hotel Santos-Dumont employed live servitors.

"What?" Puzzled, Eric approached. "Who'd be sending me anything?"

"I don't know, sir. It arrived by conveyor a few minutes ago. We knew you were still here and thought you might like to have it at once."

126

"Well, uh, uh, thank you." Eric took the parcel. It was in plain packwrap and bore only his name and address. The man remained for a moment, then left. The door shut behind him. *Damn!* Eric thought. *Should I have given him money? Haven't I read about that as a Terrestrial custom?* His face heated.

Well, though . . . He laid his present on a table and tugged the unsealer. Inside were a box and an envelope. The box held a freshly folded suit of clothes. The envelope held two sheets. On the first was written: "To his Excellency Eric Tamarin-Asmundsen, in appreciation of his gallant efforts, from a member of United Humanity."

Who— Wait, it did get mentioned while I was with those politicians and officers yesterday. A mildly racist association, naturally jingoistic about Babur. With the publicity that our escape from Hermes seems to have gotten . . . Hm, a second message. WAIT A GOD-SMITTEN MINUTE!

My son,
Read this and destroy. Leave the other note lying about so it may satisfy the curiosity of those who have a watch on you.

I am anxious to meet you, for your own sake but also for the sake of both our planets and perhaps many more. It must be done secretly, or it is useless. I will only say now that you and your men are in danger of being made pawns.

If you possibly can, cancel any appointment you have, wear the enclosed outfit, and at 2000 hours—Earth-clock, not Hermetian—go to the parking roof. Take a taxi numbered 7383 and follow instructions. If you can't tonight, make it the same time tomorrow.

"Long live freedom and damn the ideologies."

Your father,
[seismograph scrawl]
N. van Rijn

For a minute that stretched, Eric stood where he was. *Old Nick himself,* hammered through him. *You hear stories about him throughout space as if he were already a myth. Of course I intended to look him up, but—*

His blood began to sing. After the grinding voyage, the wary reception, the strenuous drabness of two conferences with highly placed Earthlings, conferences that were more like interrogations, the interview before a telenews camera, and now this . . . Why not?

He was invited to dinner at the Hermetian ambassador's home in Petrópolis. He might have been housed there, except for lack of guest facilities; the embassy had a very small budget, because hitherto it had had little to do. Hence the Commonwealth government was treating him to these quarters. Quite possibly they were bugged. Certainly he was separated from his crews, who had been sent to dwell in—what was the name?—Cape Verde Base?

Yet why should he suspect the Commonwealth? He had everywhere met politeness, if not effusiveness.

Could be I'll learn tonight. He phoned, pleading fatigue, and postponed his engagement a day. Room service brought him sandwiches and milk. (Earth's food and drink had subtly peculiar tastes.) Afterward he changed into the new garments. They were flamboyant: sheening blue velvyl tunic and culottes, white iridon stockings, scarlet shimmerlyn cloak. Even here, where colorful garb was the rule, he'd stand out. Shouldn't he be inconspicuous instead?

Somehow he outlived the wait. Dusk fell. At the designated time he stepped from a gravshaft out onto the roof. The muggy atmosphere had not lost much heat; the city's horizon-wide shattered rainbow of lights seemed feverish. Several cabs stood in line. Opposite them, a man leaned against the parapet as if admiring the view. *Is he a watcher?* The sleek teardrop vehicles bore numbers on their sides. Eric's was in the middle of the row. *How to take it without making obvious that that's the one I want? . . . Ah, yes, I know. I hope.* He paced back and forth for a bit, cloak aswirl behind him, like a person not sure what to do; then, passing 7383, he feigned the impulse that made him lay a hand on its door.

It opened. He got in. A shadowy shape crouched on the floor. "Quiet," muttered forth. Aloud, to the autopilot: "Palacete de Amor." The car took off vertically, entered the lane assigned it by the traffic monitoring system, and headed west.

The man crawled up. "Now I can sit," he said in Anglic. "They're following us; but that far off, they can't see through our

128

windows." He extended a hand. "I'm honored to meet you, sir. You may as well call me Tom."

Eric accepted the clasp numbly. He was looking at himself.

No, not quite. The clothes were identical, the body similar, the head less closely so though it should pass a cursory inspection.

Tom grinned. "Partly I'm disguised, hair dye, maskflesh here and there, et cetera," he explained. "And a standout costume, which draws attention from me to itself. Gait's important too. Did you know that you Hermetians walk differently from any breed of Earthling? Looser jointed. I've spent the past day in crash-course training."

"You . . . are a man of van Rijn's?" Eric asked. His mouth was somewhat dry.

"Yes, sir. He keeps several like me on tap. Now please listen close. I'll get off at the Palacéte while you hunch down the way I was doing. I'll give them a satisfying look at me, hesitating before I go in. Meanwhile you tell the car, 'To the yacht.' It isn't really a cab, it just looks like one. It'll take you to him. At 0600 tomorrow morning, it'll bring you back to me, I'll step in, we'll let you off at your hotel. As far as the Secret Service is concerned, you spent the night at the Palacete."

"What, uh, what am I supposed to be doing there?"

Tom blinked, then guffawed. "Having a glorious time with assorted delicious wenches after your long journey. Don't worry, I'll leave behind me a goodly tale of your prowess. At times like this, I enjoy my work. Nobody will mention it to you; that's bad form on Earth. Just be prepared for a few smirks when you tell people you're tired because you slept poorly."

Eric was spared the need to respond, since Tom said, "Get down" as a garishly lighted façade came in view. A minute later, they landed, Tom got out, the vehicle took off again.

The episode felt unreal. Eric brought his face to a pane and stared. The city fell behind him, the bay, the coast whereon he glimpsed kilometers of magnificent surf. He was over the ocean. Luna stood low ahead, near the full, casting a witchcraft of brilliance across the waves. In its presence, not many stars were visible. Was that bright one Alpha Centauri, the beacon for which men steered when first they departed the Solar System? Were those four the Southern Cross, famous in books he had read as a boy? The constellations were strange. Maia was drowned in distance.

The car canted. Eric saw a watership in the middle of otherwise empty vastness. She was a windjammer, with three masts rigged fore and aft though only the mizzen sail and a jib were set to keep her hove to. He couldn't remember what the type was called; no pleasure boat on Hermes was that big. Doubtless she had an auxiliary engine. . . . What a place to meet. The reason was total privacy—nevertheless, how wildly romantic, here under Earth's moon. Lunatic?

The false taxi came to a hover alongside the starboard rail. Eric emerged, springing to a deck that thudded beneath his feet. The air was blessedly cool. A man took his seat and the vehicle flitted off, to abide somewhere till it must return.

More sailors were in sight, but Eric knew the captain at once, huge in the pouring pale radiance. He wore simply a blouse, wraparound skirt, and diamonds glistery on his fingers. "My boy!" he roared, and stampeded to meet the newcomer. His handshake well-nigh tore an arm off, his backslap sent the Hermetian staggering. "Ho, ho, welcome, by damn! For this, you bet I give good St. Dismas candles till he wonders if maybe he was martyred by a grease fire." He clasped his son's shoulders. "*Ja*, you got some of your mother in you, even if mainly you are what they call extinctive-looking like me. What a jolly roger we raised together, she and me! Often have I wished I was not too obstreptococcus a bastard for her to live with long. You, now, you is a fine, upstanding type of bastard, *nie*? Come below and we talk." He propelled Eric forward.

A lean man in early middle age and a pregnant woman who looked younger stood at the cabin door. Van Rijn halted. "Here is David Falkayn, you heard about him after the Shenna affair, also his wife Coya—Hoy, what's wrong, *jongen*?"

David Falkayn. I should have expected this. Eric bowed in the manner of kindred among each other. "Well met," he said ritually, and wondered how he could add what he must.

"Below, below, the akvavit calls," van Rijn urged, less loudly than before.

The ship's saloon was mahogany and mirrorlike brass. Refreshments crowded a table. The quartet settled themselves around it. Van

Rijn poured with more skill than was obvious from his slapdash manner. "How was Lady Sandra when you left her?" he asked, still quieter.

"Bearing up," Eric said.

"Proost!" Van Rijn raised his liquor. The rest imitated him, sending the chilled caraway spirit down their gullets at a gulp, following it with beer. Across his tankard, Eric studied faces. Coya's was delicately molded, though somehow too strong to be merely pretty. David's was rakish in shape, rather grim in mien. *No, hold, I'd better think of him as "Falkayn." Most Earthlings seem to use their surnames with comparative strangers, like Travers, not the first name like Kindred, and he's been long off Hermes*.

Van Rijn's visage—sharply remembered from documentary shows a decade ago following the Shenna business—was the most mobile and least readable of the three. *What do I actually think of him? What should I?*

Sandra had never spoken much of her old liaison. She wasn't regretful, she just didn't care to dwell on the past. And she had married Peter Asmundsen when Eric was four standard years old. The stepfather had won the child's wholehearted love. That was why Eric had never considered seeking out van Rijn, nor given him a great deal of thought until lately. It would have felt almost like disloyalty. But half the genes in yonder gross body were his.

And . . . be damned if he wasn't enjoying this escapade!

Falkayn spoke. Abruptly Eric recalled the tidings he bore, and lost enjoyment. "We'd better get straight to work. No doubt you wonder about the elaborate secrecy. Well, we could have arranged to meet you candidly, but it would've been under covert surveillance—not too fussing covert at that. This way, we keep an option or two open for you."

"I knew you would come," van Rijn said. "Your mother proved it on Diomedes before you was born."

"We're not sure how complete your information is about the Commonwealth," Coya added. She had a lovely low voice. "The fact is, we're in the bad graces of the government."

Let me buy time, while I figure out how to tell Falkayn. "Please say on, my lady," Eric urged.

131

She glanced back and forth between the men. They signed her to continue. She spoke fast and rather abstractly, perhaps as a shield for nervousness.

"Well, to generalize, for a long time in the Solar System, underneath all catchwords and cross-currents, the issue has been what shall be the final arbiter. The state, which in the last analysis relies on physical coercion; or a changeable group of individuals, whose only power is economic. . . . Oh, I know it's nowhere near that simple. Either kind of leadership might appeal to emotion, for instance—yes, does, in fact, because at bottom the choice between them is a matter of how you feel, how you see the universe. And of course they melt into each other. On Hermes, for instance, you get the interesting situation of a state having essentially risen from private corporations. In the Solar System, on the other hand, the so-called Home Companies have become an unofficial but real component of government. In fact, they've had the most to do with strengthening it, extending its control of everybody's life. And for its part, it protects them from a lot of the competition they used to have, as well as doing them a lot of different favors on request." She frowned at the table. "This didn't happen because of any conspiracy, you realize. It just . . . happened. The Council of Hiawatha—well, never mind."

"You remind me of the final examination in the philosophy class, my dear," van Rijn said. "The single question was: 'Why?' You got an A if you answered, 'Why not?' You got a B if you answered, 'Because.' Any other answer got a C."

Smiles twitched. Coya met Eric's eyes and proceeded. "You must know enough about Solar Spice & Liquors and its fellow independents to understand why we aren't popular in the Capitol. We can't greatly blame them for fearing us. After all, if we claim the right to act freely, we might do anything whatsoever, and simply the claim itself is a threat to the establishment. When Gunung Tuan—Freeman van Rijn—sent my husband off on a private expedition during this crisis, that was the last quantum. Commonwealth agents ransacked his ship after he returned, and sequestered her. They didn't find evidence to convict him; not that David had done anything particularly unlawful. But like everybody else, we're forbidden to leave

Earth except on common carriers. And we're incessantly spied on."

Eric stirred. His words came hesitant. "Uh, given the war, aren't your interests the same as the Commonwealth's?"

"If you mean the government of the Commonwealth," Falkayn said, "then no, probably not. Nor are yours necessarily. Don't forget, I'm a Hermetian citizen myself."

And you are now the Falkayn.

"I do have my underblanket connections," van Rijn added. "So I know you is been watched since you arrived. They think: You come for an ally, yes; but how trustworthy is you? Anyways, it is in the nature of governments to be nosy."

"Don't worry," Falkayn advised. "I'm sure you'll be accepted for what you are, and accorded more rank than you maybe want. Nor will we ask any treachery of you. At this minute I'm not sure what we will ask. Maybe only that you use the influence you're going to have—a popular hero, granted special status and so forth—your influence to get us back some mobility. I believe if you think over what we've done in the past, you'll agree we aren't such dreadful villains."

The miners on Mirkheim. Their high-flying hopes. Eric nodded.

"In return," Coya said, "our group may help keep Hermes from becoming a counter in a game. Because Babur and the Commonwealth won't fight till one is crushed. That's hardly possible for them. After they've traded some blows, they'll negotiate, with the upper hand in battle being the upper hand at the conference table. Tonight it looks as if that hand will be a Baburite claw—because everything we've learned indicates their force in being is at least equal to the Commonwealth's, and their lines of communication are short where its are long. For the sake of an annual quota of supermetals, the Commonwealth might well agree to let Hermes remain a so-called protectorate. Certainly the liberation of your planet is not its prime objective."

Lorna. The home we mean to have.

"What I would like to do," van Rijn came in, "is send messages to the heads of independent companies, get them together for some kind

133

of joint action. Right now they got no leadership, and I know them and their fumblydiddles by themselves. If you can arrange for people of ours to go off to them, that will be a real *coup de poing.*"

"*Coup de main,*" Coya corrected under her breath. "I think."

Van Rijn lifted the akvavit bottle. "Better let me pour you a buckshot more, my son," he invited. "This will be a long night."

Eric accepted, tossed off the fiery swallow, and said, before he should lose all heart for the task: "Yes, we've much to tell, much to talk over, but first—This didn't get into the news, as far as I'm aware, nobody mentioned it while my men and I were being interviewed, because we'd agreed en route to avoid naming names as much as possible for fear of provoking reprisals at home, but—You recall we lost our battleship on the way out. Well, its commander was Michael Falkayn. I understand he was your brother, Captain."

The blond man sat still. His wife seized his arm. "I'm sorry." Eric's tone stumbled. "He was a gallant officer."

"Mike—" Falkayn shook his head. "Excuse me."

"Oh, darling, darling," Coya whispered.

Falkayn's fist smote the tabletop, once. Then he blinked hard, sought van Rijn's eyes, and met them unwaveringly. "You realize what this means, don't you, Gunung Tuan?" he asked, flat-voiced. "I'm the new head of the family and president of the domain. That's where my first duty lies."

XIII

The telephone image of Irwin Milner said: "Greeting, Your Grace. I hope you are well."

Like death and hell you do, Sandra thought. She jerked a nod in reply, but could not bring herself to wish good health to the commander of planet-based Baburite occupation forces.

Did he stiffen the least bit? She watched his features more narrowly. He was a squat redhead whose gray uniform differed little from that on the lowliest human among his troops. Born on Earth, he retained an accent in his Anglic that she had been told was North American. He was naturalized on Germania, he said; it was a faraway neutral, hence his service with Babur did not make him guilty of any treason.

So he claims.

"What did you wish to discuss, General?" she demanded rather than inquired.

"A necessary change," he replied. "To date, we've been busy getting the protectorate functional, the military side of it, that is."

Warcraft in orbit, whose crews are more alien to man than a shark or a nightshade, ready to hurl their nuclear weapons downward. On the ground, oxygen-breathing mercenaries, human, Merseian, Gorzuni, Donarrian—adventurers, the scourings of space, though thus far they've stayed disciplined. Not that we see much of them. They have taken over our abandoned navy facilities, plus the Hotel Zeus and a few other buildings roundabout in Starfall. He says they will spread out in garrisons, in all the inhabited parts of Hermes. He has given me no satisfactory answer as to why, when it would seem that those circling spacecraft are ample to assure our meek behavior.

"That work will go on," Milner continued. "But we're now ready to start making a sound, uh, infrastructure. I'm sure your people understand they can't have our protection for nothing. They'll need to do their share, producing supplies in their factories, food and raw materials from their lands—you see what I mean, I'm sure, madame." He scowled. "I told you before, the attack those Hermetian ships made on ours, their defiance of orders . . . Yes, yes, not your fault, madame. But if your navy had that many subversives in it, what about civilians? We might start getting sabotage, espionage, aid and comfort to enemy agents. That has to be guarded against, doesn't it?"

He paused. "Go on," Sandra said. The words sounded remote in her ears. She was tensing to receive a blow.

The first several days of the occupation had gone with eerie smoothness. Were the people stunned, mechanically tracing out routines—or how much ordinary life went on, education, recreation, lovemaking, even laughter? She herself had been astonished to find she could still enjoy a meal, be concerned when her favorite horse developed a limp, take interest in some unusual triviality on the newscast. Of course, no doubt it helped that few dwellers on the planet had glimpsed an invader. And she liked to think that her speeches had had their effect—first, on a conference hookup, to the world legislature, the presidents of the domains; afterward on television to everybody. "We have no other choice but our useless deaths and our children's. . . . We yield under protest, praying for eventual justice. . . . Our forebears entered wildernesses whose very life forms were mostly unknown to them, and many suffered or died, but in the end they overcame. In this hour we must be worthy of them. . . . Prudence. . . . Patience. . . . Endure. . . ."

"We'll have to organize for the long pull," Milner told her. "Now I'm a plain soldier. I don't know the ins and outs of your society here. But I do know there isn't another like it anywhere that humans have settled. So we're bringing in a High Commissioner. He and his staff will work closely with you, to ease the, uh, transition and make what reforms are required. He's Hermetian born, you see, madame, Benoni Strang by name."

Strang? Not one of the Thousand Families. Possibly a Follower, but I doubt it; I'm sure I'd remember. Then he must be—

"He arrived today and would like to meet with you informally as

136

soon as possible," Milner was saying. "You know, get acquainted, let you see that it's his world too and he has its best interests at heart. When would be a convenient time, madame?"

They are very polite to the prisoners, not?

Waiting, she wandered alone save for one of her hounds, across the top of Pilgrim Hill to the Old Keep. Its stone massiveness housed nothing these days but records and a museum; nobody else was in the formal gardens surrounding it. The stillness made her footsteps seem loud on the graveled paths.

Flowerbeds and low hedges formed an intricate design anchored to occasional trees. Most blooms were gone; colors other than green were only in crimson daleflower and small whitefoot, in shrubs where skyberries ripened vivid blue, in the first yellow on leaves of birch and purple on leaves of fallaron. Maia shone muted through a hazy sky. The air was mild, with a slight tang. Trekking wings passed overhead. Autumn is gentle around Starfall, despite its latitude; Hermes tilts less on its axis than Earth. Under the hill gleamed the river, the city stretched eastward in roofs and towers to the bay, westward it soon gave place to plowland and pasture and Cloudhelm's ghostly peak. She saw little traffic and heard none. The world might have been keeping a Sabbath.

But nothing ever really stopped work, least of all the forces of disruption. Soon she must go back inside and haggle for the liberties of her people. She remembered that it had been just this season and just this weather when she and Pete rode into the trouble at Whistle Creek. *Pete—* Her mind flew back across twenty-two Hermetian years.

This was a while after they met. That hour was still in the future when he would ask for marriage, or she would. (They were never quite sure which.) They were, though, seeing a good deal of each other. He had suggested she join him for some outdoor sport. She left Eric in her mother's care and flitted northeast from Windy Rim, across the Apollo Valley, to Brightwater in the foothills of the Thunderhead Mountains.

It did not belong to him. The Asmundsens were Followers of the

Runebergs, whose domain had property in these parts as well as on the coastal plain and elsewhere. However, the Asmundsens had been tenants of the estate called Brightwater for generations, managers of the copper mining and refining which were the area's sole industry. Pete was content to let his older brother handle that, while he went into business for himself, exploring the planets of the Maian System and developing their resources. (Naturally the domain took a share of the profits; but then, it had put up the original investment, after he persuaded the president and advisors that his idea was sound.)

The family made Sandra welcome, at first with the formalities due a person of her rank, but soon warmly and merrily. Having seen different cultures in her travels, she noticed what she would earlier have taken for granted, the absolute lack of subservience. If they had by birthright a single vote each in domain affairs while every adult Runeberg had ten, what of it? Their rights were equally inviolable; they enjoyed hereditary privileges, such as this use of a lucrative region; they were spared tedious detail work vis-à-vis neighbor domains; if any of them came to grief, it was the duty of the presidential bloodline to mobilize what resources were necessary to help. Indeed, they stood to the Runebergs much as the Runebergs stood to whatever head of state the legislature elected from the Tamarins. Her awareness growing keener as time passed, Sandra often wondered whether she envied more the Kindred or the Followers.

On the day that she was to recall long afterward, she and Pete took horse for a ride to Whistle Creek, the industrial community. There they would visit the plant and have a late lunch before turning back. The route was lovely, a trail along ridges and down into vales whose forests were beginning to add gold, bronze, turquoise, amethyst, silver to their green, along hasty brooks, across meadows which had heaven for a roof. Mostly they rode in a silence that was more than companionable. But for an hour Pete unburdened himself to her of certain cares. Grand Duke Robert, old and failing, had begun by seeking his opinion on interplanetary development questions, then lately was progressing to a variety of matters. Pete did not want to become a gray eminence. Sandra did her awkward best to assure him that he was simply a valuable counselor. Inwardly she thought that if somehow she *should* be chosen successor, he never would escape the role.

They entered the town in a step, for it had no agricultural hinterland or suburbs. A single paved road to the mine served it; otherwise traffic went by air. Its core was the sleek, largely automated refinery, carefully designed to spare the environment. Round about clustered the shops, homes, and public buildings of a few thousand inhabitants. The streets smelled of woods.

Today they were strangely empty. "What's going on?" Pete asked, and sent his horse clopping ahead. Presently a human noise became audible, the fitful shouting of a crowd. Heading in that direction, the riders rounded a corner and found a small park. Three or four hundred folk stood in it. Mostly they were clad in coveralls without insignia, showing them to be Travers who worked here. Shoulder patches identified Runeberg Followers; these kept apart from the rest and looked unhappy. Followers, too, were the police at the corners of the park. Evidently a disturbance was considered possible.

This was near the end of the midday break. Obviously the meeting would continue into working hours, and the management had decided not to make an issue of that. The arrangers had timed themselves shrewdly; Pete's brother was absent, overseeing the start of a new mine.

A woman stood on the bed of a truck which had set down on the yerb and spoke into an amplifier mike. From newscasts seen at Windy Rim, Sandra recognized her wiry figure, intense dark features, military-style slacksuit—Christa Broderick, Traver born but heiress of a fortune made by her sea-ranching parents. Her words stormed forth.

"—overdue to end the reign of the Thousand Families and their lackeys. What are the domains but closed corporations, whose shares are required by self-serving law to pass from generation to generation? What were those corporations, ever, but the outfits which happened to come here first, and so seized the choicest lands of an entire planet? What was the Declaration of Independence but an attempt to escape the democratization that was stirring in the Commonwealth, an attempt to perpetuate an aristocracy which even stole a medieval title for its new head of state?

"And what are you, the Travers, but workers and businesspeople, excluded from inherited privilege, denied any vote, who nevertheless provide the energy that drives what progress Hermes is making? What are you but the fraction of its population which is not caught in a web of custom and superstition, the part whose vitality would haul this stagnant world into the modern age and the forefront of tomorrow, were you not shackled hand and foot by the ancestor worshipers? What are you but a three-fifths majority?

"Oh, the feudalists are clever, I admit. They hire you, they buy from you and sell to you, they leave your private lives alone, occasionally they adopt one of you into their own ranks, above all they exempt you from taxation. I have heard many a Traver say that he or she is quite happy with things as they are. But ask yourselves: Is this not a subtle slavery in itself? Are you not being denied the right to tax yourselves for public purposes chosen by your democratically elected representatives? Are you content with the do-nothing government of a decadent aristocracy, or would you rather bequeath to your children a state—yes, I will say a commonwealth—to which everything is possible? Answer me!"

A part of the listeners cheered, a part booed, most stood in troubled muteness. Never before had the Liberation Front sent a speaker—its leader, at that—to Whistle Creek. Of course, Sandra realized, those here would have seen rallies and heard speeches made elsewhere, on their telescreens; some would have read the literature; a few might have dropped in on movement headquarters in Starfall. But she felt with shocking suddenness that there was nothing as powerful as a meeting of flesh with eye, voice with ear, body packed close to body. Then the ancient ape awoke. Briefly, sardonically went through her the thought that perhaps this was why Kindred and Followers went in for so much pageantry.

Turning her head, Broderick saw her and Pete in their saddles. They had each gotten a certain amount of publicity; she knew them by sight. At once she pounced. Yet her sarcasm was delicate. "Well, greeting! All of you, look who've come. Peter Asmundsen, brother of your general manager; Sandra Tamarin, possibly your next Grand

Duchess. Sir, madame"—and that second title reminded those who knew of Eric that he might in his turn bring foreign blood to the throne— "I hope I've not given offense in proposing some reforms."

"No, no," Pete called. "Sail right ahead."

"Perhaps you would like to reply?"

" 'Tis your speech."

Chuckles came from the Followers and half the Travers. Broderick plainly knew the charm was broken. Men and women were beginning to glance at their watches; most of them were skilled technicians who could not be absent too long without problems developing in their departments. She would have to start fresh to rearouse interest.

"I'm glad you're here," she said. "Very few of your class can be bothered to debate the issues the Liberation Front is raising. Thank you for showing public spirit. . . . *Do* you wish to respond?"

Expectant gazes turned toward the pair. Dismayed, Sandra felt her tongue lock tight. The sky pressed down on her. Then Pete brought his horse forward a pace, sat there with light shining on his blond mane and in his blue eyes, and said in a deep drawl that carried from end to end of the park:

"Well, thank you, but we're only visiting. Anybody interested in a thorough discussion of the pros and cons of this subject should fax the Quadro twelfth issue of the *Starfall Weekly Meteor*. After that, you can find any number of books, recorded talks, and what have you.

"I might say this, for whatever 'tis worth. I don't think democracy, or aristocracy, or any other political arrangement should be an end in itself. Such things are simply means to an end, not? All right, then ask yourselves if what we've got isn't at least serving the end of keeping Hermes a pleasant place to live.

"If you're feeling restless—well, belike most of you know I'm in charge of an effort to exploit the other planets, instead of overexploiting this one we inhabit. 'Tis tough and often dangerous work, but if you live, you've a goodly chance of getting rich, and are bound to have the satisfaction of knowing you did what not many persons could have done. We're chronically short of labor. I'll be delighted if you mail me your applications." He paused. "My brother will be less delighted.

"Carry on," he said into their laughter, and led Sandra away.

Later, when having skipped lunch they were riding back through the woods, he apologized: "I'm sorry. We'll have to try another time. I'd no idea this would happen."

"I'm glad it did," she answered. "It was interesting. No, more than that."

I learned a little something, Sandra Tamarin-Asmundsen remembered. *Including, maybe then, maybe a bit later, that I loved you, Pete.*

During the years between, the Liberation Front had gained strength. Much of her reign had gone into a search for compromises. Principally, Travers now had a vote in choosing municipal officers. Broderick and her kind were still maintaining that this was a mere sop; and they seemed to make ever more converts. *What will Benoni Strang be like?*

Received in her confidential conference room, he proved a surprise. Medium-sized, slim, the rather handsome features of his rectangular face ornamented by a neat mustache and a suntan, his slightly grizzled brown hair sleeked back, he spoke as smoothly as he moved. His clothes were of rich material, soft in hue but cut in the latest Terrestrial mode. He bowed to her as courtesy required a Traver do. (A member of the Kindred would have shaken hands with the Duchess, a Follower would have saluted.) "Good greeting, Your Grace. I thank you for the honor you do me." The words were traditional, though Hermetian intonation had worn away. He must have spent long years separated from the Strangs whom a city directory listed as being of his class.

Her throat tightened as if to keep her heart from jumping out. *Traitor, traitor.* Barely could she make herself say, "Be seated" and take her own carven armchair.

He obeyed. "It's a wonderful feeling to be back, madame. I'd well-nigh forgotten how beautiful this area is."

"Where else were you?" *I must find out everything about him I can. For this purpose, I may have to smile at him.*

"Many places, madame. A checkered career. I'll be glad to reminisce if you wish. However, I suspect today you'd rather get straight to the point."

"Yes. Why are you working for the Baburites?"

"I'm not really, madame. I hope to do my best for Hermes. It was not always kind to me, but it is the world of my fathers."

"Invaded!"

Strang frowned, as if wounded. "I sympathize with your distress, madame. But Babur was forestalling the Commonwealth. Intelligence discovered that the general staff of the enemy had a plan, the preliminaries already in train, to take over this system."

So you say, Sandra thought. Yet she could not help wondering.

"You can hardly blame Babur for acting," Strang continued. "And from your viewpoint, isn't it the lesser of two evils? It doesn't want to rule you; couldn't possibly; the idea is ridiculous. At most, some kind of postwar association for mutual defense and trade may prove desirable. But the Commonwealth has always deplored the fact that several colonies broke loose from it."

True enough. Our forebears did because they were evolving societies, interests, philosophies in their new homes, too strange to Earth, Luna, or Venus to fit in well with laws and usages developed for those worlds. The Commonwealth didn't resist independence by force of arms. But many of its citizens believed that it ought to.

"Madame," Strang said earnestly, "I've been a xenologist, specializing in subjovian planets and Babur in particular. I know that race and its different cultures better than any other human. No boast, a plain statement of fact. In addition, as I said, I'm a Hermetian, yes, a Hermetian patriot. God knows I'm not perfect. But I do think I'm the realistic choice for High Commissioner. That's why I volunteered my services."

"Not on any quick impulse," Sandra scoffed. "This whole operation must have been planned far ahead."

"True, madame. In a way, all my life. Since I was a boy here in Starfall, I was conscious of things deeply wrong, and thinking how the wrong might be set right."

Fear brushed Sandra and made her snap, "I've lost more time out of my own life than I like to reckon up, listening to the self-pity of the Liberation Front. What's your tale?"

Cold anger flared back at her: "If you haven't understood yet, probably you never will. Have you no imagination? Think of yourself as a child, crowded into a public school while Kindred children were getting individual tutoring from the finest teachers on the planet. Think of having dreams of accomplishment, of becoming somebody whose name will survive, and then finding that all the land worth having, all the resources, all the key businesses belong to the domains—to the Kindred and their Followers—who stifle every chance for a change because it might upset their privileges and make them use their brains. Think of a love affair that should have led to marriage, was going to, till her parents stepped in because a Traver son-in-law would hurt their social standing, would keep them from using her to make a fat alliance—"

Strang broke off. Silence filled the room for half a minute. Thereafter he spoke calmly.

"Madame, quite aside from justice, Hermes must be reorganized so it can aid in its own defense. This archaic half-feudal society is flat-out too cumbersome, too unproductive . . . most important, too alienating. The naval mutiny and flight to Earth showed that not even your government is safe from the insolence and insubordination of an officer corps drawn from the aristocrats. You have to win the loyalty of the Traver majority for practical as well as for moral reasons. But why should it care what becomes of Kindred and Followers? What stake has it in the planet as a whole? Production can no longer be divided among domains. It has to be integrated on a global scale. So do distribution, courts, police, education, welfare, everything. For this, the domains have to be dissolved. In their place, we need the entire populace.

"And after the war—it'll be an altogether new universe. The Polesotechnic League won't be dominant anymore. The Commonwealth won't be the most powerful state. Leisured negotiation won't be the single way of settling disputes between nations and races. Hermes will have to adapt or go under. I want the adaptation to start immediately.

"We're going to have a revolution here, madame. I hope you and your upper classes will willingly assist it. But be that as it may, the revolution is going to happen."

144

XIV

Hanny Lennart, serving the Commonwealth at a credit a year as Special Assistant Minister of Extrasolar Relations, declared across a continent and an ocean: "You appreciate what a difficult position your coming has put us into, Admiral Tamarin-Asmundsen. We welcome your offer to join your strength to ours. However, you admit that your government, which we still recognize, did not order you here."

"I've been told that a few times," Eric replied to the phone as dryly as he was able. Within him raged, *Will you say something real, you mummy?*

She did, and the end of suspense almost kicked the wind out of him. "I am calling informally to let you know without delay that I've decided to support the position taken by your ambassador. That is, the Hermetian government is under duress and therefore only those of its agents who are at large can properly represent it. I expect this will get Cabinet approval."

"Thank you . . . much," he breathed.

"It will take at least a month," she warned. "The Cabinet has a host of urgent problems. There's no hurry about your case, because our fleet won't move till it has reasonably good intelligence of Baburite forces and their dispositions. We don't want a second Mirkheim!"

"According to the news," Eric ventured, "quite a lot of your citizens don't want the fleet to move at all. They want a negotiated peace."

Lennart's sparse brows drew together. "Yes, the fools. That's the softest name I can give them—fools." She grew brisk again. "Pending acceptance of my proposal concerning you, I have the authority and obligation to rule on your temporary status. Frankly, I'm puzzled why Ambassador Runeberg objects so hard to your being considered internees. It's a mere formality for a short period.''

Nicholas van Rijn put him up to it, that's why. The knowledge surged through Eric that he was winning this round. But it wasn't over yet and the fight had many more to go. His mind and tongue began working at full speed.

"I'm sure he's explained to you, Freelady. We will be answerable to our government after the war. Accepting internment would imply that its status was dubious. Nor can we put ourselves under your command till we're fully recognized as allies.''

Lennart compressed her lips. "Someday I must study your curious legal system, Admiral. . . . Very well. I trust you're willing to commence unofficially developing plans with us for integrating your flotilla with our navy?''

"Our *fleet* with yours, if you please, Freelady." The tide of confidence rose in Eric. "Yes, certainly, save when I'm looking after the well-being of my men. And about them, they've been effectively interned already. That has to stop. I want a written statement that they're free to travel around on any innocent errands they may have.''

The discussion that followed took less time than he had expected. Lennart yielded to his demands. After all, they appeared minor. And the Commonwealth government was new to the business of war, unsure how best to handle its own citizens. It would not gratuitously insult the Hermetian popular heroes of the day. Van Rijn's publicists had done their job well.

In the end, Eric switched off, leaned back, and gusted a sigh which turned into an oath. His look roved from the screen on his desk, across the room to a window beyond which green meadows tilted up toward snows and the sheen of a glacier. His new lodging and headquarters was a chalet in the Southern Alps of New Zealand, into which communication and data equipment had hastily been moved. Given a few precautions, it was spyproof and bugproof. The wealthy "sympathizer" who lent it was a dummy of van Rijn's.

His elation receded before a wave of anger. *Haggling,* he thought. *Scheming. Waiting. Waiting. When do we fight, for God's sake?*

For Lorna's sake. The vision of his betrothed rose before him, sharper than any electronic ghost but powerless to speak. Two hundred and twenty-odd light-years beyond this bland sky, she dwelt beneath the guns of Babur, and he had had no chance to kiss her farewell. A pen snapped between his fingers.

Van Rijn came in from the next room, where he had been listening. "We got what we was after, ha?" His tone was unlightened by the minikin victory. "I would shout hurray and toss my hat in the air, except my heart is not in it. We still need to move fast, *nie*? Let us right away knock up a plan."

Eric wrenched attention to the merchant. "Oh, I've done that," he said.

"Ha?" The little black eyes blinked. "I come so we could be sure we talked safe."

Eric shoved back his frustration. Here was another step he could take toward his desire. "I worked it out while you were on your way. Then Lennart called, as we'd been hoping, right after you arrived.

"You go quietly with your agents to your midocean retreat, Ronga, as if for a few days' relaxation from the harassment the government's doubtless been giving you."

Van Rijn's mustaches vibrated. "Who told you about there?"

Eric felt progressively better as he spoke. "David Falkayn. Remember the night on your yacht, how toward morning, when we seemed pretty well talked out, he and I went topside for a breath of fresh air before the car came for me? He described your various private landing facilities, in case of need, and Ronga seems to me like the best bet."

That wasn't all he told, he thought. *Already then, he knew what he aimed to do and had a fair idea of how to go about it. Today I have been, I still am acting at his behest as much as I am at my own.*

"Well, now," he continued into the prawnlike stare, "each of my cruisers carries a speedster—outfitted for interstellar travel, I mean. I'll personally order one down, to land at Ronga. Some Commonwealth naval functionary will have to grant clearance. I'm wagering he'll just retrieve a listing of Ronga as bearing a civilian field suitable for that kind of vessel, and not check any further, like whose property it is. He won't dare to delay me. I've been acting mighty touchy—

you noticed how I snooted Lennart—in hopes that word will go out to handle me with velvyl waldos.

"To avoid phone taps, I suggest you visit my ambassador after you leave here—get him out of bed if necessary—and hand him my commissions of your agents as officers of the Hermetian navy. Then bring to the island, and hand to them, my orders that they're to leave the Solar System according to instructions delivered verbally. They'll take the speedster after she's touched down; you can talk her pilot back to his ship. She carries several weeks' worth of basic supplies. Can you see to it that the nonhumans have along whatever supplementary nutrients they require?

"I don't imagine the boat will meet any problems getting cleared to lift, either. The person in charge will assume I want to visit my ships in their orbits. But once away from Earth, she'll head for the deeps. Space is big enough that it's unlikely she can be intercepted, if your man knows his trade. The Commonwealth navy isn't deployed against possible outward movements, as the Baburites were at Hermes."

A laugh clanked forth. "Oh, yes, I'll get any amount of thunder about this," Eric finished. "I'll enjoy pointing out that I've been entirely within my rights. We are not interned, and as yet we are not under the Commonwealth supreme command. 'Tisn't my fault if their officer took for granted I wanted a jaunt for myself. I'm not obliged to explain any orders I issue to personnel of mine—though as a matter of fact, 'tis quite reasonable that I'd send scouts to see from afar, if they can, how Hermes is doing. Yes, the brouhaha should be the first fun I've had since you smuggled me out of Rio."

Van Rijn stood moveless for seconds. Then: "Oh, ho, ho, ho!" he bellowed. "You is my son for sure, a chip off the old blockhead, *ja*, in you the Mendelian excessives is bred true! Let me find a bottle Genever I said should come with the office gear, and we will drink a wish to the enemy—bottoms up!"

"Later," Eric replied. Warmth touched him. "Yes, I do look forward to getting imperially drunk with you . . . Dad. But right now we've got to keep moving. I'll take your word for it that nobody can have traced you to this place. However, if you're out from under surveillance, if your whereabouts are unknown, for long at a time, it could start the watchers speculating, not?"

He reached for writing materials. "Give me again the names of Falkayn's partners," he requested.

Van Rijn started where he stood. "Falkayn's? David? No, no, boy. I got others standing by."

Eric was surprised. "Of course you're reluctant to send him back into danger. But have you anybody more competent?"

"No." Van Rijn began ponderously pacing. "*Ach*, I admit I hate seeing Coya try not to show she grieves while he is gone. Nevertheleast I would send him, except—Well, you heard, that night on the boat. He will not go arrange a getting together of the independent company heads like he is supposed to. He does not lie to me about that. Give him a chance, he goes to Hermes."

"Why, yes. Should I object?"

"Tombs and torment!" van Rijn spluttered. "What can he *do* there? Get himself killed? Then what has all this pile of maneuvers been for?"

"I'm assuming he didn't boast when he told me, that dawn on your yacht, he and his gang can slip down onto the planet unbeknownst," Eric said. "Once there, yes, quite likely he will stay for the duration. That's good from my viewpoint, because his advice and leadership should be valuable. He also said it'd be harder to get a vessel back into space, but his partners have a sporting chance of being able to do it, after they've left him off. They have a record of such stunts. So they'll assemble your entrepreneurs for you. Though frankly, I've no clear idea of what you think those can accomplish."

"Little, maybe," van Rijn conceded. "And yet . . . I got a hunch on my back, son. It says we should work through what is left of the League, and maybe we find out the reasons for Babur's actions and how we can change them. Because on the face of it, they make no sense." He lifted a slab of a hand. "Oh, *ja*, I know, wars often do not. Still, I wonder and wonder what the Babur leaders imagine they can gain by imperialism against us." He knuckled his forehead. "Somewhere in this thick old noggin is fizzling an idea. . . .

"Davy will insist on going first to Hermes. Then could well be that

Adzel and Chee never manage to continue. The jeopardy cannot change its spots. Let me send somebody else than them. Please."

That his father should finally use that word to him gave Eric a curious pang. "I'm sorry," he said. "It has to be Falkayn, no matter what terms he sets. You see, I've got to carry a rose in my tail—uh, that's Hermetian—I've got to guard my rear, legally, for the sake of my own men. Falkayn has my nationality. And his partners don't belong to the Commonwealth either, do they? Then I have a right to commission them. Have you any equally qualified spacers on tap that that's true of?"

Suddenly van Rijn looked shrunken. "No," he whispered.

He's old, passed through Eric, *weary, and, here at last, forsaken.* He wanted to clasp the bent shoulders. But he could merely say, "Does it make such a difference? At most, we'll set up a liaison, first with my home, later with your colleagues. We hope 'twill prove useful." He made his next words ring. "The issue, though, will depend on how well we fight."

Van Rijn gave him a long regard. "You do not see, do you, boy?" he asked, low and harshly. "Win, lose, or draw, much more war means the end of the Commonwealth like we has known it, and the League, and Hermes. You beg the saints we do not have to fight to what we call a decision." He was mute for a little. "Maybe we is already too late. Hokay, let us go ahead the way you want."

Burnt orange shading to molten gold and far-flung coral, sunset lay extravagant over the ocean. Light bridged the waters from horizon to surf. High in the west stood Venus. Beneath a lulling of waves, Ronga was wholly quiet. The day's odors of blossoms were fading away as air cooled.

Adzel came along a beach that edged the outside of the atoll. On his left a stand of palms glowed against eastern violet. On his right side, the scales shimmered. Chee Lan rode him; her fur seemed gilded. They were spending their last hour before they returned to space.

She said into a silence that had held them both for a while: "After this is done with, if we're still alive, I'm going back to Cynthia. For aye."

Adzel rumbled an inquiring sound.

"I've been thinking about it since the trouble began," she told him—or did she tell herself? "And tonight . . . the beauty here disturbs me. It's too much like home, and too much unlike. I try to recall the living forests of Dao-lai, malo trees in flower and wings around them, everywhere wings; but all I see is this. I try to remember folk I care about, and all I have left is their names. It's a cold way to be."

"I'm glad your appetite for wealth is sated," Adzel said.

She bristled. "Why in chaos was I confessing to you, you over-grown gruntosaur? You wouldn't know what homesickness is. You can pursue your silly enlightenment anywhere you may be, till you've run the poor thing ragged."

The great head shook; and that, meaning no, was a gesture learned among humans, not seen in any land on Woden. "I am sorry, Chee. I did not mean to sound smug, simply happy on your account."

She calmed as fast as she had flared and gave him a purr. He continued doggedly, "I thought in my vanity that I was indeed free of birth ties. But this sun is dim, these horizons are narrow, and often in my dreams I gallop again with comrades across a wind-singing plain. And I long for a wife, I who am supposed to have such wishes only when a female is near me in her season. Or is it young that I really want, tumbling about my feet till I gather them up in my arms?"

"Yes, that," Chee murmured. "A lover I can be kind to, for always."

The beach thinned as it bent around a grove. Passing by, he and she came in sight of Falkayn and Coya, who faced each other with hands joined and had no vision of anything else. Adzel did not slacken his steady pace; he and his rider neither watched nor averted their eyes. Of three races and one fellowship, these four had little they need conceal between them.

"Oh, I regret nothing," said the Wodenite. "The years have been good. I will but wish my children have the same fortune I did, to fare among miracles."

"I likewise," Chee answered, "though I'm afraid—I'm afraid we've had the best of what there was. The time that is coming—" Her voice trailed off.

"You are not compelled to endure the future today," Adzel counseled. "Let us savor this final adventure of ours for what it is."

The Cynthian shook herself, as if she had climbed out of a glacial river, and leaped back to her olden style. "Adventure?" she snarled. "Crammed in a hull half the size of *Muddlin' Through*, with none of our pet amusements? Not even a computer that can play poker!"

XV

At first Hermes was a blue star. It grew to a sapphire disk marbled with white weather, darkened where its single huge continent lay, elsewhere a shining of seas sun-brightened or moon-shimmery. Later it filled half the firmament and was no longer ahead but below.

Here was the danger point. Her crew had ridden *Streak* in on a hyperbolic orbit, entering the Maian System from well off its ecliptic plane, nuclear power plant shut down and life support apparatus running at minimum activity off electric capacitors. Thus if any radar from a guardian Baburite ship fingered her, she would most likely be taken for a meteoroid from interstellar space, a fairly common sort of object. But now, lest she burn in the atmosphere, Falkayn must briefly apply thrust to give her the precise velocity required.

Readouts glided before his eyes, data on air density and its gradient, gravity, altitude, planetary curvature, the boat's ever-changing vectors. A computation flashed forth: in thirty seconds, aerodynamic descent would be feasible, given the correct amount of deceleration, and would bring the speedster down at such-and-such a point. He must decide whether to take advantage of that opportunity or wait for the next. Then less negagrav force would be needed; but the hull would grow hotter and the place of landing would be different. Acting half on reason, half on trained instinct, he pressed the button which elected the immediate option.

With no internal field to compensate, deceleration crammed him forward into his safety web. Weight dragged on his body, darkness went tattered across his vision, thunder sounded through his skull. After minutes the drive cut off and he was flying free on a shallow slant. This high in the stratosphere, stars still shone in a heaven gone blue-black.

"Are you all right back there?" he croaked into the intercom.

"As all right as any other squashed tomato," Chee grumbled from the weapons control turret.

"Oh, I found the maneuver quite refreshing, after so long a time weightless," Adzel said in the engine compartment. "I can't wait to disembark and stretch my legs." Aboard *Streak* he had had no room for anything except isometric exercises and pushups. He must vacate the recreation chamber, the only one in which he could extend himself, whenever his shipmates wanted a workout—either that or risk becoming a backstop for a handball.

"You may get in more jogging than you really want," Chee said dourly. "If somebody's detector registered our power output."

"We were over the middle of the Corybantic Ocean," Falkayn reminded her. "The odds should favor us. . . . Whoops, here we start bouncing."

The boat struck the interface of stratosphere and troposphere at a small, calculated angle. Like a stone skimmed across water, she rebounded from the denser gas. Shock drummed through her structure. For a while she flew on, almost free, rising higher toward space, then curving downward to strike and leap again . . . again . . . again. Each pass was deeper in the atmosphere, at a lower speed. The sky outside turned blue by day, starry only as she rounded the night side. A wail of cloven air swelled to a hurricane roar. Land and sea began to fill more view than heaven did.

At last she was mere kilometers above the surface, acting now as a lifting body. Falkayn tapped a button to demand her geographical coordinates, computed from the continuous signals of navigation satellites. Eagerly he compared a map in his hands. He was over Greatland, bound for a setdown in the Thunderhead Mountains. Below him stretched the sunlit desert of the continental interior, red soil rising in fantastic wind-sculptured yardangs, scantily begrown with yerb, empty of man. If he hadn't been observed yet, he doubted he would be. So he could use the engine to bring the vessel quite near Hornbeck, ancestral home of the Falkayns.

Chee's voice was a swordcut across his hopes. "*Yao leng!* Two aircraft from northeast and southeast, converging on our track."

"You sure?" Falkayn almost shouted.

"Radar and . . . yes, by all doom and hell, neutrino emission,

154

nuclear power plants. I don't think they're spaceable, but they're big, and you can bet they're well heeled.''

Oh, no, oh, no, twisted in Falkayn. *We were spotted. How? Well, the occupation force must be bigger and more dispersed than Eric realized, for whatever reason. After all, he was gone before it took over. . . . Somebody noted an energy burst high up, and queried a centrum which said it probably was nothing Baburite, and a widespread detector net got busy, and we were discovered, and the nearest military flyers were scrambled to check on us.*

He shoved out the dismay in him and asked, ''Any prospect of shooting them down when they come close?''

''Poor, I'd say,'' Chee replied.

Falkayn nodded. *Streak* wasn't *Muddlin' Through.* In atmosphere and a strong gravity field, she was much less agile than machines intended for such conditions. She had no forcefield generator capable of stopping a missile, and her unarmored sides were desperately vulnerable to rays. Before she could strike a first-class fighting aircraft, it would likeliest have blown her apart.

To attempt a return to space would be as senseless as to try combat here. Tracking devices already had a lock on her. Warcraft in orbit must already have been alerted.

The three had discussed this, and every other contingency they could think of, during their voyage. ''Okay,'' Falkayn said. ''Where'll they meet us, Chee?''

''In about another five hundred kilometers, if everybody keeps his present vector,'' the Cynthian told him.

''Give thanks for so much luck. We'll be well over the Thunderheads, a section of them that I knew as a boy. I'll land us short of our destination, and we'll bolt into the woods. Maybe we can shake pursuit. You two, leave your posts right away; no further point in your staying on watch. Chee, collect our supplemental rations.'' They could all eat most of the native life, but it lacked certain vitamins and trace minerals. ''Adzel, get the traveling gear.'' A bundle of that had been prepared in advance, including impellers on which they could fly if they did elude enemy search. ''Stand by at the personnel lock, but buckle onto stanchions. I'll be slamming on brakes quite soon.''

Trailing a sonic boom that shivered the ground below, *Streak* continued her long descent. The mountains reared ghost-blue over the worldrim, then starkly gray and tawny, then beneath the speedster, rock, crags, talus slopes, eternal snows. Peaks raked at her as she crossed their divide. The eastern heights were gentler, falling in long curves toward the Apollo Valley, beyond which lay the Arcadian Hills, the coastal plain, Starfall, and the Auroral Ocean. In the moister air of this side, clouds drifted, alpine meadows glimmered autumnally pale, the lower slopes lay mantled in forest.

Here we go! Falkayn cut in the drive afresh. With a surge of force, the spaceboat shuddered to a virtual halt, tipped to a vertical position, sank, struck. Her landing jacks bit into topsoil, found solidity, adjusted themselves to hold her steady. By then Falkayn was out of his seat. A dose of equilibrol had compensated his organs of balance for the time under zero gee. He swung himself down a companion, dashed along a corridor, found the airlock open and sped over the gangway after his partners.

They gave him the lead. He pelted across the glade where he had settled, toward the trees that walled it. The bare sky bore death. Between the trunks, shrubs and withes grew thick, stiffly resistant. Old skill came back to him and he parted them with economical movements of arms and shins. Adzel must follow more cautiously, lest he leave a trampled trail; but each of his strides was longer than the man's. Chee traveled easily from branch to branch.

Falkayn guessed they had gone three kilometers when a whistling sounded overhead. Glancing up, he saw one of the vehicles as it moved toward *Streak*. The lean shape belonged to an Avelan, produced for human-occupied planets after the Shenna scare made them arm to some degree, as formidable a war machine as he had feared. The insigne painted upon it was the linked figure eights of united Babur. It and its like had surely been bought through dummies years ago, and put in care of human mercenaries.

Relief fountained in Falkayn when it passed out of sight. It had not spied them.

"Let me take a look," Chee called. Adzel tossed her a pair of binoculars adjustable to her eyes, and she swarmed aloft.

Falkayn felt glad of the halt. He wasn't yet tired. On a clear track he could still run his thirty klicks without breathing unduly hard. But this was a chance to let his senses range around, to become part of the world instead of its being a set of obstacles.

Late afternoon light speared among boles and boughs from a blue in which small clouds wandered. The trees hereabouts were mainly stonebark, now leafless, and rainroof, whose canopies were gone yellow but would provide cover if he picked his way with forethought. The forest floor was less overgrown in this area of summer shade than it had been around his landing spot. Its new-fallen cover scrunched beneath his feet, sending up a rich, damp odor. Ornithoids flitted among bare twigs and buzzbugs danced in the sunbeams like dustmotes. A sudden powerful sense of—not homecoming—longing gripped Falkayn. Was this his country yet, or had he roamed away from it for overly many years?

No time to mope about that. Chee scampered back down. "I saw our bandit descend, and the other's hovering above, evidently at the boat," she reported. "They'll soon find nobody's minding that store."

"We had best move fast," Adzel proposed.

"No," Falkayn decided. "Not till we know how thorough they're going to be. Let's get tucked away while we can, especially you, old bulligator."

Chee returned to her post while Adzel squeezed into a thicket. Falkayn used his blaster to slash bushes and boughs, which he laid across the Wodenite's protruding tail. He himself could more readily hide—

The Cynthian zipped to the ground and across it. "School's out," she snapped. "They're coming on impellers, four men flying a search spiral. What d'you bet they've got a sniffer?"

Falkayn stiffened. Short of a cave, there would be no concealment from an instrument sensitive to the gases of breath and perspiration. Wild animals might cause delays with false alarms, but hardly enough to do the hunted any real good.

This could be the end, after all our years of luck. The thought was strange. Aloud, idiotically, he asked, "How would they happen to have a sniffer?"

"Precaution against guerrillas, or maybe guerrillas already are active," Chee said. "Only one of the flyers seems to've carried any, though. Else they'd have two parties in motion."

"Could we take to the air ourselves?"

"*Chu*, no! Where've your wits gone? We'd be seen for sure, this close to them."

Adzel spoke from the coppice: "I'll register much the most strongly when they come in range. You two proceed. Let me stay and decoy them."

"Have your brains turned to oatmeal too?" Chee snorted.

"Listen, friends, it is impossible in any event for me to escape—"

Intelligence slammed back into Falkayn like sword into sheath. "Sunblaze!" he cried. "Turn that notion inside out. Adzel, you stay put. Chee, come along with me. Guide me on a course that'll make them scent us first."

Her ears lifted. "What have you in mind?"

"Hurry, move, you jittertongue!" Falkayn said. "I'll explain as we run."

He stood beneath a rainroof at the edge of a stand of stonebark, whose limbs and twigs traced a skeletal pattern across what he could see of the sky. It hummed above him, and his hunters glided into view, well clear of the treetops. They were human but didn't seem so, the impellers on their backs like thick, paired fins, the helmets on their heads like naked bone, metal agleam in the level light. Otherwise they wore unfamiliar gray uniforms, and three of them carried energy guns whose long barrels bespoke heavy destructive capacity. The leader, who flew lower than the rest, bore a box with scanners and intake valves on its front, meters on its rear: yes, a sniffer.

That man pointed. A bolt raved from the weapon of another, scything dazzlingly across limbs that fell off and crashed downward in bitter-smelling smoke. An amplified voice boomed in accented Anglic: "Come out in sight or we'll burn the ground you're on!"

Falkayn stepped forth, empty hands raised. He was beyond fear. But every sense was at its keenest pitch, he saw each separate fallen leaf under his boots, heard it rustle, felt it give beneath his tread, he knew how a breeze whispered the sweat away from his cheeks, he drank fragrances of growth and healthy decay, it felt impossible to him that Chee's presence did not shout a warning.

The soldiers paused. "That's right, hold where you are," the voice ordered. The four of them conferred. They would naturally be wary of any ambush. However, their instrument had told of just this single man. . . .

An arboreal animal clinging to a high branch didn't count. It was inconspicuous, its fur gray with black spots, its posture that of a creature frozen into terrified immobility. Chee had rolled in the humus below the dead leaves. And the men were not Hermetians, they knew nothing of the planet's wildlife. Perhaps none of them had even noticed her.

One remained high. His companions came down to take the prisoner. As they passed near the Cynthian, she whipped her blaster from under her belly and opened fire.

The first bolt struck the sniffer, slashed through the cover and in among the circuits. He who bore it screamed and let go. The shot trailed across him, searing shut the mortal wound it made. His body continued down on its impeller, brokenly dangling.

Her second ray missed. It only got her target on the leg. But that put him out of action. He fled straight up, his own shrieks horrible to hear.

The third blazed at Chee. She had already slipped behind the trunk and was on her way groundward, springing from bough to bough across meters of air. He slewed his gun about in search of Falkayn, but Falkayn was back under foliage. Hermetian and Cynthian snapped shots from what shelter they had. The soldier retreated. In blind fury, he and his unhurt companion sent flame after flame. Where those struck, wood burst and soil steamed. Hundreds of wings lifted in panic, till cries well-nigh drowned out the flat thunder.

It was useless. Slipping from cover to cover, Falkayn was out of that area within seconds. Chee had less trouble moving invisibly. When they rejoined Adzel, she went on high and glimpsed no hostiles, apart from the one aircraft at hover. The mercenaries must have helped their wounded mate back.

"And they'll be without a sniffer till somebody brings a replacement," Falkayn said. As he had not been afraid earlier, he was not exultant now; he merely knew what he must do, and momentum carried him headlong. "We've got to be far gone before then. We'll start off now, slowly and ultracautiously. Come nightfall, which thank God is soon, we'll move fast. I mean fast." To the Wodenite: "Never mind any more noble self-sacrifices, huh? You carry me, and Chee on my back, and we *will* have a good speed without needing rest stops." *Yes*, he thought, *the old team is still working rather well*, and pointed to a landmark glimpsed between trees, an unmistakable snowpeak. "Steer yonderward. That way are my people."

XVI

Hornbeck occupied a plateau jutting from a lower flank of Mount Nivis. North beyond a forest climbed the heights, up to where whiteness forever gleamed. In the west also the horizon was ridged, but to east and south vision met just sky at the end of plowlands. The gray stone manor house stood a little apart from a thorp of lesser dwellings and other buildings. Here was the origin of the Falkayn domain, in timber and iron; though its enterprises had since spread planetwide, here was still its heart.

Walking along a road that wound among the fields, he saw them empty at this season, stubble and bare brown soil except when cattle in pastures cropped the last Earthside grass which autumn had left. The day was clear, windless, and cool; so great a silence filled it that the scrunch of his boots on gravel seemed mysteriously meaningful. Far overhead a steelwing hovered, alert for prey. No cars flew by to trouble it, nor did any move across the ground. The whole settlement had withdrawn: sending few messages to the outside world and those curt; sending few of its members there and those, closemouthed, on the briefest of errands; inviting no visitors—as if in preparation for onslaught.

Which it would soon undergo, in a form more dangerous to it than physical attack, Falkayn thought.

He and his mother had come forth, this morning after his arrival, to talk together away from last night's loving turmoil. But for half an hour they walked speechless. After the years that had passed, he could not be sure what she was thinking. He himself found he could not dwell on plans. His body was too busy remembering.

Athena Falkayn finally took the word. She was a tall woman, still handsome and vigorous, white hair falling thick past her shoulders.

Like her son, she wore a coverall ornamented by the family patch; but she had added a necklace of fallaron amber.

"David, dear, I was too happy to see you again, too horrified at the risks you've run and then realizing you did come through them safe—I couldn't say this erenow. Why are you really here?"

"I told you," he answered.

"Yes. To take over from Michael, as is your right."

"And my duty."

"No, David. You know better. John and Vicky"—her remaining two children, living elsewhere—"and their spouses are perfectly competent. For that matter, I was essentially in charge after your father died, Michael being away so much with his naval work. Or have you grown so foreign to us that you don't believe we can cope?"

Falkayn winced and rubbed his face. It was gaunt from days of hard traveling, living off the country; his party had not dared fly. "Never," he replied. "But with my, well, my experience—"

"Could you not have applied that more usefully in space, helping organize the war effort?" The glance she sent on high, where ships patrolled, was like a shaken fist.

"I doubt it," he said roughly. "Do you suppose the Commonwealth government would have any part of me? As for van Rijn—well, maybe I've made a bad mistake. Or maybe not. But . . . look, Hermes has always been at peace. The rough and tumble of history is unreal to you—to everybody living on this planet—no more than a set of names and dates we learn as children, and forget afterward because they mean nothing to us. I, though, I've seen war, tyranny, conquest, upheaval, among scores of races. It made me visit sites on Earth, from Jericho and Thermopylae to Hiroshima and Vladivostok, only there were more of them in between than anybody could have time for. . . . I know something about how these horrors work. Not much—the League's got plenty of people as well informed as I am or better—but I can claim more understanding than most Hermetians."

He gripped her arm. "Before I go on, please let some air into this vacuum I've been talking in," he craved. "Tell me what the situation is. I heard mention of a social revolution sponsored by the occupation authorities, but no details. Everybody yesterday was excited and—Lord, it did get to be one hooraw of a sentimental occasion, didn't it?

162

Plus the cursing of traitors who've stirred up the Travers. It can't be as simple as that."

"No, 'tis not," Athena agreed. "Maybe you can see a pattern, different from what I fear I see."

"Tell me."

"Well, I'm a light-year from having all the facts, and I may be shading those I do have, according to my own biases. You should talk to others, consult news records—"

"Yes, of course." Falkayn laughed sadly. "Mother, I'm fifty years old. Uh, that's forty-five Hermetian."

Her smile responded in the same mood. "And I can't feel, I suppose I can believe but I can't feel it's been that long since the doctor laid you down on my stomach and I heard what a fine pair of lungs you had."

They walked on. The road was interrupted by a plank bridge crossing the Hornbeck itself. They halted at the middle and leaned on the rail, looking down through the water to the stones on the bottom which it made ripply. The current clucked.

"Well," she said in a low monotone, "you know the Baburites came into this system and announced we were their protectorate. They meant to take our few warships, but Michael led those out.

"Michael," she said again after a second, in pride and mourning.

Wyvernflies danced above the brook, golden on gauzy wings.

"I imagine Lady Sandra needed a moonful of nerve then," she continued. "The fleet gone, her oldest son with it—what an excuse to depose her. She must have stood up to those creatures and made them see that she alone could maintain a government, that otherwise they'd inherit anarchy on a planet about which they were nigh totally ignorant. Which was true. Her purpose is to save our lives, our way of living, as many and as much as she can. If she has to compromise, well, I at least will thank her for whatever she can keep."

Falkayn nodded. "You're wise, Mother. Listening to some of those hotheads last night . . . Help me tell them there's nothing romantic about war and politics."

Athena sent her gaze toward a glacier which gleamed under the snows of Mount Nivis. "Soon afterward, the Baburites brought in oxygen-breathing mercenaries, mostly human," she said. "Happens

I've a little information about those, because the Duchess asked me to get folk I could trust to make inquiries, since businesses of our domain would inevitably be dealing with the occupiers and Lady Sandra knew I've always been close to our chief Followers.

"The humans and nonhumans are both a motley lot, recruited over a period of years—from the broken, the embittered, the greedy, the outlawed, the amoral, the heedless adventurous."

Falkayn nodded. Expanding through space with the speed and blindness of a natural force, Technic civilization had bred many such. "Recruitment alone must have required quite an organization, backed by plenty of resources," he said.

" 'Tis plain," Athena answered. "I suppose their upper-echelon officers knew part of the truth; but the ranks weren't told. The story *they* were handed was this: A consortium of investors, who wanted to stay anonymous, was quietly preparing a free-lance army, crack troops who'd hire out at high prices wherever they might. That might be on behalf of societies which found themselves meeting a threat like the Shenna; or it might be to assist would-be imperialists venturing outside of known space. There was a strong hint that the Ymirites in particular were interested in that and would find oxygen-breathing auxiliaries useful on smaller worlds—for instance, to exact tribute in the form of articles manufactured to order."

Falkayn let a corner of his mouth bend upward. "I almost have to, no, I do have to admire their audacity," he said. "Ymir was a natural choice, however; it's a favorite object of superstition."

Because we know hardly a byte about it, he recalled. *Our name for a giant planet, dwarfing Babur, whose inhabitants are traveling and colonizing through space but apparently uninterested in any close contact with us—or else have decided we're too hopelessly alien.*

"I wonder why you, the League, got no inkling of all that recruitment," Athena said. "The best estimate I can make, from what reports of conversations I've gathered—and, yes, between us, interrogations of a few kidnapped soldiers—some small guerrilla activity has begun, we disown it publicly but word does filter back to us—" She drew breath. "Never mind. Mainly, my folk have counted the occupying troops as well as possible. They number about a million.

164

Other information suggests that about as many more are being held in reserve.''

Falkayn whistled.

And yet— ''It's quite understandable why no intelligence of it reached us,'' he told her. ''A couple of million individuals, collected piecemeal in tens of thousands of places on dozens of planets, they don't amount to a particularly noticeable statistic. Intrigues are forever going on anyway.

''Maybe agents of one or two companies did get some intimations. But if so, they or their bosses didn't see fit to pass the information on to the rest of us and push for a full investigation. Communication between members of the League is not what it used to be.''

Space is too big, and we too divided.

Athena sighed. ''I've gathered that.

''Well. The soldiers were warned they'd be in isolation for years. But the accumulating pay was excellent, and apparently some fairly lavish recreational facilities were provided, everything from beer halls and brothels to multi-sense library service. And of course the planet where they were sent had its natural wonders to explore, grim though 'twas—marginally terrestroid, hot, wet, perpetually clouded.''

''Clouds?'' Falkayn said. ''Oh, yes. So nobody who wasn't cleared for Top Secret could figure out where it is.''

''Its name among them was Pharaoh. Conveys that aught to you?''

''No.''

''Maybe 'tis outside of known space altogether.''

''Hm, I doubt that. Explorers keep expanding known space, and might well come upon it. I'd guess Pharaoh was visited once and is down in the catalogues with a number, not a name, as a not particularly interesting globe, compared to most others. . . . Okay. The army lived and trained there, till lately it shipped out and found it was working for Babur against the Commonwealth and possibly against the League. Has that shaken morale?''

''I really know not. My folk—like all true Hermetians—haven't gotten exactly intimate with them. My impression is that most of them still feel entirely confident. If anything, they're glad to lash out

165

at a Technic civilization that kicked them aside. Surely the Merseians among them are. If any individuals do have qualms, military discipline keeps them quiet. That's a highly disciplined outfit.''

Athena bowed her head. ''I'm afraid I can't tell you more about them,'' she finished.

Falkayn laid his hand over hers, where it rested on the rail, and squeezed hard. ''Judas priest, Mother, what are you apologizing for? You've missed your career. You should've been in charge of Nick van Rijn's intelligence corps.''

Meanwhile he could not help thinking what an epic the gathering of the host was. Somebody very high-powered had been at work.

''Let's go on,'' Athena said. ''I need to exercise the misery out of me.''

Falkayn flinched as he matched his pace to hers. ''Yes, it must be a foretaste of hell, having to sit helpless day after day while—Am I correct in thinking the Baburites originally promised no interference in our domestic affairs?''

''More or less.''

''And then, once they were firmly based here, they reneged; and they've been pouring in additional troops, stationed over the entire planet, to deter revolt.''

''Right. They planted a High Commissioner on us who's going ahead mostly as he pleases. If Lady Sandra gives him not a minimum of cooperation, 'tis plain he'll depose her and put us completely under martial law. But the poor brave lass stays on, with Christ knows how many struggles, in hopes of preserving some representation for Kindred, Followers, and loyal Travers . . . some part of our institutions.''

''At the same time, by remaining Duchess, she does give a certain cachet of legitimacy to his decrees. . . . Well, who am I to criticize? I'm not there on the throne. Tell me about this High Commissioner.''

''Nobody knows much. His name is Benoni Strang. That means naught to you either, not? Well, he claims being Hermetian, Traver born and raised. I did manage to have birth and school records checked, and they bear that out. Bad experiences early in life seem to have turned him into a revolutionary. But instead of becoming a Liberation Fronter, he went offplanet—got a scholarship from Galac-

166

tic Developments to study xenology—and nobody here heard a word about him for the next three decades, even his relatives, till suddenly he reappeared among the Baburites. He's very familiar with them, belike as much as is possible for an oxygen breather. But he's also been in topflight human circles; he's sophisticated."

Falkayn frowned across the fields. A loperjack padded from a hedge and over the stubble, small furry shape whose freedom was untouched by ships and soldiers. "And he's taking this chance to get revenge. Or to right old wrongs, he'd say. Same thing. Does the Liberation Front cheer him on?"

"Not really," Athena said. "Their leader, Christa Broderick, made a televised speech after the Commissioner proclaimed his intention of putting through basic social reforms. She welcomed that. Quite a few Libbies promptly resigned, declaring they're Hermetians first. And later, he's made no effort to enlist her organization as such; he's bypassing it entirely. She's grown resentful. Censorship won't allow her to denounce him openly, but her public silence indicates how she now stands. His Traver supporters are moving to form a new party."

"I'm not surprised at Strang's action," Falkayn observed. "He wouldn't want a strong native group for an ally. He'd have to give it a voice, and the voice wouldn't always echo his. If you plan to restructure a society, you start by atomizing it."

"He's said, through the throne, there'll be a Grand Assembly to draft a new constitution—as our present constitution provides for, you know—as soon as suitable procedures for the election of delegates can be set up."

"Ye-ih. That means as soon as he can rig it, without being too blatant about the fact that everything's happening under Baburite missile launchers. Do you know what changes he plans to make?"

"Naught's been definitely promised yet save 'an end to special privilege.' But we're hearing so much about one 'proposal' that I'm sure 'tis scheduled to be enacted. The domains will be 'democratized' and will conduct all their operations through a central trade authority."

"A good, solid basis for a totalitarian state," Falkayn said. "Mother, I did do right to come back."

She regarded him for a while before she asked, "What do you intend?"

"I'll have to learn more and think a lot before I can get specific," he replied. "Basically, though, I'll take over the presidency of this domain as I'm entitled to, and then organize resistance among the rest."

Appalled, she protested, "You'll be jailed the minute you reveal yourself!"

"Will I? Unlikely. I'll come onstage with fanfare. What have I done that was illegal? Nobody can prove how or when I arrived here. I could have been meditating in a backcountry hermitage since before the war. And . . . the Shenna episode made me a standard-model hero. Never mind modesty—the fact has often been a damned nuisance—but a fact it is. If Strang's proceeding as warily as you tell, he won't move against me without gross provocation, which I won't give. I believe I can rally the Kindred and Followers, get them out of their demoralization, and appeal also to plenty of Travers. When the Grand Assembly is called, we'll pull some weight in it. Probably not much, but some. We may at least be able to preserve elementary civil liberties, and keep Hermes enough of a symbol of that that the Commonwealth can't bargain us away."

"I'm afraid you're overoptimistic, David," Athena warned.

"I know I am," he answered grayly. "At best, I'll hate the next few years, or however long the war lasts—separated from Coya and our kids, with the same emptiness in their lives—

"But I've got to try, don't I? We can only lose all hope by giving up all hope."

Falkayn had left Adzel and Chee in the woods before he hiked the last several kilometers to the manor. Among his earliest concerns was to get them safely tucked away without too many people learning about them, even at Hornbeck.

Athena had been able to arrange it immediately. When the Baburites made known their intention to occupy, Duchess Sandra had distributed among trustworthy households those Supermetals personnel she had evacuated from Mirkheim. Athena took charge of Henry Kittredge, the ground operations chief. She sent him to a hunting lodge off in the wilderness. None but she and a few ultratrusted underlings who brought him his necessities knew he was there. He was delighted when the Wodenite and the Cynthian were guided—on their impellers, after dark—to keep him company.

In the morning, the three of them settled down for intensive talk. Kittredge sat on the porch of the log cabin, Chee perched on a chair beside his, Adzel lay at ease on the ground outside with his head rearing above the rail. Sunlight streamed past surrounding trees, turning vivid what leaves remained, yellow, russet, white, blue. Animal life made occasional remote drummings and flutings that drifted through speckled shadows. Otherwise the air was quiet, pungent, a little chilly.

"Books, music tapes, television," Kittredge said. "Chatter whenever somebody brought me more grub. It got lonesome. Worse, it got boring. I've caught myself wishing something would happen, anything, good or bad."

"Could you not take recreation in the forest?" Adzel asked.

"I've never dared go far. I might get lost, or come to grief in a hundred unpredictable ways. This planet is too unlike mine."

Chee flicked ashes off her cigarette at the end of its holder. "Vixen has a human-habitable hemisphere," she said, "including wood-lands."

"But not like these, except in superficial appearance," Kittredge replied. "Hell, you know that, as many worlds as you've seen." Wistfully: "Me, I'd settle for just seeing Vixen again, and never stirring my butt off it anymore."

"Nor the rest of you, I presume," Chee muttered.

"I sympathize," Adzel said gently. "Home is home, no matter how stern."

"Vixen's a better place to live than it was," Kittredge said with an upsurge of pride. "Our share in Supermetals has paid for founding a net of weather stations, which we badly needed, and—Well, we've gained that much, whatever becomes of Mirkheim in the future."

Chee stirred restlessly. "It may make a difference in determining what gets done with Mirkheim if Adzel and I can continue our mission," she declared. "Have you any notion of how we might get a ship?"

Kittredge shrugged. "Sorry, none. No doubt it'll depend on how things are going elsewhere."

"You must have some idea about that," Adzel urged. "You've spent considerable time here watching broadcasts, and must also have talked to Hermetians at length *viva voce.*"

Kittredge raised his brows. "Talked how?"

"Never mind him," Chee advised. "He gets that way occasionally."

"Well, I'm a total foreigner to this planet," Kittredge said. "And you two, what do you know about it, starting with its type of society?"

"A fair amount," Adzel assured him. "David Falkayn discussed it with us, over and over. He had to."

"Yes, I suppose he would," Kittredge said compassionately. "Well, then, as near as I can discover, the Baburites, through their human honcho, intend to mount a revolution on Hermes—from the top, though doubtless they expect to get support from the bottom. The whole scheme of law and property is to be revised, the aristocracy abolished, a 'participatory republic' established, whatever that means."

Adzel straightened his neck and Chee sat stiffly upright with her whiskers dithering. *"Chu-wai?"* she exclaimed. "Why in cosmos would the Baburites care what kind of government Hermes has, as long as they're in control?"

"I think they intend to stay in control," Kittredge answered. "Also after the war—for which purpose they'll have to have a pro-Babur native régime, since otherwise too much of their strength would be tied down here." He tugged his chin. "I figure this takeover of theirs is not just to forestall the Commonwealth's doing the same thing."

"Which was a poison-blooded lie from the first," Chee snapped. "The Commonwealth never had any such intention, and the Baburites can't be too stupid to know that."

"Are you sure?"

"Quite sure. Van Rijn would have gotten at least an intimation, and told us. Besides, we come straight from the Solar System. We've seen what disarray the war effort is in, there—military unprepared-

170

ness, political uproar, a substantial party howling in terror for peace at whatever cost . . . The Commonwealth is not and never has been in shape to practice imperialism."

"Then why in the name of all that's crazy did the Baburites invade Hermes? And why do they want to keep it in the empire they'd build around Mirkheim?"

"That is a mystery," Adzel said, "among other mysteries, largest of which is the reason for Babur's launching a campaign of conquest in the first place. What does it hope to gain? As a world, a sophont species, it can only suffer a net loss by replacing peaceful trade with armed subjugation. Napoleon himself remarked that one can do everything with bayonets except sit on them. Of course, there may be a small dominant class on Babur which stands to make a profit—*Hro-o-oh!*"

He bounded to his feet. Chee snatched for the blaster she wore holstered. A car had appeared above the trees.

"Easy, easy," Kittredge laughed, getting up himself. "It's lugging in extra supplies to feed you two."

Adzel eased. Chee did so more slowly, as she inquired, "Isn't that a bit risky? An occupation patrol might notice."

"I asked the same question," Kittredge assured her. "The lady Falkayn said the family's always let its servants use this lodge when they're off duty if it's not otherwise in demand. Nothing unusual about them flitting here for a few hours."

The car landed in the open before the cabin and the pilot got out. Kittredge recoiled. "I don't know him!" Chee's hand snaked toward her gun.

"I'm a friend," the stranger called. "Lady Athena sent me. I've brought your food." He approached, short, stocky, weatherbeaten, plainly clad, with a slightly rolling gait. "My name's Sam Romney, from Longstrands."

Introductions were made and hands shaken. Kittredge fetched beer and everybody settled down.

"I'm a fisherman," Romney related. "An independent shipowner, but I've done most of my business with the Falkayns, we've gotten pretty close, and in fact, uh, a lad of yours from Mirkheim is currently being supercargo on a herder of mine out at sea. The

Hornbeck pantries can't supply a bonzer your size, Adzel, not without making a conspicuous hole on the shelves. So last night Lady Athena sent a messenger asking me to come with a lot, explaining roughly how matters stand. She also thinks, and I believe she's right, she thinks it might be useful, when nobody knows what'll happen next, it might be useful for you to have outside contacts.''

"Perhaps," Chee muttered, coiled herself on a cushion, and started a fresh cigarette. Whatever harm had been done, was done.

Adzel gave the newcomer a searching look. "Excuse me," he said, "but are you of the Traver class?"

"Sure am," Romney replied.

"I do not mean to impugn your loyalty, sir, but I had been given to understand that considerable conflict exists on Hermes."

"The Travers on this manor can be trusted," Kittredge pointed out. "Otherwise I'd've been clutched weeks ago."

"Yes, of course, the phenomenon of the faithful retainer is reasonably general," Adzel said. "And obviously Captain Romney is on our side. I merely wonder how many more like him there are."

The seaman spat. "I don't know," he admitted. "That's one hell-wicked thing about having the enemy amongst us, we can't speak our minds out loud any longer. But I can tell you this, plenty Travers never swallowed that Liberation Front crock. Like me. I begrudge not the Kindred and the Followers an atom. Their ancestors earned it, and if they maintain it not, they can still lose it, fair and square. Besides, once a government starts dividing property up, where does it stop? I worked hard for what I have, and I mean for my youngsters to have it after me—not a cluttle of zeds who can't be bothered to do anything for themselves save fart in unison when their glorious leader says to.''

He took out a pipe and tobacco pouch. "Also this," he continued, "several Libbies have told me, because you know people will talk now and then regardless, confidential-like, several Libbies have told me they're not happy either. They want not change pushed down everybody's throats by those creepie-crawlies; and Babur's using a traitor like Strang to do it makes the whole affair stink worse. And they, the Libbies, that is, they've not been invited into any conferences. Strang's given them a glop of praise for the, what's he say, the noble ideals they've long upheld—*ptui!*—he's given them a few fine words, like a bone thrown to a yellow dog, but that's been it.''

Having stuffed his pipe, he applied fire before he ended: "Oh, we've got a fair-sized minority of yellow dogs, who're overjoyed at the prospects before 'em. I'll say to her credit, Christa Broderick, the Libbie leader, Christa Broderick's not among those. But what means that, save that the only thing she has left to lead is a powerless rump of the old organization? Maybe the Duchess will keep some small voice when the Grand Assembly gathers. But not Broderick, no, not Broderick.''

Adzel met Chee's eyes. "Partner," he said, "I suspect we had better make sure that before he reveals himself or does anything else irrevocable, David talks with Lady Sandra.''

XVII

The image of Benoni Strang stated: "I am calling you about Elvander's Birthday, madame."

For a moment Sandra could not brace herself. She had had to do that too often, until now she sat back and waited in weariness for the next blow. Then thunder resounded outside, she heard anew the trumpet of wind and march of rain, it was as if Pete rode by. She straightened in her chair and replied coldly, "What of it? The date is still a month off."

"We're wisest to be beforehand, madame," Strang said. "My request is that you announce there will be no public celebrations of the holiday this year, in view of the emergency—that demonstrations of any kind are forbidden."

"What? On our planetary day?"

"Exactly, madame. The danger of emotions avalanching is too great. Citizens may quietly observe it at home if they wish; but we can't allow any large private parties either. Churches must be closed."

No real surprise, Sandra thought. Yet her earliest memory was of her father holding her high above a crowd on Riverside Common, to see the fireworks cascade upward off a barge draped in flags. The water was alive with their light. "What if I don't issue your proclamation?" she challenged.

Strang frowned. "You must, madame. For the sake of your people. Riots, which could lead to actual attempts at overthrow . . . the military would have no choice but to open fire." He paused. "If you do not issue the order, I will. That would seriously undermine your authority."

What authority?

Nevertheless, this polite, grisly game we play, you and I, is all that postpones—what?

"A massacre would lose you much of your support," she warned.

His mouth tightened beneath the neat mustache. "Your use of an emotional word like that shows that an incident might necessitate extreme measures on the part of my office, madame."

"Oh, I'll cancel the festivities. Belike nobody would be in a mood for them anyway."

"Thank you, madame. Ah . . . you will consult with me on the wording, won't you?"

"Yes. Good day, Commissioner."

"Good day, Your Grace."

Alone, Sandra rose and sought an open window. She had not turned on fluoros, and the storm made her conference chamber gloomy, a cave wherein only a few visions stood out, shimmer of a polished wood panel, dulled colors of a picture, curve of the Diomedean battle-ax. Freshness blew in, though, loud and raw. Rain struck the garden like spears and hid sight of the world beyond its wall. Lightning flared, making every bare twig on the shrubs leap forth under a sheet-metal sky; thunder rolled across unending reaches while murk returned.

She would not ride forth today. She had been doing that every morning, taking her best-beloved horse over Pilgrim Hill to Riverway, along the Palomino to Silver Street, thence to Olympic Avenue and back, a distance of several kilometers—always alone—to let the people see her, for whatever comfort that might give on either side. Folk often bowed deeply or kissed their hands to her. But too few would be out in this weather to make the gesture worth the effort.

I want to, however, I am parched with wanting. Though not through Starfall. West instead, on Canyon Road into the countryside, at a gallop straight against wind and rain, gallop and gallop without stop, hoofs smashing skulls of Strang and his men, then beyond them into the hills, the mountains, the deserts, a leap off the horizon and out among the stars.

A buzzer sounded. She untied her fists, strode to the intercom, and pressed accept. "Yes?"

"Madame," said the voice of her entrykeeper, "Martin Schuster is waiting to see you."

"What?" She came back to herself. "Oh. Yes. Send him in."

Whoever he is. I know only that Athena Falkayn sent me a message asking me to receive him in private, which is why I happened to be here when Strang—her gullet clenched—*called*.

The door opened for him and closed again. He was like her in being tall, blond, and middle-aged. When she looked more closely into the lean countenance, she choked down a cry of startlement and stood rigid.

He bowed. "Good greeting, Your Grace. Thank you for receiving me." He kept a touch of Hermetian accent if not of phrasing, for, as she knew, throughout the years he had not been long at a time on Earth, nor on any other world where Anglic was spoken. "What I have to say is confidential."

"Right." Her heart fluttered. "This room is spyproofed." As he hesitated: "Since the occupation, I've assigned guards and technicians to full-time duty, making sure it stays secure."

"Fine." Their gazes locked. "I think you know me."

"David Falkayn?"

"Yes."

"Why have you come back?"

"To help however I can. I was hoping you, madame, could give me a few ideas about that."

Sandra's gesture was jagged. "Welcome. Sit. Care you for refreshment, a smoke, aught I can offer?"

"Not now, thank you." Falkayn remained standing till she had taken her seat. She fumbled forth a cigar from a humidor beside her chair, bit the end off, and started it going.

"Tell me your story," she said.

"Eric reached Sol unharmed," he began, and continued. She seldom interrupted his succinct narrative with questions.

When he was through, she shook her head and sighed. "I admire your courage and resource, Captain Falkayn, and maybe you can be of help. That's dreadfully far from certain, though. At best, between us we can fight a delaying action, buying temporary concessions from Strang with our cooperation in laying the foundations for his eventual dictatorship. Naught can really save Hermes but the defeat of Babur.''

''Which will take years if it's possible at all, and lives and treasure and social disruption beyond reckoning,'' he said. ''The Commonwealth is confused, dismayed, and lacks will. The League is paralyzed by its own feuds. I think after a while the Commonwealth will fight all-out, largely because the Home Companies want that. They see Mirkheim as their entry into space on a scale that'll make them competitive with the Seven. But they can't conjure up a determined populace and a powerful navy overnight. Meanwhile Babur will—who can tell what? Yes, madame, I doubt we on Hermes can count on rescue from abroad.''

''What would you advocate, then?'' She drew savagely on her cigar. The smoke bit her tongue.

''Political maneuvers, as you've been carrying out and I may be able to join you in. Simultaneously, covert organization of armed resistance, to operate out of our enormous hinterlands. We just might make the cost of supporting Strang more than it's worth to Babur, which has little to gain here.''

''Whatever the real reason was for Babur overrunning us, won't that continue to obtain?'' she argued against all her dearest wishes. ''And never underestimate Strang. He's surely foreseen that we may try what you suggest, and taken steps. In his evil way—not that he sees himself as evil—he's a genius.''

Falkayn stared past her, out the rainful window. ''You must know him better than anybody else on this planet,'' he said.

''That's not well. He's as dedicated as a machine, and no easier to get near. I wonder if he ever sleeps. Why, shortly before you came in, he called me personally about banning public events on Elvander's Birthday. He could have told an aide to make the arrangements, but no, he had to see to it himself.''

Falkayn smiled a little. ''I must study him, try to get a notion of his style. I'm told he makes no speeches, and hardly ever delivers a statement in his own name.''

''True. He's no egotist, I must admit. Or . . . rather . . . he's interested in the substance of power, not the show.''

''I don't even know what he looks like.''

177

"Well, I can play back our conversation." Sandra was vaguely relieved to rise, walk across to her phone, and punch the button. She wasn't sure how to respond to this man, home-born but far-faring, famous but a stranger, who had come to her out of the storm.

The screen lit, the familiar, well-hated features appeared, Strang said, "Good morning, Your Grace—"

"*Yaaah!*"

The yell ripped at her eardrums. She whirled and saw Falkayn on his feet, crouched crook-fingered. "Can't be!" he roared. And then, a whisper: "Is."

"I am calling you about Elvander's Birthday, madame," said the recording.

"Turn it off," Falkayn asked hoarsely. "Judas priest." He looked around him, as if seeking among the shadows. "What else can I say? Judas priest."

It was as if a tendril of the lightning ran up Sandra's spine, but cold, cold. She went stiff-legged back to him. "Tell me, David."

"This—" He shook himself violently. "Does Strang have a twin brother, a double, anything of the kind?"

"No." She halted. "No, I'm certain not."

He began to pace, hands wrestling behind his back. "A piece of the puzzle, a keystone, an answer?" he mumbled. "Be quiet. Let me think." Neither of them noticed his breach of manners.

She waited in a chill draught from the window while he prowled the room, his lips shaping unvoiced words or now and then a nonhuman oath. When at last he stopped and regarded her, it was strangely right that he stood beneath the ax.

"This is information that has got to get to Earth," he thrust forth. "To van Rijn. Immediately. And secretly. How can you smuggle a message out?"

She shook her head. "There's no way."

"There must be."

"None. Think you I have not wanted it, have not sat with my officers trying to imagine how we might do it? This planet is meshed in radar sweeps, detectors, and ships. Your friends could never have gotten off it alive. You reached atmosphere by masking yourself as a

meteoroid, yes. But you know what happened after that. And
. . . meteoroids don't rise.''

Falkayn's fist smote the wall. "Listen. What I've learned could
determine the whole course of the war. If we get it to van Rijn in time.
That's worth virtually any sacrifice we can make.''

She took hold of his arm. "Why?''

He told her.

She stood long silent. "You see I don't have a complete solution to
the riddle,'' he added. "I'll leave that for Old Nick to work out. He's
good at such things. I could even be wrong, in which case our effort
will have gone for zero. But you see why we must make the effort.
Don't you?''

"Yes.'' She nodded blindly. "A wild gamble, though. If aught
goes awry, we've lost more than our lives.''

"Of course. Nevertheless,'' he hammered, "we must try. No
matter how fantastic our scheme, it's better than nothing.

"Surely communication goes back and forth between Strang and
the Baburite high command. If we could hijack one of those boats—''

"Impossible.'' Sandra walked from him, back to the window.
Wind whooped, rain rushed, thunder went like enormous wheels.
Winter was on its way to Starfall.

He came up behind her. "You know something,'' he accused.

"Yes,'' she answered beneath the noise, not turning her head. "I
do. But oh, God, my people—and yours, your mother, brother,
sister, spaceship comrades, everybody left behind—''

It was his turn to fall mute, and afterward to force: "Go on.''

"I still have the ducal space-yacht,'' she told him, drop by drop.
"Strang has more than once suggested I might like to take a cruise to
relax. I've ever answered no. His meaning is obvious. I can flee to
Sol. He'll not oppose that.''

"No, he wouldn't,'' Falkayn agreed low. "It'd give him the
perfect excuse to seize total control, with the support of the extremist
Hermetian Liberation Fronters. Quote, 'The Grand Duchess, like her
son before her, has defected to the enemy, intending to lead back a
foreign force that will crush our glorious revolution.' ''

"There'd be no leadership for Kindred, Followers, and loyal

Travers. They'd feel I'd betrayed them . . . and erelong they could become the subjects of a reign of terror."

"I see you've read your history, Lady Sandra."

Once more they stood dumb.

"I'd still be here," he said at last. "I'd proclaim myself and do whatever I was able."

She swung about. "Oh, no," she denied. "Oh, no, David. I'd take my entire immediate family, including Eric's fiancée, because this would make it doubly plausible to Strang that I intended to run. But you . . . you'd come along under your false name, substituted for one of my regular crew. I can't leave you."

"Why not?"

"You could stay incognito, useless, when we've need of your talents in space. Or you could invoke your prestige, try to fill my role . . . and provoke the terror for certain. Strang would know we'd conspired. He'd feel he must strike fast and hard. Whereas if you're not on hand, if the aristocrats in fact are leaderless and dismayed, he *may* think it politic to spare them the worst."

"If he doesn't—"

"I said it before, David. Everybody at Hornbeck must remain, save you."

His gaze yielded to hers. After he had long been hypnotized by the floor, she barely heard him: "If we do help short-circuit a total war, we'll save lives in the hundreds of millions. But they'll be lives that we never knew."

He lifted his head. "So be it. Are you game, Sandra?"

An early snow decked the land when the yacht *Castle Catherine* lifted from Williams Field. Beyond ferrocrete, cradles, buildings, and machines, the country lay blue-shadowed white, altogether hushed, rolling away westward to the panther forms of the Arcadian Hills. Above, heaven was unutterably blue. Breath smoked from nostrils, footfalls rang loud.

High Commissioner Benoni Strang had provided Her Grace with an honor guard of his soldiers. They presented arms while she and her crew passed by them. She touched her brow in return salute. All proceedings were correct.

Likewise was the paperwork which had led to this day. Her Grace had expressed a desire to visit the outer planet Chronos, enjoy the beauty of its rings, mountaineer and vac-ski on its moon Ida. Clearance was naturally granted.

She, her children, Lorna Stanton, and her men boarded. Nobody paid the men any special heed, though it was alive on their faces that they knew where they were really going. The gangway retracted behind them, the airlock shut. Soon engines hummed, negagravity took hold, the hull rose like a snowflake borne on a breeze, until it was so high that it gleamed like a star and then blinked out.

Past the guardian vessels *Castle Catherine* accelerated, outward and outward in the ecliptic plane. The sun dwindled, the Milky Way beckoned. At a sufficient distance, she sprang over into hyperdrive and overtook the light that fled from Maia.

There was no pursuit.

When it was clear that she would go free, Sandra sought Falkayn in private, laid her head on his breast, and wept.

XVIII

Hanny Lennart appeared uncomfortable. Eric suspected that that was less because of having to rebuke him than because of the surroundings where she must do so. Leading the navy of a world which the Commonwealth still recognized as sovereign, he could not well be given a formal reprimand. She had asked him to join her at lunch and he had promptly chosen the Tjina House, off a list that van Rijn had supplied earlier.

The last of twenty-one boys set down his dish of condiment, bowed above hands laid together, and withdrew from the private room. The diners would ring for further service when they desired. It was a lovely day along the Sunda Strait, and a wall had been retracted to let sea-cooled tropical air flow in. Gardens fell in thousand-hued terraces toward the water, palms rustled, bamboo swayed. Out on cobalt blue glided the stately torpedo shape of a cargo carrier and the winging sails of sportcraft. Unseen, a musician drew softness from a wooden flute.

Eric took a long swallow of beer and began slathering his curry. Lennart gave him a disapproving look across the table. "This much luxury feels indecent in wartime," she said.

"What wartime?" he retorted. "If we were bestirring ourselves, I might agree."

"Patience, please, Admiral Tamarin-Asmundsen. But I'm afraid that's a quality you lack. It's what I want to speak to you about."

"Carry on, Freelady." Thought of Lorna, his mother, his planet made the food suddenly ashen. "I'd like to have the Solar strategy explained to me, if any. I don't have to sit here stuffing my gut. Rather would I be out raiding."

"This government cannot condone your acting independently."

"Then let it integrate us with its forces and give us work to do!"

Lennart puckered her lips. "Quite frankly, Admiral, you are responsible for the delay in that. After your connivance at David Falkayn's escape—"

"What escape? I'm tired of repeating that he and his fellows went as commissioned Hermetian officers, on orders from me, to gather intelligence . . . because the Commonwealth has persistently neglected that elementary operation."

Lennart gave way a little. "Let's not quarrel." She constructed a smile of sorts. "I argued on your behalf, argued that you could not really be blamed for wanting news about your home, nor for your now obvious liaison with your father. Yes, I wanted you to become part of a unified command as soon as possible."

To become subordinate, you mean, subject to court martial if I misbehave again, Eric knew.

"Well, Admiral," Lennart proceeded, "what I wish to discuss today is the additional difficulties you have since created for me, for all your friends. Your appearances before civic groups, your speech on the *Issues* show—they have alienated high officials. They give the impression of a chronic troublemaker, if you will excuse the language."

"Why, yes, Freelady, I am a troublemaker, or hope to be," he said. "For the Baburites, that is. I've urged that we move. If we're not ready for another pitched battle, we can still make life fairly miserable for the enemy. We can harass his commerce, we can dump megatons on his bases, till he sees 'twill pay him to disgorge Hermes and negotiate an agreement about Mirkheim."

Lennart's expression bleakened. "There can be no compromise. Otherwise Babur has gained by its aggression. It must be made to yield on every point—especially on Mirkheim, which precipitated the whole war. For that purpose, we need to build more strength than we have at present. This cannot be done overnight. Meanwhile we have to keep our forces guarding the Commonwealth against the kind of tactics you describe."

Eric thought of crowds wild with fear, demonstrating in favor of just such a policy, as well as influential commentators, businesspeople, politicians. . . . Pressure on the government, yes. But how much of the pressure was being engineered? The Home Companies had an overriding interest in protecting their properties from attack, in manufacturing unlimited armaments at fat profits, in getting the citizenry into the habit of being closely controlled by a state wherein they exercised much of the power; and the devil might have Hermes for all they cared.

Yet why did Dad talk me into making those speeches, antagonizing those authorities? He had a purpose of his own. At the time, I was too impatient, too angry to probe him. Protest came natural to me. But now I begin to see we'll have to talk further, he and I.

He couldn't continue the minuet. "Freelady," he growled, "these arguments have been batted back and forth till the meaning's knocked out of them; they've become slogans. Let's drop them. Are you and I hopelessly at odds, or can we reach an agreement?"

"You do not put it very diplomatically."

"My food's getting cold." Eric began eating.

Lennart picked at hers. "Well-ll . . . if you insist on being blunt—"

" 'Tis why we're here, not? Go ahead."

"Well, then, quite simply, if you will be discreet, refrain from further public statements, prepare yourself and your following to cooperate in our larger mutual purpose—if you will prove you can do that, then I believe, I do not promise but I believe, in due course I can persuade the high command to enlist you on the terms originally proposed."

More delay. Which Dad prodded me into causing. Why?

"What is the alternative?" he asked.

Redness splotched Lennart's skin. "You cannot expect that the Commonwealth will indefinitely grant shelter and assistance to a violator of its hospitality."

Eric scowled. "I'll not take time to analyze that sentence, Freelady. But I will wonder aloud precisely what 'the Commonwealth' is. An individual, receiving another individual as a guest? Or a government? In that case, who makes up the government, the real power, and why have they received us, and why like they not my presenting a different point of view from theirs to the people at large? I thought this was a democracy."

He raised his palm. "Enough," he said. "I don't mean to irritate;

184

and I am prepared to be realistic. You'll admit my first duty is to Hermes, that if the freeing of Hermes isn't going to be an objective, my men and I have no business in your war. But I'm willing to try working for that quietly, laying it before cabinet ministers, corporation chairmen, and union leaders rather than the public.''

Lennart relaxed a trifle. "That would probably be acceptable."

"One small thing," Eric continued. "Your navy has sequestered a spacecraft belonging to my father's company. I want her released to me, assigned to my force."

She was surprised. "Why?"

"No great matter. She's my father's, and I feel under some filial obligation to him."

Actually 'twas Coya who begged me to insist on this. Muddlin' Through *isn't really van Rijn's, she's David's.*

Though . . . did Old Nick put her up to that bit of sentimentalism? Muddlin' Through *does have more capabilities than most ships.*

Lennart clutched her fork tightly. "That's another matter you and I must handle today," she said. "We on Earth knew of your parentage, but hoped Freeman van Rijn would have no attraction for you. You had never seen him. At first those hopes seemed fulfilled. But suddenly you were collaborating with him, doubtless after furtive contacts. We are quite disappointed."

"Why? Should I have disowned him? Was I ever required to file reports of all my comings, goings, and meetings? Is he not a citizen in good standing of the Commonwealth?"

"Only technically, Admiral Tamarin-Asmundsen, only technically. His has been a pernicious influence."

Which is to say, he's taken a forefront position in combating the growth of statism. Also, from time to time he's cut the Home Companies out of juicy deals.

"You can explain why at your leisure, Freelady," Eric said, resigning himself. "First, though, what about yon vessel? Blame my request on my primitive colonial hankering for tangibles."

Lennart pondered. "You would have custody, not he?"

"That's right. I'd arrange for her commissioning in the Hermetian navy. Which will bring her under the Commonwealth when our forces are integrated." *If.*

185

"Hm. . . . I see no major objection. It's not my department, but I could make a recommendation. In return—"

"Yes. I stop stumping." Eric filled his mouth. Now the food tasted good. Lennart would lecture him during the whole meal, but he needn't pay close attention. Instead, he could daydream about bringing Lorna here . . . sometime.

Nicholas Falkayn was born in his great-grandfather's mansion in Delfinburg, which was then passing through the Coral Sea above the wrecks of an ancient battle. Labor was long, for he was big and his mother slender. Since her man was away, she denied admittance to everyone save the medics, who noted that she often had half a grin on her face, as if telling the universe to put down its pride.

Afterward she received her new child gladly. She was nursing him when van Rijn hurricaned into her room. "Hallo, hallo, harroo!" the old man boomed. "Congratugoddamnlations! Is that the pup? Ah, a whopper. He has the family looks, I see—never mind which family, Adam's maybe, they are all crumpled red worms at this age. How is you?"

"Restless," Coya complained. "They won't let me out of bed till tomorrow."

"I got some conosolium," van Rijn told her in a stage whisper, and slipped a bottle of brandy from under his jacket.

"Well, I don't know. . . . Oh, he may as well start learning early. Thanks, Gunung Tuan." She took a hearty swig.

He studied her, pale features in which the eyes still seemed too large, dark hair spread across the pillows. "I am sorry I did not come sooner. I could not get free of business."

"It must have been important."

"To the other osco. A little trader what supplies me with a particular offplanet spice. Jula, you ever heard of it? Tastes like chocolate soap to me, but they like it on Cynthia. The war, the ban on travel, he was threatened with bankrupture. I could not just give him a loan over the phone because of the tapioca-brain antitrust laws. Better he should crawl broken to the government and beg for a crust, *nie*? So we met and talked personal; and things is now hunky-dinghy."

"That was good of you."

"No, no, bah, is a bad time, and a worse time coming. If we do not stand together, we will have to stand for anything. Never mind such fumblydiddles. How you do, bellybird?"

She had long ago accepted the fact that he would never stop using the nickname he had bestowed when she was a baby. "I'm fine. My parents called an hour ago. They said to give you their regards."

"Swat my regards straight back at them." Van Rijn took a turn about the chamber. Sunlight, slanting inward, cast wave reflections on the wall behind him. "They is nice people," he said, "but like their whole generation, they do not understand an image is not enough. We is been too intellectual too long, here on Earth."

Coya kept silent. Nicholas tugged lustily at her breast.

"*Ach*, my apologetics," van Rijn said. "I should not have criticized. Everybody does his or her foolish best. But the touch of a hand—especial when Davy is gone from you—" He poked a finger toward the infant, who, temporarily sated, rolled his head that way and blew milk bubbles at him. "Ho, ho, already he has got the art of making political speeches!"

"Davy," Coya whispered. Aloud: "No, I will not bawl, no matter how he's been cheated. But Gunung Tuan, what do you think may be happening to him?"

Van Rijn tugged unmercifully on a ringlet. "How can I tell, a futtersnipe like me? Too many unknowns, darling, too many unknowns."

She half lifted the arm which was not holding her child. "Haven't you thought your way toward any answer? Provisional, yes, yes, but an answer?"

Van Rijn grimaced, banged his great bottom down on a chair, and took a long drag on the bottle he carried, which afterward he offered to Coya. She signed refusal, intently watching him.

"We got a mystery here," he said. "Some parts is plain to see, or ugly to see. Others—" He gave a shrug like a mountain shedding a snowpack. "Others make no sense. We got many paradoxes and no paradoctors. You heard me talk about this."

"Yes, but I've been so concerned about Davy, and later this kid here. . . .Talk. Please. No harm done if you repeat things. I need to be able to imagine I'm somehow working on Davy's behalf."

187

"Hokay," van Rijn sighed. "We go down the list." He ticked points off on his hairy fingers.

"Item: How did Babur arm for war? And why? Nobody could have foreseen Mirkheim; that was only the trigger to the landslide, what caught Babur splatfooted too and maybe made it act before it had really intended.

"Item: A couple companies of the Seven had been having dealings with Babur over the years. Why did they get no hint of that arming? Oh, *ja*, the dealings was small and unoften, and the planet is huge and strange. But nothingtheless—"

"Item: What makes Babur so sure it can win? And why is it been so contemptuous of the League as to arrest your husband when he came peaceful like? Babur is not really such a mighty place. Most of it is desert.

"Item: Looks like Babur has got lots of oxygen-breathing mercenaries. You tell me how hydrogen breathers recruited those, secretly, over the worlds and the years. No, Babur had help—also with research, development, and production for its war machine— but whose, and why?

"Item: What makes Babur think it knows enough about us aliens that it can fight us and, eventfully, negotiate whatever kind of peace? Who's been telling it things?

"Item: Why should Babur occupy a neutral, small-populated, terrestroid planet—"

The phone at the bedside chimed. Coya swore and accepted. The image of van Rijn's executive secretary burst onto the screen. "Sir," he stammered, "sir, news received, a—a—a ship from Hermes, the Grand Duchess aboard, she's broadcast an announcement that she's the Hermetian government in exile . . . and—and David Falkayn is with her!"

Glory exploded in the room.

Later came grimness, as they who were there got to wondering.

XIX

A third of a century had blurred Sandra's memories of Earth. She recalled the hugeness of megalopōlitan integrates, but had forgotten how daunting it could be. She had experienced totally synthetic, totally controlled environment, but only now did it come to her that this was in its way more alien than the outer planets of Maia. And in her earlier visit she had been a tourist, free to flit around, available for every adventure that came along; she had not known how heavy were the chains which Earth laid upon the prominent. Each hour was appointed, each meeting a ritual dance of words, each smile measured for its public effect. She was shown some of the remaining natural marvels, but she could only look, she could not scramble down a trail into the Grand Canyon or cast off her clothes and plunge into Lake Baikal. And everywhere, everywhere guards must accompany her.

"Who would want power, here, at this price?" she lamented once.

David Falkayn had grinned wryly and replied, "The politicians don't have that much. They put on a show, but most of the real decisions are made by owners, managers, bureaucrats, union chiefs, people who aren't conspicuous enough to need all that protection or all that secretarial prearrangement of their days. . . . Of course, the politicians think they lead."

So it was immensely good to be back among her own, aboard her flagship, the cruiser *Chronos*, cramped and sterile though the interior was. Orbiting independently around Sol, the Hermetian flotilla counted as Hermetian soil. After an unpleasant argument, she had even gotten the secret service left behind. And the men and women aboard were bred of the same lands as hers, born to the same skies, walking with the easy gait and talking with the slight burr that were hers, standing together in a loneliness that she shared.

Yet her heart stumbled. This day she would again meet Nicholas van Rijn. No matter that that was in her territory—to prevent electronic eavesdropping, if nothing else—she felt half afraid, and raged at herself for it. Eric, waiting beside her, should have been a tall comfort, but was instead almost a stranger, flesh of this stranger she must receive, reluctantly come from Earth and his Lorna. The spacemen in their white dress uniforms, their double line flanking the airlock, had also gone foreign to her; for what were they thinking behind their carefully smoothed-out faces? Ventilation muttered, touching her with a coolness that said her skin was damp.

The inner valve opened. There he stood.

Her first thought was an astonished *How homely he is*. She remembered him bulky and craggy rather than corpulent; and he did not belong in the lace-trimmed sylon blouse, iridon vest, purple culottes he had donned for this occasion. Behind him, in plain gray tunic and slacks, Falkayn was downright cruelly contrasting. *Why, he's old*, Sandra knew, and her embarrassment dropped from her. The stranger was no longer her son but that girl who had once been headstrong.

"Good greeting, gentlemen," she said as if they were anybody with whom she meant to confer.

And then van Rijn, damn his sooty heart, refused to be pitiable but grabbed her hand, bestowed a splashing kiss upon it, and pumped it as if he expected water to gush from her mouth. "Good day, good day," he bawled, "good nights too, cheers and salutations, Your Gracefulness, and may joy puff up your life. Ah, you is a sight for footsore eyes, getting better and better with time like a fine cheese. I could near as damn thank the Baburites for making you come shine at us, except they brought you trouble. For that they will pay through the noses they isn't got but we will make them buy from us at a five hundred percent markup. *Nie?*"

She disengaged herself. Cold with indignation, she presented the captain and ranking officers of the ship. Eric took over the making of formal excuses to them, since they were not invited to the wardroom for drinks before dinner. They had already been apprised of that; van Rijn's message had asked for a conference in secret. Mechanically they accepted the courtesy due them, their attention mainly on the merchant, the living legend. Could *this* be he? And what hope for Hermes might he have in his pocket?

He took Sandra's arm when she led off their son and Falkayn. She resented the familiarity but couldn't think how to break loose without a scene. He dropped his voice: "I would say, '*Weowar arronach*,' "—the phrase from the Lannachska language of Diomedes was one they had made their own during their first year together— "but is long ago too late. Let me only be glad you was happy afterward."

"Thank you." She was caught off balance anew.

They entered the wardroom. It was not large, but was outfitted in stonebark wainscoting and cyanops leather as a sign of home. Faint odors of them lingered. Pictures hung on the bulkheads, Cloudhelm seen from a wooded Arcadian hilltop, dunes in the Rainbow Desert, the South Corybantic Ocean alive with night phosphorescence. A viewscreen gave a wild contrast, the spaces which encompassed this hull, millionfold stars, billionfold Milky Way, Earth a globule almost lost among them, fragile as blue glass. Eric stepped behind the miniature bar. "I'll be your messboy," he said. "What'll you have?"

It broke a certain tension. *Gets he that skill from his father?* flashed in Sandra. *I've never been quick to transform the mood of a group.* Seeing that the men waited for her, she chose an Apollo Valley claret. Van Rijn tried a Hermetian gin and pronounced it scorchful. Falkayn and Eric took Scotch. It struck Sandra as funny—or symbolic, or something—that that should have been hauled the whole way from Edinburgh to Starfall and back.

They settled themselves on the bench which curved around the table: she, Eric, Falkayn, and, to her relief, van Rijn at the far end. But when she took out her cigar case, the trader did likewise, and insisted she have a genuine Havana. She found she had also forgotten how good that was.

Silence fell.

After a minute or two, Eric shifted in his seat, took a gulp from his drink, and said roughly, "Hadn't we better get to our business? We're here because Freeman van Rijn has a word for us. I'm anxious to know what."

Sandra tautened, met the old man's eyes, and felt as if sparks flew. "Yes," she agreed, "we've no right to dawdle. Please tell us." Her look sought Falkayn's. *We know*. And Eric's. *You and I talked about this too, after we had first embraced on Earth*.

Van Rijn streamed smoke from his nostrils. "We ought to put on a scene like from a *roman policier*, where I dump a kilo of clues on the rug and we fit them together in the shape of the villain, us having a guilting bee," he began. "But you has a fair-to-muddling notion of what must be the answer. Mainly we is got to decide what to do.

"Let me lay everything out before us anyways, to make sure we is thinking the same."

For a few breaths he sat quiet. The murmurs of the ship came to Sandra like a single thrum from a plucked string that was stretched close to breaking.

Van Rijn said: "Bayard Story of Galactic Developments, leader of the delegates of the Seven In Space to our council in Lunograd, is Benoni Strang, High Commissioner of Babur on Hermes. There is the fact what makes all the rest tumble into place."

"I suppose not, in spite of the pictures and other evidence Mother brought, I suppose not that could possibly be wrong," Eric ventured with a caution she recognized as new to him.

Van Rijn shook his head. "No. Resemblance is too close. Besides, the identity does explain so much else."

"Especially the help Babur's gotten," Falkayn put in. His tone was that of a judge handing down a sentence. "Armament, military and political intelligence, recruitment of mercenaries, direction of the entire campaign thus far—by the Seven."

"Not as a whole, surely," Eric protested, as if the shock had just now reached him.

"Oh, no," van Rijn said. "That secret could never have kept, it would have spoiled and stunk up the galaxy, did any except a few top managers know—and, of course, the human technicians they engaged and held strictly isolated. Surely, too, not many Baburites is been told."

He laid a fist on the table, big, hairy, knobbly, with power in it to smash. "Makes no difference," he stated. "Policy, orders come from the top down. The Baburites treat the League with contempt because their supreme chiefs know the League is broken from within.''

''But what an enormous effort,'' Eric wondered. ''Research, development, construction, decade after decade till a whole giant plane was ready to launch its hordes—how could that ever stay unknown? Why, the cost would show up on the accountants' tapes—''

''You underestimate the size of operations on an interstellar scale,'' Falkayn told him. ''No underling, even a highly placed underling, can keep track of everything a big company does. Spread over several companies, the expense could easily be disguised as statistical fluctuations. It was never overwhelmingly great. Babur undoubtedly supplied most labor. Raw materials came from there as well, and from uninhabited planets and asteroids. Once the basic machine tools were built, comparatively little of the Seven's original capital was tied up. Various persons must have been getting paid fortunes, to get them to live a goodly chunk of their lives cut off from their own civilization. But a fortune to an individual is small change to a major corporation.''

He added slowly: ''We had an important clue to the whole thing quite some time ago. The Baburite warships seem to have electronic systems certain of whose parts can't be manufactured there, others of which deteriorate in a hydrogen atmosphere. They aren't obliged to; they could do better. We put it down to sloppy engineering, the result of haste, and quite likely the lords of Babur still believe that's the case, if anybody on that planet with scientific training has been given time to stop and think about the matter. But actually . . . the Seven would want to have a hold on their allies, something to keep them subordinate till the objectives of the Seven have been achieved. Why not leave them in chronic need of vital replacement parts which are supplied from outside?''

''The revelation of Mirkheim precipitated action,'' Sandra said. '' 'Twas simply too mighty a prize to let slip. But what is the real goal, of Babur and the Seven alike? Why go to war at all? That's what I still can't grasp.''

"I am not sure anybody will ever grasp why mortals make war," van Rijn answered somberly. "Maybe someday we will find a sophont species what is not fallen from grace, and they can tell us."

Falkayn addressed the woman: "Well, we can use logic. Successful imperialism does in fact pay off for its leaders, in wealth, power, the sense of glory . . . yes, and often the sense of duty carried out, destiny fulfilled."

"Better we stay with honest greed," van Rijn remarked.

"In the case of the Baburites," Falkayn continued, "we can't be certain till a lot of intensive xenological research has been done—unless we can get hold of Strang's files on them. But we do know they resented being shoved aside in the scramble for a place on the frontier. Influential ones among them may well have decided that nothing but *force majeure* would win their species its due. And don't forget, Babur was united rather recently, by the conquering Imperial Band. I suspect the wish to go on conquering acquired a momentum, as it's done in most human cases. Also, again like human history, I suspect the rulers saw foreign adventures as a way of giving their empire a common purpose, of securing their grip on the lately acquired lands.

"Be that as it may, Babur *was* ripe to be coaxed and helped into overrunning its stellar neighborhood. I wouldn't be surprised but what Benoni Strang was the man to whom the idea first occurred, and who persuaded the masters of the Seven to undertake it. He seems to've started his career as a scientist on the planet."

Sandra nodded. Before her rose a vision of her enemy, the fire beneath his armor of courtliness, the often faraway look in his eyes, and words he had now and then let slip.

"And the motives of the Seven?" she asked, though she and Falkayn had talked this over for hours while they fared Solward.

"I already tried to list a few reasons why humans run amok," he reminded her.

"There is this too," van Rijn added. "The Home Companies is become near as damn the government of the Commonwealth. At least, the government does nothings they don't want, and everythings they do want. I, an independent, see the threat in that; but I am not

194

hungry for power myself, I simply want people should let me be to play my little games.

"The owners of the Seven feel different. Else they would not be organized as they are. They must dread the day when the Home Companies do actively move out into space. Against that, what better than to be operating a strong government of their own? Except nothing exists ready-made out there. So they have to build an empire. Then they can afford to let the whole conspiracy be known."

"In alliance with Babur . . . yes, it makes a creepy kind of sense," Eric said. "The two races would not likely fall out with each other; they don't want the same real estate, save the kind that Mirkheim represents, and they could agree to divvy that up. Meanwhile Hermes, under totalitarian rule, would be the human power base in those parts."

He slammed the table. "No!" he shouted.

"That is agreed," van Rijn said. "What we is here today for is to grind out what we can best do. Is everybody clear on what the situation computes to? Hokay, we roll up our sleeves and get down to the nutty-gutty."

Sandra sipped her claret as if its taste of vanished sunshine could give strength. "You do not want to inform the Commonwealth," she foreknew.

"Positive not," van Rijn replied. "They see the weakness, they strike, they win—and who gets Mirkheim? The Home Companies."

"They'd move to utterly crush the Seven," Falkayn supplied. "I don't believe the empire in space that they'd win would be less vicious . . . or more likely to set Hermes free. Oh, they'd make Babur withdraw. But the temptation to impose a 'caretaker' government which'd build a corporate state in the Commonwealth's image and be properly subservient in its foreign relations—they could scarcely resist that."

Van Rijn turned toward Eric. "That is why I got you to stall the co-option of this force into Sol's," he explained. "I only had a hunch then it was best you keep your freedom of action. Now we know it is."

This too had been in Sandra's mind for endless days. Yet voicing it still felt like stepping onto a bridge which her tread must cause to break behind her. "You propose we leave, to carry out our private campaign."

"*Ja*. Not direct attacks on Babur. We hit holdings of the Seven. They got little defense for those. We can give them choice, either they pull away support from their allies so both must make peace with us, or else we ruin them."

"Let's not be overhasty," Falkayn urged. "For instance, it'd be worthwhile, it'd save lives in the long run, to alert as many independent League members as possible, and get them to join their fighting craft to ours."

"Then they'll want a part in writing the peace," Eric objected.

"Yes," Falkayn said. "Don't you think it's best if they do? That way we might salvage a little stability, a little decency."

In the meantime, Sandra thought, *the agony of Hermes goes on. But I myself dare not speak against it. I've not the wisdom to know a better way.*

Does anybody?

Again they stood in Delfinburg, David and Coya, and from a balcony of van Rijn's house looked across a nighted sea. In the room behind them, their children slept. Before them was a shadowy drop down to the yacht harbor where boats lay phantomlike at piers. Beyond, under a high wind, waves rushed to break in whiteness, rise, and march onward. Above arched a moonless sky where the stars fled among ragged clouds.

"The third time you're going," she said. "Must you really?"

He nodded. "I couldn't leave Adzel and Chee fighting alone on my planet, could I?"

"But you can leave us—" She caught herself. "No. I'm sorry. Forget that ever crossed my mind."

"This time will be the last," he vowed, and drew her toward him. Neither of them spoke: *The last indeed, if one never comes home.*

Instead, she told him, "Right. Because afterward, when and wherever you travel, you're taking me along. Me and the kids."

"If I go anyplace, sweetheart. After all the hooraw, I should be quite content to settle down on Earth and let the tropics toast my bones.''

She shook her head so the dark hair swirled. ''You won't. Nor will I. If nothing else, it's no world for Juanita and Nicky. You don't imagine the war will cleanse it, do you? No, the rot can only grow worse. We're getting the hell out while we still can.''

''Hermes—'' He was mute for a while. ''Maybe. We'll see. It's a big universe.''

The wind whistled cold. Chill also, and bitter, was spindrift cast off the booming waters.

XX

Abdallah Enterprises, of the Seven In Space, guarded its centrum on Hopewell against possible banditry from without and sabotage from within. But the former seemed so unlikely that a single corvette orbited the planet, whose successive crews had never encountered a worse problem than filling the time until they were relieved.

The destroyer *North Atlantis* sped inward to engage. Despite the risk, Eric found he must beam a warning: "Get out of our way before we attack you." Astounded profanity replied, then a brace of missiles and an energy beam.

The Hermetian vessel glided sidewise on thrust. The torpedoes maneuvered still more agilely, but now she had a good sight on them. A lightning storm of rays struck outward. The missiles disintegrated in fire-fountains, momentarily dazzling athwart the stars and the serene disc of the world. She did not reply in kind, for Eric wanted to conserve munitions not readily replaceable. Instead, he ordered her conned near the foe, until he was in range for energy weapons. "Kill," he said, and nuclear-powered flame leaped forth.

The corvette accelerated to escape. With less mass, she could change velocity faster. *North Atlantis* followed doggedly, smashing or warding off missiles, absorbing blast-cannon shots in armor plate, unleashing fresh bursts of her own whenever the shifting configurations of battle brought her close enough. After hours, the survivors aboard a ruin knew they could not break free, and signaled surrender.

"My compliments on your gallantry," Eric responded, "though you might ask yourselves if your cause was worth it. You may take lifeboats to Hopewell. I advise you do not bring them down at Abdallah City."

He already knew, from communication, what had happened there.

Accompanying him on his voyage, *Muddlin' Through* had left him to his warfare and herself entered atmosphere.

Falkayn uttered the broadcast words that he knew would bring him into peril of his life. "Attention, attention. . . . Your owners have conspired with the rulers of Babur to bring war. . . . The Free Hermetian navy is about to demolish your company installations. Evacuate immediately. . . ."

Aerial vehicles swarmed aloft. But *Muddlin' Through* was not the specialized speedster through the void, well-nigh helpless above a planet, which *Streak* had been. Trade pioneers must be prepared for trouble in any environment. The spacecraft descended in great spirals, from which again and again she swooped to dodge a missile or blaze at an opponent.

Before Falkayn, as he sat in the pilot's chair, land and sea revolved crazily, clouds streamed past through day-bright azure, fighting machines flashed across vision like wind-flung raindrops. This was no space combat, which computers alone could direct. Movements were too fast, actions too unforeseeable. He meshed his intuition with Muddlehead's logic, sank his personality into his ship, and steered. Engines growled, air outside shrilled. His nostrils caught a thundery tang of ozone.

"Hoo and ha!" van Rijn's voice bawled from the weapons control turret. Gleefully he tracked, sighted, fired, manning the entire system, sending vessel after vessel to its meteoric grave. "Oh, ho, ho! Casting bull's eyes at me, is you? Smack right back at you with a wet loincloth! Ha-ah, that was a near miss at us, good shooting, boy, only not quite good as this, by damn! Whoo-hoo! Brocken and brimstone, here goes another!"

In the end, *Muddlin' Through* hung alone; and there was silence in heaven about the space of half an hour.

Underneath her stretched a land that had been rich. Miners, builders, industrialists had ripped and befouled it till its river coursed poisoned among dumps and slag heaps, pavements and waste outlets, bearing death to the sea. Few human colonists of Hopewell had protested. This was not Earth, they still had plenty of room, nobody need make his home in the place that ground forth prosperity.

Besides, the local government belonged to Abdallah Enterprises. In the middle of the desert it had created, the centrum raised splendid towers above many-colored sleeknesses. Looking down, Falkayn thought, *This was a grand era in its way. I too will miss it.*

Cars fled in flocks. At his height they were like midges. He must make an effort to remember that each one bore fear, bewilderment, crushed hopes, longing for loves who were elsewhere and terror on their behalf. War scrubbed such peculiarities out of consciousness. He had not heart to speak further to this world, but let a recording repeat itself. "Free Hermes is striking at the Seven, Babur's allies. Our campaign will end when the war against the Commonwealth and the occupations of Hermes and Mirkheim do. Convey our message." He reflected that someday his wife and children might be likewise fleeing; for when would civilization in the future know safety?

His time allowance was generous. Nothing had stirred for fifteen minutes when he ordered a torpedo released.

Fifty kilotons sufficed. A fireball blossomed and lifted, smoke and dust roiled after to rise in a monstrous pillar that spread out in an ice-fringed toadstool cap, reverberations toned through the spaceship, and when sight came back, a crater lay in the land, from which a few twisted frameworks lifted like dead men's fingers.

"Take orbit at ten radii," Falkayn directed, "and we'll wait for *North Atlantis* to finish her business."

After Hopewell was once more a blue-and-white loveliness among the stars, he met with his shipmates, van Rijn and engineer Tetsuo Yoshida. The merchant was still gleeful. "Halloo, harroo," he chortled, "how I feel youthed! We had what Aristotle called a cathartic, *ja*, and gives me an abysmal appetite. Suppose I quickroast a nice Virginia ham with sweet potatoes and Caesar salad—and what would you two like for lunch?"

"Later," Falkayn said. "I'm not hungry."

Van Rijn considered him. "Your conscience is panging, ha? But that is silly, boy. We is vented a lot of beast in us by bashing what well deserved bashing. Is it a sin if we enjoy? Me, I wish we could make more raids."

Yoshida lifted his brows. "I would not object personally," he said, "but unless I am mistaken, Freeman van Rijn, you gave your fellow planners a promise to confine yourself to this single action, if they would agree to your doing that much."

He's too valuable to risk, Falkayn remembered: *first as a leader of our overall strategy, afterward as our chief negotiator. My job from here on is to convey him safely to the headquarters he will set up, and then act as his special advisor and deputy.*

Damn him, though, he's right. Being in battle ourselves was something we inwardly needed. Even I, even I.

"*Ja*, is true," van Rijn grumbled. "So we got weeks, maybe months where we do hardly nothing but sit snuggled in our own fat. You got ideas how we can put our minds to some good use in between happenings?"

"Poker," said Muddlehead.

Experts agreed that it would take considerable time and money, and no few lives, to start Mirkheim producing afresh. However, immensely precious stocks of metals and supermetals lay already cast in ingots, awaiting shipment out. The Baburite occupation force received instructions to let the Stellar Metals Corporation have this on a profit-sharing basis. Stellar, in turn, contracted with Interstar Transport to carry it to the numerous markets.

In the deeps of space, ships which had been lurking and watching drew alongside the freighters, matched hyperdrive phase, and signaled a wish to send people aboard. Suspecting no evil, the captains did. But those who entered, grinning, were armored and armed. In each case, they took swift possession.

Crews were sent off in lifeboats, bearing word that Free Hermes was confiscating both cargo and carrier. The losses to Timebinders Insurance were staggering—and also to Stellar and Interstar, for their coverage extended to less than half of these values.

Men landed in wilderness areas of the planet Ramanujan and flitted inconspicuously to rendezvous in the city Maharajah. On an appointed night, they converged on a cluster of towers which were the core of XT Systems. Overpowering the guards, they set explosives to wreck equipment which would take years to replace and destroy data stores which could never be replaced. Prisoners whom they released afterward said they had identified themselves as a commando of Free Hermes.

XT had been at a nexus of the global economy. As such, it had made the government its servant. Now massive unemployment came, bankruptcies, dislocations, civic upheaval. The cry arose for legislators whose loyalty was to Ramanujan itself, and Parliament dissolved on a vote of no confidence.

Sanchez Engineering was engaged in an ambitious project on barren but mineral-rich St. Jacques, which would make its resources readily available to the humans dwelling on its sister world Esperance. The leaders of the colony, who were nobody's hirelings, had written a stiff penalty for nonfulfillment into the contract.

Suddenly the technicians called a strike, alleging that the war posed too great a hazard. In vain did the directors of Sanchez reveal what detectives learned, that the union bosses had taken a whopping bribe. No legal proof was available, at least not without disastrously prolonged litigation; and if this went against them, the persons accused need only withdraw themselves from Esperancian jurisdiction.

"The answer's easy," said their spokesman around his cigar to the board chairman of Sanchez. "Use your influence to end the fighting."

But at best, the corporation would remain gravely injured.

Galactic Developments owned a moon of Germania, which it had made into an entrepôt for that stellar neighborhood. There, after a short, sharp battle, landed ships, whose crews efficiently looted the treasures before lifting back into space and bombarding the installations.

They did not even pretend to be Hermetian. They were from the independents Sindbad Prospecting and the Society of Venturers, out to punish the Seven for an unholy alliance with Babur.

The Germanian space police made no move throughout. Later the

202

government denied complicity, declared it had been taken by surprise, and took charge of the remaining assets which Galactic Developments had in this system "pending an arrangement which, in view of the present emergency, will be more in the public interest."

The Seven struck back. Baburite warships accompanied theirs. The announcement was that Babur thus exercised its right and duty to suppress piracy. Few beings believed it.

Hammer blows fell on bases of the hostile companies. But these, forewarned, had for the most part been abandoned. Damage was thus comparatively small. The character of the typical independent operator—else he would long since have entered one of the great combines—was such that he counted it as an investment. He might go broke; but if not, his gamble should pay off richly. A share in Mirkheim, reduced competition from the Seven, plunder along the way . . . he saw opportunity before him, and jumped.

Privateers and Hermetians alike could resupply on a hundred different worlds, attack wherever they chose, and vanish back into vastness. Babur had no such advantage. Seeing the forces of the Imperial Band dispersed and under fire, the Commonwealth naturally launched probing assaults of its own, which intensified with time and lack of effective response. As for the Seven, the whole intricate structure whereon they had based their might was crumbling. After Timebinders Insurance stopped payment on claims, they knew they must make what terms they could.

Spring was full-blooming in Starfall when the patriot army stormed it. The attack was two-pronged. Christa Broderick's city and farmland followers, who throughout the winter had held themselves to sniping and sabotage while they gathered strength, appeared in the streets. They fell on all the mercenaries they could find, surrounded such strongholds as the Hotel Zeus, and commenced bombardment. Meanwhile the guerrillas whom Adzel and Chee Lan had been leading in the Arcadian Hills and the Thunderhead Mountains entered from the west and moved to take Pilgrim Hill. A wild variety of cars, trucks, and buses had carried them from their fastnesses over the

203

valleys, protected by atmospheric fighters which the ducal navy had sent down. Now that navy was in combat with the enemy's guardian ships—off behind a cruelly soft blue sky—and the fight for the city must be waged on the ground.

Must be. As long as the occupation forces refused to surrender, it was necessary to dig them out, body by body. A nuclear warhead fired from orbit would annihilate them, if the Free Hermetian fleet was victorious, but at cost of the city. The hope that their side would win in space, and thus hold the entire planet hostage, kept Benoni Strang's men in battle—that, and the fear of retaliation among those of them who were native born and had freely served his revolutionary régime.

Adzel trotted along the esplanade. It thudded to his hoofs. In the crook of an arm he carried a blast rifle. Perched on his shoulders, Chee manned a heavier energy weapon. Most of the troop loping wolfishly behind bore slugthrowers, tools for hunting such as every outback household possessed. The artillery that trundled among them—cannon, mortars, rocket launchers—used chemical explosives. It had been furtively made in hundreds of small factories and home workshops, according to plans retrieved from public data banks before the first Baburite soldier landed.

Coordinating the whole effort, across the world and at last with the armed return of Grand Duchess Sandra, had been the truly difficult task. The anger to power it was already there, in many a Traver as well as in Followers and Kindred. Government by terror does not work on people used to liberty, if they have hope of deliverance. And Strang's most rigid censorship could not keep hidden the fact that Babur's cause was waning.

Overhead in sunlight, flyers dueled. Seen from below, they were bright flecks, unreal as stars. Reality was the hardness underfoot, sweat, harshly drawn breath, the taste of the fact that soon one might be dead but there was no way left to turn back. On the right flowed the Palomino, brown and murmurous, its opposite shore rising in green slopes where villas lay scattered and fallaron trees bloomed golden. On the left, older houses stood close-ranked, deserted, their windows blind. Ahead swelled the hill, steeps and terraces, gardens and bough-roofed walks, to the gray bulk of the Old Keep. Beyond it lifted the lattice of Signal Station and a pastel glimpse of the New Keep. Sounds of gunfire drifted from the east.

"You're shivering," Chee said to Adzel.

"Today I must again make myself kill," the Wodenite answered.

John Falkayn quickened his pace and drew alongside. Like the other humans, he was unkempt, grimy, and gaunt, clad in whatever rough clothes he happened to own, his uniform a blue band wrapped around the left biceps. Sewn to it was the insigne of a colonel, cut out of sheet metal. He pointed. "We should turn off up yonder path," he said. " 'Twill bring us around to a grove of millionleaf which'll give us some cover."

"Aye." Adzel took that direction.

Bullets began to whinner past, followed by the crack of their rifles. A man in the ranks screamed, clutched his stomach, went to his knees. His fellow irregulars drew further apart and advanced crouched, zigzag, as Chee had drilled them. Several flung themselves prone to return the fire before hurrying on.

It grew heavier when they reached the bosquet, a buzzing that ripped through foliage, thudded into wood and sometimes meat. Energy beams flashed from the Old Keep and back against it, trailing thunder and acridness. Adzel trotted about, calming his men, disposing them in formation. An occasional slug, nearly spent, bounced off his scales. Chee crouched low, a minute target, wasting no shots of her own across this distance.

"The enemy are concentrated in the stout stone building," Adzel said. "Our first move will be to neutralize it."

"Destroy, you mean?" John Falkayn said. "Oh, merciful Christ, no. The records, the mementos—half our past is in there."

"Your whole flinking future is here," Chee snapped.

Positioned, the artillery cut loose. Guns roared, rockets whooshed, explosives detonated in racket, smoke, and flinders. Slowly the Old Keep crumbled. At last from the wreckage stepped a Merseian waving a white flag.

"Kittredge, have your unit secure this place," Adzel said. "The rest of us, on to the New Keep." He lifted his weapon and charged. Men howled as they followed. *"Namu Amida Butsu,"* he whispered.

"Ya-ah!" screamed Chee. Her gun began to throw its bolts. They crashed lurid around the barricade which blocked the main door. A cyclic slugthrower hailed forth its reply. Adzel staggered. Chee swiveled her weapon past the right side of his torso and centered her fire. Flame geysered. A burning man climbed over the barricade, mindlessly shrieking, fell on the turf outside and sprattled like an overturned beetle, still burning. Adzel recovered and pounded onward.

He reached the rude fortification. Timbers, tables, sandbags, rocks came apart beneath his flailing hoofs. He leaned across and laid about him with his clubbed blaster. From his back, Chee sent narrow beams, finickily aimed. Surviving defenders broke and fled.

Adzel pursued them down echoing corridors. A squad dashed from a side room. His tail sent them tumbling. "Come on, you sons!" John Falkayn shouted to his troops. "Is he going to do it all?" They entered like a tidal wave.

Grim small battles ramped throughout the edifice. From its rotunda, the attackers recoiled. There every entrance had an obstruction, behind which men crouched shoulder to shoulder, firing—Strang's Hermetians. Dead lay thick in the halls after that charge; the wounded begged for help which nobody could bring.

In a room where councillors had met, Adzel and Chee gathered their officers. Blood smeared the Wodenite's scales and dripped from between them, scorch marks dulled his flanks, the dragon head was blackened by smoke. "I think we should offer them amnesty if they will lay down their arms," he said.

John Falkayn spat. "When my sister's husband died under their arrest, God knows how? Never."

"Besides," Chee observed, "if I'm not much mistaken about human affairs, you'll have trouble enough after this war without them in your body politic."

Assent rasped forth. "Very well," said Adzel. "However, I refuse to send unsupported infantry again. And if we destroy the structure from outside, as we did the Old Keep, we'll exhaust ammunition that will be needed in the lower city, not to mention killing disabled people of ours. Suggestions?"

206

Chee bounced in her saddle. "Yes," she said.

The enemy occupied the galleries beneath the dome . . . but not the outside of it. The Cynthian climbed that and planted a shaped charge which blew a hole. Perched on the edge, she sprayed the interior with fire. The soldiers in gray uniforms must seek shelter away from their breastworks. Adzel led a rush across these, and fighting became hand-to-hand.

The Wodenite himself found Benoni Strang dying of a gut shot, recognized him from pictures, and bent down to learn what he could and give what comfort he might. Cradled in those great arms, the man looked dimly upward and gasped, "Listen. Tell them. Why should you not tell them? You're not human, it's nothing to you. I brought everything about . . . I, from the first . . . for the sake of Hermes, only for the sake of Hermes. A new day on this world I love so much . . . Tell them. Don't let them forget. There will be other days."

The ducal navy was victorious in its home space because, while it had considerable help from the independent merchants, Babur had recalled much of its Hermetian force to the sun Mogul. This was after the Seven had—piecemeal, in chaos—withdrawn as allies.

Thereafter the defeat of Babur would have hinged only on time and determination; and the lack of replacements for rapidly deteriorating parts of ships would have made the time fairly short. The Imperial Band did not surprise van Rijn when they declined a finish fight. Thirty years before, they had shown the intelligence to cut their losses on Suleiman. Nevertheless he admitted gaining astonished respect for them when they sent messengers directly to him. Had they all along known that much about Technic civilization?

The meeting took place near Mirkheim, between a pair of ships. *Chronos* came battle-ready from Hermes, bearing him and Sandra. (David Falkayn and Eric Tamarin-Asmundsen stayed behind in command of the united fleet, prepared if need be to exact vengeance.) The Baburite vessel humbly bore no weapons. They orbited amidst uncountable diamond suns while images passed back and forth between them.

207

The little being stood foursquare before the scanners and spoke into a vocalizer. To Sandra it no longer appeared ugly. And was it just her imagination that found sorrow in the flat syllables?

"—We were used. We understand that we ourselves were among those who used us. . . . Let you and we make peace."

"What of the Commonwealth?" she replied.

"It mounts its onslaught. But as yet it is not strong."

"Hold on," said van Rijn, and switched off sound transmission. He turned to the woman. "The boojer speaks right. The Home Companies would fight a total war if possible, so they may gain what the Seven has lost. But if we, Hermetians and independents, stop fighting, if we use our influence against more war by anybodies, *ja*, hint that we and Babur together will resist—the public wish to go on spending lives and money should puffle away on Earth and Luna till not even the Commonwealth government can continue."

Troubled, she said, "I can't believe in suddenly putting ourselves on the side of these . . . creatures. After what they've done."

His words came whetted. "Can you instead believe in more people killed? And is not a question of getting buttock to buttock with the Baburites, what would freeze ours and sizzle theirs anyway. Is simply a question of we stop hostilities quick, on terms everybody can live with, and then lean on the Commonwealth to squash its 'unconditional surrender' clabberbrains."

Sandra paced around the bridge. How her muscles longed for a horse, a surf, a trail among glaciers. The viewscreen gave her mere immensities. Van Rijn sat like a spider, puffing a churchwarden pipe whose reek stung her nostrils. In the viewscreen frame the nonhuman shape waited patiently.

"What should we propose today?" she asked.

"We is talked about it before often enough," he answered. "Now that we see how anxious Babur is to make a deal with us, I say let's pick these quidbits out of our chaffing.

"The Commonwealth government can never recognize the independents as rightful agents, no more than it could ever really recognize the League. *Hemel!* Something besides another government having the right to decide things? Much too dangerous. Might get folks at home wondering if they do need politicians and bureaucrats on top of themselves.

"So: You, heading the Hermetian state, has got to front for us. Like you originally proposed, Hermes takes over Mirkheim, under a treaty that says you license legitimate companies from everywhere. A reasonable tax on that ought to repay what you lost in the war, plus a little extra for buying offplanet goodies like heavy industrial equipment and Genever. Babur disarms. Its fleet will soon be no use anyways, without supplies from outside; and the Commonwealth would not make peace if Babur was going to reengineer its forces. Hermes, though, will guarantee its safety plus a fair share in Mirkheim." Van Rijn chortled. "Babur becomes your protectorate! Musical chairmanships, *nie*?"

Sandra halted, folded her arms, caught his gaze, and inquired pointedly, "What about yourself? You and your buccaneer companies?" *O Pete, be with me now.*

But he made no demand, he only looked off into the Milky Way and said, rough-toned, "Is not your problem. Give those of us that want, a chance at Mirkheim, and everything else is a bone we gnaw between ourselves. Many bones must go dry before what is dead can rise again."

He smote his knee. "Ready to start bargaining on this basement?" he challenged.

Dumbstruck, she nodded. He swung back to the stranger.

XXI

Early during the triumph and toil, reunion and wrangling, merrymaking and mourning, there was held a private party at Windy Rim on Hermes. It was to say farewell.

Two of those who came would soon be departing together, for Sol aboard *Chronos*, David Falkayn and Eric Tamarin-Asmundsen. However, they had been separated for weeks, each busy with different shards of the huge confusion. This was their first chance to talk at length since shortly after the armistice. Following dinner, they drew apart from the others for a while.

The room they chose was a study, enclosed in wood panels of beautiful grain, shelves of codices in leather bindings, ancestral portraits, a gun rack, a desk whereon many high decisions had been written. A window stood open to the young night. Air drifting in was cool, fragrant with blossoms, alive with the sound of the river in the canyon below.

Falkayn hoisted his tumbler. "Cheers." Rims clinked. The men settled down in deep armchairs and drank, a taste of peat smoke from the birthworld of their race.

"Well," Falkayn said, "so you're the new Hermetian ambassador."

"Oh, no," Eric replied. "By all accounts, Runeberg conducted our affairs very competently throughout the war. We want to keep him on. My title will be special envoy, head of our negotiators with the Commonwealth."

"Why you? No offense, of course, but what experience have you had at that sort of thing?"

Eric grinned crookedly. "I wondered too. In fact, I objected with a deal of noise. But Mother insisted. 'Tis a matter of politics. I *am* the

210

heir apparent, the biggest name Hermes could send save for her, and she's got her hands full and overflowing here. That should carry weight on Earth—a token that we're determined about the peace settlement we want. And, uh, it should help at home likewise, that the Grand Ducal house is still concerning itself with crucial matters.''

"I see.'' Falkayn studied the homely, strong countenance. "Also, and this time no flattery, I think you're a good choice, you'll be much more than a figurehead. The blood of Sandra Tamarin and Nicholas van Rijn . . . yes.''

Eric flushed. "Maybe. Still, I'm not trained for diplomacy, I know not the ins and outs and roundabouts. . . . David, friend, will you help me? Can you?''

"How?''

"Oh, advice and—I know not. You do.'' Eric dropped his glance. "If, uh, if you'll not be too busy yourself.''

"I'll have plenty to keep me out of mischief, for certain. In effect, I'll take over the Solar Spice & Liquors Company, try to keep it afloat through all the hooraw to come.'' Falkayn sipped, set his drink down, and reached for his pipe. "On second thought, that'll keep me in mischief.''

Eric stared. "What about Freeman van Rijn?''

"Damn him, he'll be charging around through space, probably for years to come, mending broken fences and, I have no doubt, making new ones out of pieces stolen from the competition. I wish—Ah, well, I can't do that anyway, me a family man.'' Falkayn loaded tobacco before continuing. "But yes, Eric, I'll find time and energy somewhere to give you what help I can. Your job is more important than mine. In fact, I might not choose to do mine, if I didn't think it had some value to yours—I mean to getting back some stability throughout what we are pleased to call civilization. A strong private company under the right leadership can contribute toward that end.'' He started fire and puffed smoke. "For a while,'' he finished.

"What imply you?'' Eric asked.

Falkayn shrugged. "I'm coming to share Gunung Tuan's opinion. The wound to the old order of things is too deep, and I don't see anything to replace it that'll be worth having. We can buy time, you and I, maybe as much as a few decades before our splints and bandages give way. Meanwhile you can batten down on Hermes. And I . . . I can look for a place to begin afresh.''

"I never knew you so glum, David,'' Eric said in a distressed voice.

Falkayn smiled, a genuine smile though not that of a young man. "Why, I'm basically optimistic, as you should be. Come the necessity, I expect we and those we care about will respond like survivor types. And until then, we can find a lot of happiness.'' He leaned forward and lightly punched his companion's shoulder. "Think. You're going to Lorna and marry her. I'm going to Coya and our kids.'' He raised his glass. "Here's to the lot of them.''

"Here indeed,'' Eric responded with regained eagerness.

"They're what life is all about, right?'' said Falkayn, and drank.

Van Rijn and Sandra wandered out onto the terrace. Light fell soft from the house, soon losing itself in clear darkness. Above bulks of trees and hilltops reached a sky full of stars, Milky Way, glimmer of a nebula and of a sister galaxy. They reached the parapet and lingered. Beneath them ran the river, dimly agleam, a breath from it blowing upward. The water belled.

Van Rijn slurped from his beer tankard and threw a sidewise glance at Sandra. She stood tall in a deep blue gown that seemed to make her part of the night. Unbound, her hair flowed below her shoulders and gave back what glow there was. "By damn, but you is a looker yet!'' he exclaimed. "You is got too much stuff in you for being just a sovereign.''

She evaded his intent by replying, while she gazed outward, "I may not be that much longer.''

"I heard you got some shatterbrained list of demands dumped on your head.'' He was very lately back from Babur, where he had been overseeing the dismantling of the Seven's facilities. She had requested it, knowing how few men would be able to make sure that nothing was kept slyly in reserve, somewhere in an entire planetary system.

"It took the form of a petition. But the real meaning's unmistakable. Christa Broderick's organization has tasted victory, and does

212

have a claim on our gratitude. Also, the revolutionary terror weakened Kindred and Followers, the whole structure of the domains."

"You is still got plenty who is personal loyal to you, *nie*? Including the navy."

"No doubt," she said. "But do I, does anybody in his right mind want to see Hermes a police state ruling a population of helots? The upper classes would have to sacrifice their own freedoms to maintain that, you know.

"Every side will bargain, and maneuver, and orate, and distort the issues beyond telling what shape they ever had. Because more than two sides are involved. I can't guess how many factions will spring up. The quarreling will belike go on for years. In the end, however — Well, it does give me hope that Broderick agrees we can't hold a constitutional convention till we have a firm peace. Then I fear we must. My guess at the moment is that Hermes will nominally still be a duchy, but in practice a republic.

"It may be for the best. Who knows?"

"I doubt it will make much difference in the long running," van Rijn said. "Autocrats, plutocrats, timocrats, bureaucrats, technocrats, democrats, they all tell everybody else at gunpoint what to do. We is bound into an age of crats." He sighed like a receding tide. "Was a good holiday from that while we had it, *nie*? Till mankind went and spoiled things. Back to school, children of Adam. Maybe after a few more whippings you will learn water not only flows downhill, it reaches bottom."

She turned her head toward his promontory of a profile. "Mean you the Polesotechnic League is done for?"

He nodded heavily. "*Ja*. Oh, we will keep the name. That is what I will dash about for, like a toad in a pot, to patch the old garment so it will hold off the coldest winds till those who is close to me has reached a safe port where they won't need so many metaphors. Afterward I suppose will still be held solemn councils of the League for another century, till some Napoleon type without no sense of humor comes along and ends the farce."

Almost of itself, her right hand reached to touch his left, which gripped the parapet. "How can you be sure, Nick?" she asked mutedly. "Yes, the Seven are crippled, they may well go under. But the Home Companies are if anything stronger than ever, and likewise your independents, not?"

He gave her a wry look which lasted. "Where does the strength come from?" he said. "For the Home Companies it is the Commonwealth, which is been kicked into starting a big military establishment and will not forget that kick. The independents, they is allied with *you*.

"In both cases, like what the Seven was trying for, a government.

"Don't you see, the League was once a free association of entrepreneurs what offered goods and services but did not force them on nobody. It is not private outfits what fights wars and operates concentration camps, it is governments, because governments is those organizations what claims the right to kill whoever will not do what they say. Corporations, unions, political parties, churches, God knows what, it makes no matter who gets hold of the machinery of government, they will use it and use it and use it.

"*Ach*, we mortals is not wise enough to trust with power.

"The League . . . it was split before this trouble came out in the open. Now it is had a civil war. Its first. Strang seduced the Seven into that, but he could not have done it if they had not already had their legs spread. We can temporary fake the shadow of what was, but the body is gone. And the spirit went before then, away back when men who had been free began grabbing for control over other men."

Van Rijn's vision lost itself in the night. "No more important private decisions," he predicted. "Instead, authority takes over. Slogans substitute for thinking, beginning with the intellectuals but soon percolating down to the ordinary working man. Politicians appoint themselves magicians, who by passing laws and jacking up taxes and conjuring money out of thin air can guarantee everybody a soft ride through life. The favored businesses and institutions divide up the territory and strangle out anybody what might have something new. For every shipwreck what government brings about, the cure is more government. Power grows till its appetite is too great for filling on a single planet. Also, maybe troubles at home can be exported on bayonet points. But somehow, the real barbarians is never those that is fought, until too late. . . ."

"War. War. War.

"I would advise we pray to the saints, except I wonder if the saints is left us."

He tossed off half the contents of his tankard. "Whoo hoo, but I is been talking! Like yonder stream guggles into the sea, what stays just as salt as it always was, ha?" He laughed. "We should not waste good drinking time God has given us. See, a moon is rising."

Sandra tugged his sleeve till he faced her. "Believe you seriously what you were saying, Nick?"

"Well, might not be too bad on Hermes for the next couple generations, if you can put your new régime on a short leash."

"I mean in general. . . . See you," she forced out, "I've had somewhat the same thoughts and—What intend you to do about it?"

"I told you. Patch up how best I can."

"But afterward? If we get an afterward in our lifetimes."

Suddenly, strangely shy, he looked away. "I don't know. I expect the patching will be fun, you understand. Else maybe I would not try, old tired man like I am. Later—is an interesting question. Maybe later Muddlehead and me—I will be using *Muddlin' Through*, and should ought to have many a stiff poker game aboard—maybe we will lead a little expedition quite outside of known space, for whatever we may find."

"I envy you that," she blurted.

He swung back. "Why, by damn, sweetling," he exploded, "why you not come too?"

She raised her hands as if to fend him off. "Oh, no, impossible."

"Bah!" He made a chopping gesture. "How would you violate conservation of energy if you did? Conservation of momentousness, perhaps. But suppose in five, ten years you abdicate. Let Eric take over before time turns him doddery. You take the Long Trail with me!" He drained his tankard, clashed it down, and slapped her bottom. His right hand waved widely across heaven. "A universe where all roads lead to roaming. Life never fails us. We fail it, unless we reach out."

She drew back from him a little while she laughed a little. "No, do stop, Nick. We came not together for discussing absurd plans—or politics or philosophy—only for being together. I need a drink."

"Me too," said van Rijn. "Hokay, we will drink that moon down and the sun up, we will sing rowdy songs and try if we can dance a galliard to a Bach oratorio, we will not be solemn fools but honest ones, only you will remember what we spoke of." He offered his arm. She took it and they returned to the house of her fathers.

Adzel went lurching along a cliffside path to the river, a five-liter mug in his grasp which his freedom fighters had given him. He had repeatedly filled it with martinis. You could hear him singing a kilometer away, "*Baw-aw beedle eet bee dum bee baw,*" like a cheerful thunderstorm. At the water's edge, he saw Chee Lan seated on a rock, and halted. "Ho. I thought I would find you here."

The Cynthian dipped her cigarette holder to him. The glow at its end traced a tiny red comet-streak. "And I took for granted you'd arrive when you'd tanked away enough to get sentimental," she purred. "You big blundlebumber."

Adzel loomed slightly unsteady athwart woods, water, sky. Dawn was close. Overhead, between canyon walls that still were hulks of night, the stars were paling and whiteness mounted to eastward. The stream shone, glinted, swirled over bars and foamed past stones, on its way among boulders and gnarly trees. Its voice clanged laughter-ful from cliff to cliff. He took long breaths of the cold moist air which flowed above, the odors of upland summer.

"Well, our last chance," he said. "Day after this, we embark on our courtesy rides home to our planets. I look forward, yes, obviously . . . but those were good years. Were they not? I will miss my partners. I told Davy so. I got a phone patch through to Muddlehead at Williams Field and told it so too. It answered that it is not programmed to be touched; but I wonder, I wonder. Here comes your turn. No mercy, small person." A hand descended, amply large to close around her. Quadrupedal, holder jaunty between her teeth, she arched her back to receive the caress, which was very gentle. "Come to Woden sometime," he urged. "Your folk have spacecraft. You will be investing in such ventures, and getting hog-rich. Come visit me."

"In that gravity and glare?" she snorted.

"That wild bright openness where the winds run loose, horizons

216

endlessly before us but also flowers underfoot, a land that is the living Nirvana— *Aiyu*, Chee, I know I babble. Yet I would like to share with you as much of it as you can feel.''

"Why don't you come to me instead? We could rig a set of impellers for you to get a hint of treetop faring.''

"Do you think I can appreciate it?''

"I should hope you'd have that much wit. Light across a sea of leaves, but down below full of shapes and mysteries, a cry of color on wings and petals, a glen where a rill comes joyful—'' The Cynthian shook herself. *"Dood en ondergang*, you've got me doing it!''

Adzel smiled around his fangs. ''At least we are agreed we should make an occasional rendezvous, to swap lies about bygone times,'' he said.

Chee discarded her cigarette butt, ground it out on the rock where she sat, and considered whether to add more narcotic to what she had already taken. Emerald in the mask of her face, her eyes went to Adzel's stein; her tail waved away prudence and she recharged the holder from a pouch at her waist.

After she had struck fire, she stated rapidly: ''Let's be rational for a moment, if you will pardon the expression. I think we will be rejoining forces in years to come, you and I, simply because circumstances won't allow us to enjoy our otium. We can't go home to what we left when we were young; it may still be, but we aren't, nor is the rest of the cosmos. We'll be wealthy, powerful, me more in absolute terms but you more relative to your society . . . while outside, the order of things that the Earthfolk brought goes tumbling down into the Earthfolk's flaming hell.

''Old Nick knows. He'll be doing what he can, maybe just because he never left a game while a chip remained to him, but anyhow doing what he can against the evil days.

''Cynthia, Woden—will we sit by and allow them to become victims after we're snugly dead? Or will we spend our money and knowledge working to make them ready?''

She blew smoke at the huge head. ''I don't relish the prospect,'' she admitted. ''Ya-ah, how I curse it, I who imagined I'd retire to domestic comfort and expensive fun! But we'll be conferring, Adzel, for the rest of our days, yes, yes, we will.''

A rippling went the length of the dragon. "I fear you are right," he said. "I have had such forebodings myself, though I tried to dismiss them because they bind one to the Wheel. . . . Well, certain things matter more than one's immediate salvation."

Chee grinned, a flash in the strengthening light. "Let's neither play noble," she replied. "We enjoyed the trader game as long as that lasted. The power game is less amusing, and at best it merely serves to hold off what is worse. Regardless, we can enjoy it too. And, who knows, could be that our races will build us a monument after they've started a whole new course of history for all the planets."

"Oh, we'd better keep a sense of proportion," Adzel cautioned. "We may perhaps help them survive. What they do a thousand years hence—return then and see. Reality is more big than we can imagine."

"Of course," Chee Lan said. "And now suppose we drop the subject, go join the rest, and have a last round of jollity before breakfast."

"Excellent thinking, old shipmate," Adzel answered. "Hop aboard." She leaped to his outstretched arm and thence to his back. Above the cliffs, a few eastern clouds turned red.